Island

Also by Jane Rogers

Separate Tracks
Her Living Image
The Ice is Singing
Mr Wroe's Virgins
Promised Lands

Island

Jane Rogers

THE OVERLOOK PRESS
WOODSTOCK & NEW YORK

Thanks to the Arts Council of Great Britain for their Writer's Bursary which helped to keep me while I wrote this novel.

J.R.

First published in the United States in 2000 by
The Overlook Press, Peter Mayer Publishers, Inc.
Lewis Hollow Road
Woodstock, New York 12498
www.overlookpress.com

Library of Congress Cataloging-in-Publication Data

Rogers, Jane.
Island : a novel / Jane Rogers.
p. cm.
1. Mothers and daughters—Fiction. 2. Brothers and sisters—Fiction.
3. Revenge—Fiction. 4. Islands—Fiction. 5. Murder—Fiction. I. Title.
PR6068.O346 I8 2000   823'.914—dc21   00-058016

Manufactured in the United States of America
FIRST EDITION
1 3 5 7 9 8 6 4 2
ISBN: 1-58567-076-6

For Milla

Contents

MURDER IN RUANISH

Mrs Phyllis MacLeod (50) was brutally murdered in her own home on Thursday night, in an apparently motiveless attack. She was discovered by her lodger, Miss Nikki Black, who called the police. On their arrival paramedics pronounced Mrs MacLeod dead: cause of death was blows to the head with a heavy object. Her son Calum (27), also from Ruanish, confirmed that no valuables were missing from the house.

'I have never seen anything so brutal as this senseless attack on a sick, defenceless lady,' said D. I. Sinclair. Mrs MacLeod's front door was found to be unlocked.

(*Aysaar Reporter*, 8 October 1997)

1 · Lies

When I was twenty-eight I decided to kill my mother. Things were going wrong and I was looking to put them right. They went from bad to worse and I was unwilling, basically, to see the slide continue. I needed to take control.

Nikki Black's my third name. The Cannings called me Lily. Sweet white name, little Lily Canning, little girl lost. Then the birth certificate said I was Susan Lovage. But I'm not as white as a Lily, not as blunt as a Susan, I'm nobody's Lovage. And with no father in the case – *unknown* neatly printed in his space – I fathered myself. Black.

The other serious contender was 'Ruth'; the healer I saw in Hereford recommended Ruth, but to me it smacks of pity. Rueful, you'll rue the day. 'There's rue for you, and here's some for me.' An Ophelia clone. I don't think so. Ruth's a bit open too. Ruth, truth. Nikki's better guarded. I'll go for Nikki I told her and she said it would unleash different psychic powers. Different how? I asked. Nikki is more dangerous, she said. OK fine. Dangerous suits me. Not that I believe a word of it, obviously.

Nikki Black. With teeth. The spelling matters.

The beginning.

Lily Canning lived with Mummy Canning and Daddy Canning in a nice house in the suburbs of Birmingham, and it was a happy family with spade and bucket summer hols just like the reading books. But the mummy and daddy fell out and Mummy Canning ran off with her driving instructor. Little Lily was five years old, just starting school. Daddy Canning was a busy man with an important career in banking so one day he sat Lily down and told her something that would be better for her. It would be better for her, he said, to have a mummy. And now Mummy Canning was gone and not coming back, it would be better for her to know that Mummy and Daddy Canning weren't her *real* mummy and daddy but had only adopted her. And now he would give her back to somebody else so they could find her a new mummy who would look after her properly and not run off. Because how could he on his own, when he had to be at work all day? It wouldn't be fair to her. And in another house there would be brothers and sisters to play with. It would be much better for her.

Lily Canning was taken to a children's home (the first). There she was a very naughty girl and fought with the other children and wet the bed and scribbled on her books at her new school. They told her she would never get a new mummy if she behaved like that; which was just about the only fucking true thing they ever told her.

Lies

I'll keep it short and simple. Lily Canning was fostered; no good; taken to another children's home. Went into the class of Mrs Plant at junior school who taught her to read and told her she was clever. Mrs Plant, who knew a thousand fairy tales off by heart and told them each day after dinner, filling Lily's head with lost children miraculously found, and happily-ever-afters. Lily settled down, reformed, got herself adopted again aged ten. Thank you Mrs Plant. But was 'sneaky, secretive, you don't know what she's thinking, not open like a child should be' after a trial period with new mumsy and dadsy. Silly Lily! She tried too hard. Pleasing and thanking for everything, trying to say what they wanted her to, just so they would want to keep her. So that they would like her! Thinking goodness would bring rewards. Silly sneaky Lily.

To children's home (the third). Smashed things up. Stole the little kids' money. Accused the houseparent of sex abuse when he told her off. To children's home (the fourth). There were quite a few moves around then, predictable stuff.

At fourteen I got clever again, and was fostered by the Marshalls. Moved up to the top sets at school. You don't have to be *nice* to be clever. You don't have to be *liked* to be clever. You can be clever all on your own.

The Marshalls had a fat slow daughter called Louise, she was a year older than me. She used to sit in her room and sulk. They had a pretty cosy corny house, with flowery wallpaper and matching curtains; a dresser with crystal glasses arranged on it, and bits of hand-painted pottery. Oxfam calendar on the wall; they went to church. They were as nice as pie. Suck it up, I told myself, suck it up while you can, Nikki girl, all that middle-class cosiness. They'd be in front of the telly of an evening, Mr and Mrs, with a glass of wine each and her doing something useful at the same time, ironing or putting church newsletters in envelopes or sewing buttons on. The endless useful things these virtuous women do! She had her little photo gallery like they all do that she had to show off to me:

'Sharon, she was with us for a year, she did ever so well at school. She's at college now', and 'Philippa. She was so shy she wouldn't speak to anyone at all. D'you know what we did? We started leaving little notes for her – *what would you like for tea?* and *have you got any homework tonight?* and *would you like to go skating on Saturday?* and she wrote us little replies. And then one day when I came in I started unpacking my shopping and I said to her, "Philippa, read me what you've put on that note, would you love, I've got to get this food in the freezer." So she read it aloud to me! And after that we got her talking.'

How bleeding wonderful.

They thought I was great. I was. Compared to their pudding of a child. I charmed them. I chatted intelligently at meals and passed the spuds before they asked for them. I watched the news and made remarks about world affairs. I read five library books a week. I talked to the woman.

The man might as well've had a lobotomy, he pottered about the house and got himself off to work at eight and home again at 6.30 and cleaned his car and watered his roses and never spoke a word. That's where the daughter got it from. The mother was desperate. She wanted drama. Emotion, danger, excitement. What the poor old bat wanted was a bit of life. So I started confiding in her, the sort of stuff she wanted. What did I tell her? Oh – about being abused at the home in Hereford. About the girl who killed herself, who shared my room. About my social worker having an affair with the houseparent at the last foster home but one, and not believing anything I said because she had to pretend I was lying about that too. About being raped by those two boys after school, and the deputy head who said he just wanted to help me and put his hand up my skirt. About dreaming about my mum and thinking how happy I would be with her and how good I was going to be because I knew one day she'd try to find me and be pleased about how good I was; how I woke with tears in my eyes.

Oh she loved it, poor pale woman in her ghostly eventless life. I can see her now, leaning forward on her elbows on the kitchen table, then reaching across to pat my arm and take my hand: 'Oh Nikki, I'm so glad you feel you can talk to me. It's so good for you to get all this unhappiness out into the open.' Parasite. Sucking up distress, slurping up the juice of it.

Upstairs of course her fat sad daughter's stuffing her face with choccies (they gave her £10 a week spends and she never went out) and making herself puke. Mrs wanted us to be friends. I could hear her nagging fat Louise when I was virtuously doing my homework. 'She's had such a hard life, Louise, you really should try and be kind to her. And she makes the best of it, showing an interest in everything – you would enjoy her company you know, if you made a bit of an effort.'

She took us to the cinema and left us to see a film together. Louise ate a sack of Opal Fruits and four Mars Bars. She took us skating but Louise wouldn't go on the ice. They sat together in silence eating toffee, watching me.

She had so much sympathy for me, that woman, she wanted to adopt me. She talked to me about it. 'I know you're nearly fifteen now and some would say grown up, but I just want you to know that you should always feel at home here, I really want you to think of me as family, as someone who'll always be there for you. You mustn't think everyone is like those awful people in Hereford; there are people in life who know what love is, and who are loyal.'

What a lovely time I had. Until Louise got to the point where the domestic supply of biccies and cakes and what she could buy with her spends wasn't enough, and started nicking from Mum's purse to supplement her binges.

I was the first to hear of it, of course.

'Nikki,' says Mrs, her big brown doggy eyes shining with seriousness. 'No one's going to blame you or be angry, no one's going to be upset. What's important is that you should be honest with me. That's the most important thing. I don't mind what you've done, I understand. But I do want you to tell the truth. Now did you take some money from my purse?'

I had the devil's own job to persuade her it wasn't me. She wept at me, she pleaded with me, she set Lobotomy Man on me to ask me to own up and be forgiven, she held my hand for hours, she offered me money, as much as I wanted, as long as I'd promise never to steal again . . . In the end I lost interest and told them to look under Louise's bed. She'd got all the wrappers there, everything. 'Haven't you heard her chucking up?' I asked them. 'I thought you knew she had a problem.'

Ha. They were pretty sorry for themselves. And surprise surprise all those heartfelt words about always being someone I could turn to melted away. Suddenly there was palpable coldness. And closed doors downstairs, and negotiations with my social worker on the phone. Suddenly Louise was downstairs and I was upstairs, and

Lobo Man was heard to raise his voice. He said the same word twice, I heard him. 'Cuckoo,' he said. 'A cuckoo.'

Mrs Marshall had her very own little drama to focus on and she didn't need me at all any more. And so I moved on.

The social worker lectured me. 'You mustn't tell lies. You lose sight of the truth and you don't know what's real–'

Can't see any harm in that myself. Can't see what's so great about the truth, that I should need to keep it in sight. Lies make the world go round. People need something to get their teeth into. D'you want the whole world blank and silent? Absence is nothing to talk about. You can't talk about a gap.

You mustn't tell tales. Way back, Mummy Canning said that. 'Telltale tit/your tongue shall split/and all the little birdies/shall have a little bit.' I used to imagine that: a flock of them with their sharp little beaks circling flapping swooping in, pecking at thin strips of my tongue, pulling, digging their claws into my chin and heaving like the thrush on the lawn tugging a worm out of the earth.

I like tales. Those fairy tales from junior school Mrs Plant. I like it when Fir Apple and his sister turn into a pond and a duck to escape the clutches of the wicked old cook. I like it when ugly Rumpelstiltskin helps the miller's daughter spin straw into gold. I like the princess who weaves shirts from nettles for her seven enchanted brothers to release them from the shapes of swans. (They're in such a hurry she has to give the youngest his with the sleeve unfinished and he turns back into a fine young prince except he has a swan's wing for an arm. Imagine.) I like frogs that turn into princes and old women that turn into maidens and fish that can speak and grant wishes. *I like to lose sight of the truth.* Truth is shit.

2 · Fir Apple

Fir Apple was the first tale Mrs Plant ever told us. I was new I was in a twin desk at the front of the class with no one in the other half. They used to fight not to sit next to me. When I was nervous I needed to pee and then I couldn't wait. I wouldn't have sat next to me either, given the chance.

I'll tell you about Fir Apple. He was found at the top of a fir tree, in a huge dark forest. That's how he got his name. He was a tiny baby all alone at the top of a tree in the middle of a deserted forest that spread over the mountains all around. Lying on a high feathery branch that trembled in the wind. Lying there crying with his voice so small and weak you could barely hear it for the soughing of the wind in the boughs and the cawing of the rooks in their nests.

But as luck would have it . . . (O listen)

Fir Apple

As luck would have it . . . (it still makes my stomach turn over)

As luck would have it a woodcutter is making his way home through the lonely forest after a hard day's work. Looking up he spies a strange dot of pinkness in the branches. Then he hears the baby's thin wail. And he sets down his axe and his bundle, and straightway begins to climb the tree. A fir tree is dense and hard to climb but he forces his way up through the scented prickly branches, up up up until at last he can stretch out his arm and pluck little Fir Apple from the branch. Where he was dropped, it should be told, by an eagle who had snatched him from his mother's arms whilst she slept, in a far distant land.

The woodcutter wraps Fir Apple in his jerkin. 'Poor child,' he says, 'I'll take you home and you can be a playmate for my young Lizzy. Our old cook will take good care of you.'

So Fir Apple and Lizzy grew and played together closer than ever any brother and sister, for wherever you found one you would be sure to find the other. Never were two children so happy together. Said Mrs Plant. O listen. Never were two children so happy.

One day Lizzy noticed that the old cook was toiling back and forth, back and forth to the well, drawing buckets of water.

'Why do you need all this water?' she asked.

'If I tell you you must keep it a secret.'

'O I will,' Lizzy replied. (But she didn't.)

'In the morning when your father goes into the forest I shall boil up all the water and drop in young Fir Apple, to make a tasty stew.'

When the two children were in bed that night, Lizzy whispered to

Fir Apple, as they were always used to whisper – 'If you'll never leave me, I'll never leave you.'

To which Fir Apple replied, 'Not now nor ever.'

Then Lizzy whispered to him the old cook's plan. And the two children decided to escape together. Very early next morning while the cook was in the kitchen lighting the fire under her huge pot of water, Lizzy and Fir Apple climbed out of the window and ran away into the forest.

When the cook found them gone, she was furious. What would the woodcutter say when he came home? She sent three servants to chase after them.

Deep in the forest Lizzy and Fir Apple heard the servants running crashing through the trees. Fir Apple began to cry but Lizzy said, 'If you'll never leave me, I'll never leave you.'

'Not now nor ever.'

'Then quickly, do you turn into a rose bush, and I shall be the flower that grows on it.'

In an instant the children vanished; as the cook's servants burst into the clearing all they saw was a rose bush with a single bloom. So they made their way back to the cook and told her they had searched the forest far and wide, and found nothing but a rose bush.

'You fools!' screamed the cook. 'You should have cut the bush down and carried the rose back to me. Go and look again!'

Again the servants chased through the forest, and the children heard their footfalls. Fir Apple clung in terror to his sister.

Fir Apple

'If you'll never leave me, I'll never leave you.'

'Not now nor ever.'

'Do you turn into a tall tower, and I will be the clock upon it.'

In an instant the children were gone, and in their place stood an elegant clock tower, nearly as tall as the trees that surrounded it. When the cook's servants came by they saw from the clock that it was dinnertime, and ran back to tell the cook they had found no children but a tall tower with a fine round clock.

Then the cook was furious and screamed at the servants, 'You should have knocked down the tower and brought me back the clock. You fools, I can't trust you to do anything, I must find those children myself.' So she ran off into the forest. But the children heard the sounds of her approach, and Fir Apple clutched Lizzy's hand tightly.

'If you'll never leave me, I'll never leave you.'

'Not now nor ever.'

'Do you turn into a pond, and I will be the duck swimming upon it.'

In an instant the forest was transformed, a beautiful blue pond appeared with one snow white duck swimming across the water. But the cook was clever, she fell to her knees and quickly began to drink the pond dry. Then the duck swam right up to her and pinched her nose with its beak, dragging her under the last of the water. Very soon she drowned.

Then Lizzy and Fir Apple ran through the forest to reach home before the woodcutter. They lived happily together for the rest of their lives.

Mrs Plant asked us to draw a picture for it, and I tried and tried to do a duck on a pond and it looked like a duck in a circle or a duck on a line. I couldn't draw water. At last I gave up and drew the wicked cook with her boiling pot, squiggles of steam coming out and sharp orange flames beneath. I got a star for it but it wasn't the picture I wanted to draw.

3 · A plan

Why did I decide to kill my mother? The reasons are quite simple.

When you're young you think other people can help you. Parents if you have any. Friends. Teachers. Doctors. Drink, tablets, coun-selling. Maybe they do help some people. But actually the fix is to know what you want to do and do it. Being unhappy, asking advice, trying to escape, analysing it; none of that progresses you. To progress you need to lift up your foot and take a step.

I thought, I want to kill my mother. And I will.

I've been accused of being selfish and unfeeling. Amongst other things. I've been accused of being a lot of things actually: liar, whore, thief, attention-seeker, immature, disloyal, unstable, immoral, mad and a waster of my own talents. All these things were or had been true, from time to time. Perfectly true. Which was another reason for my plan.

Because there was an author of that person (me; selfish, unfeeling, etc). And she had never been called to account. She had never been asked to explain herself or excuse herself or even to identify herself. So I decided to find her out.

Now, reasons for planning to kill her: when my mother Phyllis Rose Lovage gave birth to me she did not hug me. She did not wash me. Feed me. Dress me.

She did not love me.

She wrapped me in a towel and during the night or early morning put me in a cardboard box on the doorstep of an inner London post office.

She walked away.

(Wrapping me in a towel is part of it too. If she hadn't wrapped me in a towel – if she'd had the courage of her convictions and not merely not loved me but *hated* me, and put me naked in the box – then I would have died of exposure. Which would have been more honest of both of us.)

Further reasons: when asked by police, she claimed not to know my father. She told them she did not want me back.

All right. The reasons boil down to two: 1. She had me. 2. She left me.

Q. Why did a number of young women who'd been in care figure amongst the Wests' victims? I read an article claiming Fred and Rosemary chose them specially, knowing no one'd come looking for them. But I know the reason: upon invitation, those girls *chose* the Wests. They went *chez* West thinking it was a nice place, a proper home, a farm where you could ride horses and write poetry,

A plan

a *family*. Where you could be taken in and loved. Even when they were there for a bit maybe they couldn't see any different, thought it was an alright place to be. Because *they didn't know any better*. They didn't know the difference between a loving family and a house of murderous perverts.

Well how could they tell? I learned about families from books. Families with mummies and daddies and birthday surprises, and picnics and super summer hols. In books I had a jolly band of mates and we were always setting off to follow the mysterious man with the limp or to investigate the night-time flashlights at Smuggler's Cove; we tumbled back tired and happy to scrumptious tea prepared by Mummy; we were gravely thanked by parents of tiny lost children/owners of mischievous puppies/mayors of imperilled towns. When we got into really serious trouble often Daddy came and talked to the policeman or explained to the cross colonel or arrived just as it was getting dark to give us a ticking off with a twinkle in his eye and drive us safely home. We had boldly gone and spread decency and honesty amongst vicious aliens; we'd unearthed ancient treasure after breathtaking dangers, always remaining one vital step ahead of the crooks. OK it was crap. At least it was happy crap.

What is it like? Being brought up in care?

It is like the boy in *The Snow Queen*. He gets a splinter of ice in his eye. It changes everything he sees to cold and ugly.

That's what it's like, and you can accommodate, to a degree; it's all you know. Just as the blind-from-birth know that others have *seeing* but can't really visualise (sorry) what that is; so the ice-splinter-eyed know that everyone else has *something* but they can't quite imagine what it might be.

15

It's like a ghost limb. I felt my disability. I was tormented by discontent. Well, it wasn't merely discontent. It took more than that to galvanise me. It was the other stuff, the bad stuff.

I don't think you need to know about that. Not yet, anyway. After I blew it with fat Louise and her tragedy-junkie mother, I went down. But I came up again, bounced back. I'm good at it – I fly I soar I swoop I glide. They tried to make me shift schools again but I went to see the head and wept. I loved his school, I didn't want to leave it, I promised to work hard, I promised to stay away from Louise (why would anyone want to go near her?) Was it fair that I should be penalised for her disorders? Look how often my life had been disrupted – ten different schools, nine different homes, how could I have a chance of fulfilling my academic promise? I'd been dealt a poor hand by fate – surely he wasn't going to increase the odds against me?

By the end he was practically stroking me; of course I could stay on, he personally would speak to my social worker about getting me into a home locally; he would keep a special eye on me.

I was a good girl then; worked hard, stayed after school, did all my homework. After O levels I did my A levels, my life was going swimmingly. I developed a crush on the geography teacher who fucked me in the science prep room every Thursday at 4.30 (while his wife was doing yoga) but that wasn't particularly clever because I thought he liked me. I found he was doing it with Tessa Watson on Tuesdays (while his wife was swimming) so I told him I was going to tell the head. He gave me £234 altogether over the rest of the year, to keep me quiet.

I moved to a new set of foster parents in my lower sixth. They did their best to knock me off balance but even they didn't manage.

A plan

They were full of bullshit about freedom and responsibility. Gave me a doorkey and told me to name my own coming in time – fine, no big deal, why should I get excited about being able to walk in a door at 2 a.m. instead of sliding open the window at the kids' home and climbing over the ledge? But they told me my room was private. They told me no one would go in it. And I was naive enough to believe them.

Their house had more lights than a theatre: ceiling lights and wall lights and table lamps and night lights and security lights. That family was permanently on stage acting free and responsible and adult. Nowhere to hide. My room was white and beige. 'Light and airy, spick and span!' said Jill the latest social worker who dumped me there and ran.

After a week the woman left the vacuum outside my door. 'Your room, you clean it when you like. Candice and Zoe do theirs once a week.'

At first I did. Plugged the vacuum in under the bed, hoovered the beige carpet, sucked the dust off white windowsills and skirting boards with the little brush attachment. Then I started dumping stuff on the floor. Clothes, schoolbooks, papers. They were still there when I came back at night. Dirty knickers under my PE kit under my history books; magazines and tights and apple-cores and even coins I dropped, lying in the same place day after day. God, I began to love that room. I wrote my name in the dust on the windowsill. I had such a pile of clothes on the end of my bed it was a weight to slide my feet under, I wrote notes and lists of groups I liked, clothes I wanted, letters to people I hated, poems about sex and death, I nicked a ton of library books, and they were on the chair and chest of drawers and windowsill and floor. She never came in. Only once she knocked on the door and asked for a bath towel back, it was on the floor sopping wet and I told her I'd put it in the wash. She didn't say anything. I knew exactly where everything was, I could put my hand on it with my eyes closed. You could do major surgery on the floor anywhere else in that house, it was so squeaky clean, and my room was encrusted and complicated and not like them. I asked if I could put stuff on the walls and she gave me Blu-tack. I put up pictures from magazines and things I drew and beer mats, I filled the walls completely so there were no gaps, no white, no beige. I had skulls and mushroom clouds and bands and bits of faces, one whole wall was lips and eyes and nipples and strips of black. When they were out I took food up, biscuits, apples, crisps – so I wouldn't have to go down if I needed a snack. I had a rubbish heap in one corner. I kept my fag ends and ash in a big screw-top jamjar so they wouldn't smell it, under my bed, and some vodka and a few things I'd nicked, perfume and jewellery, in a cardboard box of second-hand clothes I'd started buying off the market to sell on to girls at school. When I went in the door and shut it and just turned on the little bedside lamp (I put blue tissue over the shade) the room was dim and mysterious and cluttered and runkled and smelt of itself. It was mine, completely mine.

I went on the school trip to France. A week. When I came back my room was clean. The floor was clear, the surfaces were empty. The dirty clothes were washed and put away in the drawers. The empty walls had been repainted cruddy magnolia. All the papers and books were on the shelves. The cardboard boxes had gone and the nicked perfume and jewellery was arranged on the dressing table like it was mine. The vodka and fags were gone. She'd wiped me out. I suppose she did it after every girl that stayed there. Every

un-house-trained creature. Mucked out the room, washed the surfaces, sprayed it with air-freshener.

I sat in it breathing in the new paint and carpet shampoo until I
knew they'd all gone to sleep then I pissed on the bed and put on
my uniform and took my suitcase to school. I sat on the steps for
the night and after the caretaker the head was the first person
there. I told him I couldn't ever go back to that house and I would
never talk to anyone about what had happened to me there. All I
wanted was to work hard for my exams and better myself. He got
me back into the kids' home that night.

I got two Bs and a C at A level and a university place in Sheffield.

I was a clever girl, I could do all the stuff those mummied and dad-
died kids could do. I did my essays, went to lectures, got my
spending money nicking books and selling them on to other stu-
dents – I nicked my room-mate's boyfriend and then I nicked her
CD player and camera (redistribution of wealth). She shouldn't
have left the door unlocked anyway, it's lucky for her that more
didn't go. I was OK, I was good, I was good for quite a while, I was
coasting along nicely until I suddenly lost it.

This seems to be the pattern. I know it from before. I swoop I glide
I fly

I fall.

Never at the right time or in the right place (what would be?) and
once I'm down it's harder and harder to get up. Like one of those
seagulls with tar on its wings. People pretend to be your friend but
when you go down no one really wants to know. My room-mate
moved out which just goes to show how right I'd been to nick her
stuff; the boyfriend went back to her. I was left to the mercies of

the student counsellor. She kept me going for a couple of months before she lost interest too. Once things start to go down they go and go. I stopped turning up for my barmaiding at the Crown. I didn't get it together to nick any books. I didn't go to lectures. I ran out of money. You go through the holes in the net. I had nowhere to stay in the vacation, I hadn't latched on to anyone, I hadn't . . .

It happens over and over again. In different ways. When I had the job at the housing association and a nearly normal life and even friends; I stopped sleeping so I lost the job. I stopped earning so I couldn't pay the rent. I lost the flat so I went to live with friends and lost my friends. This is what I mean. The whole house of cards collapses . . .

You have no control over up or down or when it's going to change. It's tedious.

4 · The pigeon

You think I'm tough, eh. *I* think I'm tough. Yeah. But I have – I have a–

A tendency to slip. Slip slide slurrup slam headlong down into – OK. How to describe it? It's another state. It's crap. I can't describe it to you but I have to tell this story.

Do I have to tell you?

Yes, obviously. Well sometimes I'm afraid.

Will that do?

Afraid. You understand? Frightened. Fearful. Got the message? Sometimes I get – Fear.

Like this. I feel it coming on. Like you see the shadow of a big building slanting across the street in front of you and you keep walking and you step from sunlight into the shadow and you think it's OK, I'm still on the pavement, same ground beneath my feet same sky above my head same traffic roaring past – but–

it's not the same.

It's not the same. You're entering the shadow and you feel the chill – I feel the chill, I feel the way the earth is turning I feel ordinary comfort sliding away over the rim I feel abandoned – I feel – Fear.

It comes on. I can't tell you why. A typical instance of it coming on: the day I saw the pigeon. I took a short cut across the park and I saw a pigeon trapped. It was nothing – insignificant, utterly and completely insignificant.

But it's how the shadow falls.

There was a pigeon trapped, in the park. They put thread like fishing line across the flowerbeds. Its feet were tangled in it. When I saw it it was standing very still, then it flapped, hard. When it stopped it looked at me with its glittering eyes.

I was on the path. I stopped. They'd been working in the park, I suppose because it was spring. Dug up the flowerbeds, put in some ugly little polyanths. And this line, crisscrossing above the soil, staked. It must be to keep the birds off, I never saw it before. There was a tractor turning on the football pitch, dragging something over the muddy grass. A cloud of birds following it. Pigeons and seagulls everywhere. But this one was trapped.

I watched to see if it would flap itself free. No. It was making things worse. The line was tight around its scrawny leg, cutting in. You can amputate a finger like that. Tie a line around it tight. Wait for the end to drop off, kids used to play it at school.

The pigeon

I looked for other people. Two briefcases going to the office. They didn't see me, never mind the pigeon. A bleary-faced woman in a blue cleaner's overall. People going to work. What would you say? 'Please can you rescue this pigeon?' 'Rescue it yourself you silly bitch. If it matters to you.'

What's one pigeon the less? They're vermin. Carry diseases. Deface city buildings. The council poisons them, they have to. That's why they put the line. To stop pigeons eating the seedlings. Trap them, make an example. There were no other pigeons near this flowerbed. Leave one and it scares off the others. Scarecrow. Scarepigeon.

It flapped dementedly, its wings beat up small lumps of soil, it heaved its body upwards. The foot could have just sliced off. I wished it would. So the pigeon would be gone.

To rescue it I would have to step over the little green hooped railings, step carefully between the crisscrossing lines of thread, bend down in the middle of the garden and touch the pigeon. It stared hatefully. Its beak was sharp for pecking. I think they carry rabies, I've heard that. I hadn't got any gloves.

My face was red and my heart was beating, I could feel it shaking my ribcage. A woman came by with a baby in a pushchair and a young kid in uniform. I turned away so she wouldn't see my face. The kid said, 'Mum!' and I knew he'd seen the pigeon but she was telling him off and didn't stop.

I decided to find a park keeper. A gardener. With proper thick gloves, with gauntlets. He could free the pigeon, it was his job. I went on along the path and part of me thought I won't come back then I won't have to see it flapping and heaving again, or sitting still and staring. Once I get to the gate it won't be important.

There weren't any gardeners. Only the tractor down on the football pitch, across a wasteland of boggy lawns. When I got close I'd be shouting over the noise of the tractor, at last he'd turn the engine off in exasperation and lean out. '*What?*'

'A pigeon,' I'd say. 'I'm sorry but it's trapped—'

'A fucking pigeon?' He'd stare at me then turn his engine on again.

I went back along the path. If I'd had some scissors. Or a penknife. I could have cut the thread. I wouldn't have had to touch it.

Perhaps it was dead. It would die quite quickly of exhaustion. I hoped it was dead already.

But there was a man crouching in the muddy flowerbed. He glanced up at me. He had the pigeon in one hand, his fingers grasped around its body and folded wings. With the other he was untangling the line from its foot. The bird stared. It did not move its head or peck him. The line was around a wing as well; the man cursed quietly as he turned the bird over and tried to free it. I was embarrassed, ashamed to stand and watch him. I moved back the way I came. When I looked over my shoulder at last he was standing on the path again. He was holding out his arm and letting the bird go, it flapped at shoulder height like it had forgotten how to move through the air. Then it was rising. Flying up.

That's it. It slips. An incident like that and I feel the whole thing slipping, I am in the picture but there's a dotted line around me. Cut around the dotted line. I am cut out.

Night-time is worst of course. I'm exhausted. Raw, jangled, wanting only to curl up and close my eyes. Wanting nothing so much as the warm enclosed huddle, peaceful black oblivion. Check the windows, lock the door, switch off the lights, pretend the flat is safe. But as soon as I close my eyes I hear noises. A hedge, a thicket, a forest of noises springs up around me. And I'm listening, watchful and alert, for the thing behind them. Straining after the one noise I can't quite hear. I lie still for a long time, while the noises become more and more deafening. There's no way out of this, I don't sleep, I won't sleep, whatever I do won't make any difference but still there comes a point when I can't lie passively any more being assaulted by the racket around me while my inner ears strain to aching after a hidden sound – I have to heave myself up in my bed (heavy; the body is heavy and dull, the legs stiff, they ache when I try to bend them. The body weighs me down, it has a hollow sensation around its middle as if food might comfort it. I know it won't.)

There is a routine of silencing: alarm clock's tick to be wrapped in a jumper, wristwatch in a T-shirt, a folded sheet of paper to be wedged in the side of the window frame. I open my bedroom door, check the lock on the front door. The fridge's hum has become a roar which drowns out everything else; I switch it off. The radio has been left switched to *tape*; its red light is still on and it emits a low exhalation of dull static like the roar of a gas flame. Pull out the plug. Next door's TV is deafening, when I touch the party wall I feel it vibrating with the sound. Someone upstairs flushes a toilet and the intensity of the noise drenches me with sweat, I am hot then cold, my hollow head echoing and reverberating with sound. Outside the steady drone of traffic has become isolated incidents, the distant whine of a motorbike crescendoing to blast force then elongating itself into distance and vanishing. But as I track each moving sound and supervise its exit from the picture it is replaced, overlaid, interfered with by other, new intrusions – a shout, thudding footsteps, the roar of aircraft, the dripping of taps, the slamming of doors and pressure of wind against the panes, the crackle of electricity in the wires and gurgle of water in the pipes, the settling and shifting of the building's bricks and mortar the pattering hail of falling dust motes the stampedes of house mites the thundering waterfall of my own blood roaring past my ears.

I turn off everything I can find. Unplug all the sockets. Listen. Strain.

There is a faraway sound, behind these walls of noise. I can almost – I think it's someone screaming. A car floods the place with noise and then recedes, I can almost – if I hear that scream again . . .

I pull back the curtain a couple of inches. There's no one there. Just empty pavement and road. It's quiet and still. I wait. It's waiting. Like a stage set. Something will happen. I am frozen here, waiting, staring into the dark street. I'm getting cold.

I back myself onto the sofa, I can still see out from here. I pull the cushions over me. Things are quieter now. I am holding them out by force. I don't let myself be distracted from the street. What is it? What?

My eyes are burning. They ache to close. Just for a second or two. But they fly open when I blink. The eyes closing will make it come. The thing in the street. I have to watch out for it. Me watching keeps it out. I haven't any choice, I must sit here paralysed, eyes glued to the empty night-time street only by my force of will can that emptiness be maintained can horror be held at bay can the suffocating press of nightmare be held outside the edges of my field of vision.

5 · On mothers

It's quite pathetic isn't it? Fear. It's on the whole contemptible. Courage is what people should have. Courage is attractive. A person sitting rigid and incapable with fear deserves to be the butt of jokes.

I am well aware of this. I don't find it attractive either. I don't just embrace it, I don't just fall into it without a fight, I don't pretend to myself it's *nothing*.

Later – not at the time because there's no brainpower spare to do it, but after an attack – I have tried to figure out the precise mechanics the twisted logic of the thing. If I relax my vigilance the bad thing will happen. Doesn't that suggest the bad thing is in me? My relaxation releases it. I have to stay awake to hold it in. But is it in or out? Am I holding it captive or at bay?

At last I make myself get off the sofa, stiff, pins and needles, aches. I deliberately turn my back on the window and make my feet go up and down over the floor to the bathroom. Take four paracetamols from the tub with the childproof lid I stabbed holes in with a tin opener because it wouldn't unscrew. It is quarter past two. I go back to bed, I close my eyes and my ears. But I don't sleep.

The night passes slowly. The first earsplitting car goes by after a long period of middle distance hum. Then another. Premature chattering from a disoriented bird. A milk float's electric whirr. Soon it will be morning.

No one else does this. No one else waits, frozen, glazed, staring at the dark. A rabbit in headlights is the nearest thing. But the rabbit's freeze is finite. The lights blaze through his eyes, fill his head in a starburst explosion, roar of engine, violent heat – it's over. A minute, less. How long will you sit here Nikki? Waiting for it to happen, staring at the dark? Another week? A month? A year?

I am so angry I am shaking, my clenched fists ache, my eyes flood with red hot tears. You cannot do this. You cannot sit here for the rest of your life. *Anything* would be better.

Every time I manage to fly I end up going down like a stone to the bottom. Why? I call it Fear. Which is childish, I know. But child-ish is the point, isn't it?

I'll tell you how I've worked it out. This may be wrong – it may well be wrong. The point is it makes sense to me. I've looked at mothers. Women with their children. I watch them a lot, in places where they're commonly found. Playgrounds are good; I sit on a bench with a fag and watch them push their children on the swings, release them down the slides, hover below them on the climbing frames. Listen to what they say:

'Hold tight!'

'Don't fall!'

'Don't let go!'

'Be careful!'

'That's high enough.'

'*Not* head first.'

'I'll catch you. Jump. I'll catch you.'

These are the kinds of things mothers say. If you're at the top of the slide and it's very high you don't have to be afraid; a mother will be it for you.

'Hold tight! Sit down! Slow yourself down with your feet.'

I hear other things they say at other times, litanies of mother-speak:

'Don't be late.'

'Lock the door.'

'I'll meet you/wait for you/pick you up.'

'Be careful on the road.'

'Wrap up warm.'

'I'll leave the landing light on.'

Island

'Don't forget to turn off the gas.'

'It'll be alright.'

'Mummy's here.'

'Sleep well.'

Mothers to their children. What are they doing? Worrying. Taking care of. *Fearing for.* It's simple, isn't it? Why do I fear? Because my mother never did it for me.

If a mother does it for you you're free to fly. Swing high on the swing, Mother can worry about what if you fall. Mother knows you're fragile, vulnerable, tiny; she knows how practically nothing you are, just a tiny smear of flesh squeezed out of her. She knows you're mortal – so you don't have to.

That's what I think. That's where successes come from. Mother-fear. Mothers who've done the proper thing and taken on all the cold sweats and shadows. Mine, the bitch, left me to do all my fearing for myself.

That's why I thought I'd kill her. Catch her and kill her. Give her a good dose of fear beforehand, a bit of paying back – then kill her and free myself to fly.

Going along in life is like skating or cycling, if you keep going you're fine. It's when you think about it or slow down, that's when it's dangerous. Which thought makes me superstitious. Are you superstitious? Most of my superstitions are to do with birds. Good birds: duck, sweet white duck on a pond. Swan, heron, lapwing, owl, Canada goose, kestrel, kite. Bad birds: magpie, obviously. Pigeon (filthy, string-tangling vermin), starling, crow, seagull, hen, white goose, tit. That's not true, I don't care about tits one way or the other. Or sparrows. They're too common. Or robins because they're too friendly. The rest are all true. A heron means it's a blessed day.

The superstitions are to keep it going, keep my balance, stay up. Or signs that I may fall and lose it.

I have spent long periods of time going along with hardly any problem. My first year at university, for example. But I always know the fall is imminent. And when it comes it's hard to go back up. I thought ironing *her* out might iron me out and stop me going down.

You might as well believe me. Why would I lie? What would be the point in writing down a load of lies?

I suppose I've always thought the truth was quite important. Not easily available, a scarce resource; but *necessary*. At some level. This was another reason for killing my mother, in fact. The necessity for truth. But I'll stick to my original point. (It's important to note though that really it's only liars who have a proper respect for truth. I mean, all the lies I've told, they've mainly been to protect the truth. There's underlying truth then there's the passing needs of the moment, reality which isn't true in any way and doesn't need to be dignified with the name. For example, I say, 'My new coat was a gift from a rich friend, she persuaded me to try it on and then said it suited me so well I must have it and she paid.' When in reality I nicked it. Well – do I deserve to have a coat bought for me? If I went shopping with a rich friend, wouldn't she have bought it for me? D'you want me to say the truth is I'm a thief and I will never get given anything? The lie is a temporary measure. Until the facts come around a bit.

This is a tangent. I've just thought of another example though. Affairs. You tell one person you love them and want to be with them always, you tell another person the same. These are necessary lies. Because if you told either of them about the other, they'd kick you out of bed. And anyway it's the truth, in fact what you told them was the truth. Truth isn't consistent with what's possible, is it? I mean the truth is people would like to live for ever, always be happy, be rich and good looking with strings of lovers and wonderful showbizzy careers. That's the truth. Whereas what people get is illness, dying, misery, poverty, ugliness, divorce and jobs cleaning toilets. What's the truth? The truth is what people *want*. Liars are basically idealists, liars are saints and prophets. Jesus was a liar.

Stories tell lies. That's why they're good. Someone's *made it up*. You start to read and it's full of lies, the ugly duckling turns into a swan, the goodies beat the baddies! Justice prevails! Hooray for lies.)

Now let's get it over and done with: Fear.

I have always suffered from Fear but it's not a constant state. It comes and goes. When it comes it paralyses me. When it goes I'm fearless. Again, I can give you proof of this. I have swum in bottomless black water in a Scottish loch. I have ridden at 90 m.p.h. without a helmet on a motorbike. I don't mind spiders. For a dare I have crossed the Mancunian Way at rush hour with my eyes closed. I have been in the back of a stolen car driven by a drunk. I can do fire-eating and juggle flaming brands, thanks to a six-week fling with an alternative clown. I have hitchhiked on my own from Newcastle to Southampton.

So I'm not afraid, OK? In the normal sense. Not timid, nervous, twitchy, looking out for danger. I mean, there's a *thrill*. The motor-bike going like an arrow through the dark so fast your lungs can't catch the air and your heart dances in its cage – fantastic. Danger doesn't worry me.

But. When I have Fear (choosing my words; as in, have a cold, have pneumonia, have a breakdown, have Fear) I am incapacitated.

Now one thing I've noticed is that no one else is. Unless they're *very* good at hiding it. Unless they're all much better liars than I think and when they crawl into work and say 'My back was out all last week' they really mean 'I was a helpless jelly in the face of non-specific terror and couldn't move.' I don't think so. There would be a cult of it, wouldn't there? People who have Fear. Like migraine sufferers and manic depressives and schizophrenics and anyone who suffers from an altered state. It is an altered state (I'm loath to give it status. It's shit. But – it is an altered state.) I am different when I have Fear. But there is no clan of fellow sufferers I can turn to for support.

So naturally then arises the question, why? Why does this supposedly healthy apparently normal reasonably intelligent young late-twentieth-century female, alone in all the world, suffer from Fear? From clinical Fear?

OK. In what way do I differ from the billions of other young women alive in the world? I look for discrepancies between my own and the common experience, attempting to narrow it down. Hey presto, I've found one! I have no mother.

Lots of people have no mother. Their mother dies or runs off with a taxi driver or gives them up at birth.

Island

OK OK. But subtract from that number all the ones who had a *bit* of mother: say were aged five when she died or eight when she ran away, or were adopted from birth by a proper mother-substitute who could be bothered to hang on to them for a whole childhood long. Subtract from that all the ones who had a parent; the ones with no mothers but with fathers. Or even grandmas, or aunties or stepmothers, *anyone* to love them.

Subtract from that anyone who was ever loved as a child. OK?

How many would be left? A few million I suppose. Subtract from that all the people whose lives are so wretched that they are permanently preoccupied by the struggle to stay alive: street kids in Bombay and Mexico, starving refugees from war-torn/drought-ridden/flood-devastated third world countries on the news every night. If you have to think about catching an insect to eat because you've had no food for five days and three soldiers have just raped you, the lack of a mother is not necessarily foremost in your mind. I imagine.

But for me it is. Due to me living in a prosperous first world democracy where the state has shouldered the responsibility of keeping me clothed and fed and a roof over my head every time no individual human wants to. Which you could see in itself as a crime couldn't you. If you go back to nature for example; a young creature rejected by its parent – left alone in the wild – will die. Unless another adult creature comes along, takes up the orphan and lavishes it with love. (It's true. Wolves and monkeys have adopted human babies, ducks have adopted swans, a collie bitch suckled a lion cub – it's *true*.) Nature's solution is: die or get another mother. What the hell right has a government got to interfere with nature?

I hope you're following my argument. I've had time to see the pattern in my own life (flying swooping falling sinking; flying swooping falling sinking) and to realise that I am powerless to change it. I can't try *not* to have Fear. It comes. It's just there one day. Like the edge in the air one winter's morning. Frost. It's not possible to push it away.

I can't stop it – even when I've analysed it; even when I've put my finger on what caused it. (A counsellor I once had swore by that: 'Articulate your distress. Get it out of your system.' Well no, actually. Articulating it doesn't remove it. Strange to say it doesn't go into a big speech bubble and float harmlessly off into the ether, it doesn't come out of me as easily as *words*. For christ's sake. It's *in* me. I am unlovable. Impossible to love. No one has ever loved me not even my own mother.)

Oh yes; I forgot. When presenting you with the figures for people who have no mother-love, I should have excluded those who have some retrospectively, those whose abandoning mothers have made the effort to trace them twenty years later or sent a card or even made a phone call. Because what any of those shows is an iceberg of love and anxiety under the pinpoint of the contact; a phone call after twenty years indicates to me nineteen years of agonising about whether to do it or not, and a final overwhelming of all other considerations by the absolute desire to hear the lost child's voice.

Absolute desire. Imagine.

Anyway. You must consider how I felt trapped. When you understand it all and you've worked it all out and even articulated your distress and realised it doesn't help; if you're twenty-nine and faced with the prospect of being damaged goods for the rest of your life say another fifty years of flying swooping falling sinking; of enduring altered states, of having Fear; of never getting out of your own head with its own particular problems (getting out of your head is another thing I should talk to you about with reference to chemicals but not to interrupt just now) then you can fall into a depression. I did. I became pissed off. I didn't want to spend the rest of my life having attacks of Fear. Yes I thought of suicide. But it makes me very angry the thought I should have to kill myself for someone else's bad behaviour.

Who put me in this situation? *She* did. And once I'd killed her, I thought, the problems she created for me would quite likely perish with her. She would have an excuse for not loving me (being dead): she would have got her just deserts for not loving me. And having given an eye for an eye I might resume myself like a phoenix, self-authored, recreated, I might fly, swoop, *fly*. Fly and fly and fly and shed that Fear for ever.

Now. Getting out of your head. To qualify: I required to get out of my head because in my head was Fear, or the danger of having Fear, and no visible escape from that cycle.

Getting out of your head (sic) tends to be done with alcohol or drugs. That's what other people do, those who feel the need. They get out of their heads and they laugh and sing and dance and feel OK. They lose control – deliberately. They chemically disinhibit themselves.

When I am flying I'm in control. When I was doing my A levels; when I started work at Yewtree Housing; I was in control. When I have Fear I am not in control.

On mothers

I spend my life being vigilant – guarding against the oncome, the creeping up of Fear. If I got smashed wouldn't I lay myself open? Prostrate myself naked in front of it yelling *Come and get me?*

I would like to get out of my head and escape fear of Fear. But I can't think of anything worse than willingly losing control and letting Fear in. And I'm afraid (I said I wasn't didn't I? I said I am not nervous timid afraid etc. it wasn't true) I am afraid that the me which is tightly constructed would unravel. I want to get out of my head, but not to nowhere. Not to find there's nowhere, no other land to stand on.

I'm afraid of drugs. I'm afraid of losing it. I'm so afraid that when people joke about how pissed they were I start to feel sick. After one drink my whole body goes hot and cold like an early warning system, I couldn't drink more if I wanted to, my throat constricts. When I see someone smashed I feel horror and disgust.

It's not something other people like (why should they? Look. I'm not asking you to like me. I'm telling you the truth, I'm telling you about a change. A kind of transformation. It is lucky I planned to kill her or none of this would have happened. You don't have to like me to see the way things have changed, sea changed. Do you?)

No one likes a person who doesn't drink or do drugs. A no-fun abstemious teetotalling creep; foul, I agree. I just daren't. I've never told anyone that before, and that's the truth.

6 · Falling

You might say this was predestined. It happened because I caught the fag end of a TV documentary in the pub. Ten minutes later and I'd have missed it. And then I wouldn't have had a clue. Before I decided to kill her you see, my position was *fuck her*. She doesn't want to know me, I don't want to know her. I'll never give her the satisfaction of imagining I've wasted even ten seconds' thought on her.

But I happened to arrive for work early. And there was this worthy female bleating on about adoption. With a couple of live *oh-yes-please-expose-my-private-parts-to-six-million-viewers* guinea pigs. Adoptees. Trying to trace their mamas. And the first thing they did was to write to the Office of National Statistics in Southport, and that's how they got their birth certificates.

Falling

You don't have a birth certificate, you see. Not like any other human being. All you have is an adoption certificate, a nice little fake, a bit of plastic panelling tacked over the void.

So I thought well it's a gift. A nudge. I'll write to them and see. What the hell. I might be the illegitimate daughter of Mary Whitehouse, you never know.

It was drip-feed for about a year then because I wasn't pushing and people in those places are basically paid to be retarded newts. Then there's the bureaucratic obstacle course; I even had to see a counsellor and convince the sucker I was sane.

However, in the end I got my hands on two photocopies: the birth certificate (Susan Lovage) and a page from someone's notepad, social worker or police, about finding me. The date at the top was 1968 October 3. The day after my birthday.

I was found in a cardboard box on the doorstep of Camden High Street post office. Found by the cleaner at 6.30 a.m. I was wrapped in a towel and I was newborn.

So where did my mother expel me? In a bed in a nearby house? Squatting in the bushes in the park? In a pub's back-yard toilet after closing time?

When did she put me there? Midnight? 3 a.m.? Or was it someone else, maybe? Her *mother*. Yes, what if she had a mother, who helped her get rid of me?

She chucked me away but didn't want me to die. That's the puzzle. The towel, the box, the post office. Maybe she even knew how early the cleaner came. Chose the post office above the bank or the greengrocer's, for that reason.

Or was it because she *really* wanted rid: not just chuck me in the bin; post me. Send me *far*.

They alerted the local hospitals. She pitched up at Casualty that afternoon, bleeding too much. Was she alone? It doesn't say. It says she couldn't keep me, she gave me for adoption. Gave. They got her name and address on a birth certificate and through that they got a name for me. It's the Susan is the only question. Her choice? Oh sure. Most likely the name of the cleaner who found me. Or the policeman's girlfriend. The worst name anyone there could think of and put on for a joke.

It's a crap name anyway. Her date of birth was 18 January 1948. She was *twenty*.

When you watch a woman with a baby she's always looking at it. On a bus for example, or just sitting in the park. She'll talk to someone but her eyes will rest on the baby, like the moon and the earth, she can't escape its gravity. She's constantly checking it, making sure it hasn't got its sheet in its mouth or its hat strings strangling it or its hands cold or its nose snotty or flies in its eyes.

Not my mother.

You see them with their knuckles clenched tight around the buggy handles battling round small shops, eyes alert for baby snatchers.

Not my mother.

You see big fat pregnant cows patting their bellies with compla-cent dozy smiles, planning names and clothes.

Not my mother. Push it out and get rid. Couldn't wait to get her eyes *off* me. OK if she was a kid. OK if she was fifteen. But *twenty*? Cunt.

Falling

She dumps me on a doorstep in a box; another bit of rubbish. She hasn't even got the courage to stuff me in a bin to die.

From then onwards I went down. Down down down down down. I stopped sleeping, I was pacing my room all night listening to the noises, then I fell asleep in the day and missed my shift at the pub. I missed a few and he sacked me. It didn't matter because I wasn't spending anything – I wasn't going out, I could survive on my giro. But the landlady gave me a month's notice. People sniff out weakness, don't they, if you're just hanging on by your fingertips, nothing gives them greater pleasure than to unclasp your fingers one by one and prise you off. What did she want me out for? She wasn't going to use the room. I paid my rent, I was quiet and tidy, I never lost my key. She said she didn't know I'd be around so much in the daytime, she liked people to work. Well whoopee-doo, she didn't work. Just hung in there like a great bloated leech sucking up cash from her tenants. I wasn't in a good state for finding another place, there didn't seem to be much available and one house I rang was always engaged and at another no one ever came to the door. I was blurry and dizzy I told her I wasn't well, which completely pisses me off now, that I was reduced to appealing to that old shark for sympathy. I made myself feel better by planning how I'd leave the room but it was difficult because I was at the top of the stairs and she always knew as soon as I came out. Also I needed my deposit back. Bitch. I had to content myself with flushing a gigantic sanitary towel down the toilet. It was an easy toilet to block.

But I was falling. I hadn't got anywhere to go. I was out on the street in the morning and nowhere to lay my head that night, and a rucksack and a bag weighing me down.

Island

There's nothing more disgusting than being pitiful. Asking for things. I had to find a floor to sleep on. I rang Karen, the other barmaid; I rang caring Bill from the last home; I rang that bastard Vince who dumped me for no reason and I knew perfectly well in advance that each of them would have cast iron reasons why it was impossible for me to curl up on four square feet of their floor for a night or two. *She* made me this; the one you can walk away from.

Oh ha ha. Don't go thinking I'm sorry for myself. I'm not that soft. I see them in their little relationships and families, maintaining their values and their property and their gene pool. At least I'm not hypocritical enough to want any of that shit. But I didn't do anything to Vince. I was nice to him.

Phoning was the most I could do, the whole of outside was so big and light and noisy and I'd hardly been out for days I was in that state where I knew all I must do was sit it out last it out endure the Fear until it rolled on over me. I had to go in somewhere I was exposed as a peeled shrimp. I went into the big marble mouth of the library, shuffling under my rucksack and bag, like those old codgers who go there for the day out of the cold to sit over a newspaper and stink. I stayed till hunger drove me out and when I went I left my rucksack there as if I'd just gone to get a book so I wouldn't have to carry it.

This is what it reduces you to. I went to university you know. I got away with pretending to be one of them, I wrote essays I talked to tutors I sat in the union bar I took notes in lectures. I screwed boys who'll be lecturers themselves by now. I was a perfectly convincing student and then I went down.

When I did resurface I couldn't go back because it was a joke. All these middle-class kids *playing*. Playing house, playing being poor/drunk/smashed/in love/broken hearted/naughty/off the rails/irresponsible/behind with their work. All cavorting in their self-invented fucking dramas and all precisely on course; with Mummy and Daddy and money behind them, through the nice straight little Uni channel where with any luck they'd pick up a well-qualified spouse from the same socio-economic bracket as well as sound qualifications for themselves – and out into the charmed world of graduate employment and starter mortgages and a car from proud Daddy on graduation day and on and on into their cushy stifling protected little lives. Once you blow out of something you see it clearly don't you. A charade. I would have gone back to puncture some of them if I'd had the chance. But the money and the energy and the perseverance required are all daunting. When I'm flying they're all there – at my fingertips, at my feathertips. But from down in the depths they're unreachable.

What I realise now looking back on that day at the library was that it was the pits. I couldn't even imagine what might happen next. My head was puffy with Fear. But coolly now what could I have done? Only two choices. Sleep in a shop doorway or pick up some pervert in the street and offer to go home with him for £10. I was destitute. I was twenty-nine and destitute. My inheritance. Thanks Mum.

But then came the proof I'd bottomed out. I fell. Coming down the marble steps in the library my foot slid away from under me and I fell. I fell backwards on to the base of my spine then I bump-bump-bumped down the remaining twelve stairs. My head snapped back as I bumped and I was knocked out. I suffered con-cussion, whiplash, spinal bruising and a hairline fracture to a vertebra. I know in detail the stages of the fall, the specific injuries sustained, because three doctors and two lawyers went into them extremely thoroughly. The stairs were wet, the cleaner had forgotten to put out a warning notice; an elderly man who hurried to my assistance also slipped and fell. It was a cut and dried case, the library was liable and owed us both compensation. It didn't matter it didn't even hurt, it was a relief to be scooped off and carted to hospital and tended. I didn't even realise for a while that I'd get money as well. It took its time grinding through the system but eventually there came an offer of £12,000.

They kept me in hospital for six weeks because of my back; I had to lie flat. And that's when I decided to kill her. I finally realised the futility of a life where whatever enterprise you embark on, after a short time the ground under your feet will run out and you will fall over the edge and disappear.

The plan to kill her gave me a path, it mapped out my course. The hospital chaplain (don't you love these things? Out of the pages of a Victorian novel; he sits by your bed and talks about god's love, he tells you how to get your benefits. If you are the only person in your ward with no visitors he clings to you like a burr) answered accommodation ads for me and even went and looked at a couple of rooms. He had a nice ground floor room all fixed up for when I moved out, and I was signed on to the sick for three months. I didn't have to do anything but work at my plan and wait for my compensation to arrive.

I traced her from the address she'd put on the birth certificate. It was surprisingly simple. A second address in Manchester surfaced. I wrote and got a reply. Her parents had lived there till '89.

Their new address was enclosed. When I could walk I went to Manchester.

I was walking with a stick because of my back. It seemed to have a good effect on people. They wanted to help me. (One day they'll help me, the next they'll kick me in the teeth. Why is there hope then no hope? There were temperature graphs on the ends of the hospital beds going up and down like mountains, high low high high highest low. A switchback, a ride on a bucking bronco, being dragged screaming and unwilling from the heights to the depths and never knowing when the high will come again or how long last so I can't even begin to relish it only know it'll end – that's the life she's given. Me.)

The house was in a leafy suburb, Edwardian semi-detached. A prosperous pile. Two-job two-car two-children-and-an-au-pair territory. Needless to say no one was home. The security alarm winked redly over the door. I tried the neighbouring house. It was dingier, peeling paint, thick net curtains; a twitching at the corner of one. An old face peered at me. I smiled brightly and he came interminably slowly to the door. Opened it three inches on a chain. I was sweet I was a charmer.

'Oh thank you for coming to the door, I wonder if you can help me? I'm trying to find the Lovages, I've been working at my family tree and we're second cousins, I've been to their old house and they gave me the address next door to you, do you know if–' His brain was as slow as his legs, I had to give him the bright patter three or four times before any of it sank in.

Creaky croaky noises in the dark behind him and there was an old woman too peering and muttering. No give on the safety chain. Who can blame them? I'd have been in there in a flash, battering and mugging them, filling my pockets with their family heirlooms. Filthy pair of ancient dung beetles. It turned out the old Lovages (Granny and Grandad? Who would've knitted me mittens and held my hand to feed the ducks?) had been shunted off to a home. Were infirm/incapable/possibly dead (some wittering and grumpy mishearing between my aged friends here, she assumed they were dead because there'd been no Christmas card this year; he said why did she always forget Mrs Lovage had Parkinson's which wouldn't have got any better with time would it and how could she have held a pen?)

The son, young Mr Lovage (uncle?) lived next door now with his family but he and his wife both worked and–

'And his sister?' I chipped in cheerily. 'I especially wanted to know about Phyllis Lovage, the Lovages' daughter?'

He turned to his wife to confer but he had to glance back to check I wasn't nicking the doorknob or the leaves off the privet. I smiled and twinkled gratefully and he turned away again. Then shook his head. No, they'd never seen her.

'He did give us an address once, when he was–' he turned to the invisible crone – 'Didn't he give us a relative's address when he went on holiday just in case?'

'Oh, if you had her address I would be so thrilled – you see she and my mother used to play together when they were young – my mother's not well and it would bring her such happiness . . .'

Wasted effort because he retreated from the door and shuffled back into the hall to join his wife who was vaguely scuffling in a mountain of newspapers, envelopes and telephone directories balanced on an ancient black chest. I put my foot gently against the door to stop it banging shut in my face. Each time she put something down in the heap after peering at it short-sightedly, he'd pick it up and carefully read it from beginning to end. They wouldn't find it, even if it was staring them in the face. I would have to come back to the brother in the evening and who knows why Phyllis never showed her face there? Disgrace? Family feud? He'd want a better story than my current one – he'd have known his sister's friends. The old guy shook his head. He began to shuffle back towards me.

'Could I help?' I tried. 'I'm a very fast reader.'

'I think you'd better ask Mr Lovage, he'll be home around 6.30.' Hideous drooling old idiot with my mother's address pulsating in your hall, I'd put my hand straight on it, I'd know it–

'Did you try the address book dear?' croaked the female. Of course he didn't you stupid bat he was looking for a piece of paper. She turned the pages of a big address book with her claws.

'L-L-Lovage. Mabel and Peter. Yes, in Altrincham – that's the home . . . Phyllis. This'll be it will it? Phyllis MacLeod but she's under the Lovages, I can't think of any other Phyllis can you Harold? We've got a Scottish address for her.'

Oh glory be and patience rewarded. They creaked and they croaked as they looked for a pen.

'Here! I've got one in my bag – here–' and she copied it out like a snail on Valium and finally it was passed into my hot sticky hand. A *this will be your lucky day; open to check your bonus number!* envelope with the address of one Phyllis MacLeod spidered on to the back. Unfamiliar unpronounceable place names. MacLeod. MacHaggis. MacTartan. Married to a Scot. Who was oblivious to my existence? Nice little surprise for him as well as her, then.

When I got back to the station I phoned Directory Enquiries with her name and address and *they gave me her number*. She was still there. I dialled and a woman said 'Hello?' I asked for Phyllis MacLeod. 'Speaking.' Middle aged middle class not Scots it was her. On the end of the line, my mother. My ignorant unsuspecting mother. So easy to find, it was meant. She hadn't even bothered about me enough to cover her tracks. She hadn't even gone ex-directory. Chucked me away and never even considered I might be dangerous. Her indifference conjured, *entreated* my plan.

7 · Calum's treasure

It turned out my mother lived on an island. An island in the Hebrides, a small tear-shaped island called Aysaar just off another bigger island. She had certainly distanced herself. You wouldn't drop in casually, on the off-chance. Perhaps she thought distance would be enough to keep me away.

I gave up my room; not knowing how long it would take and not wanting to waste money. No point in hanging onto a faceless old room. When I came back it would be a new start. Why should I come back here at all?

If you book the rail ticket in advance it's 20 per cent cheaper, which was £17 off the price of the sleeper. Never once have I caught a train I booked in advance. It was another thing I imagined the death of my mother might facilitate. The catching of booked trains.

Island

I missed my train because I had left a box of books at Patsy's years before and she rang to say she was moving and had nowhere to put them. In desperation I took them in a taxi down to Yewtree Housing offices because there used to be room on top of the metal cupboards in reception but it turned out the metal cupboards had been removed to create more seating space for clients (*clients* = homeless). There was no one there who knew me so they wouldn't keep the books and I ended up going back to my room and putting my rucksack in the taxi too and belting down to the station and taking the box of books to left luggage. There was a queue of half-wits there and an old git with Alzheimer's who wanted to know how long I was leaving the books because they charge in advance. Also the box was too big. By the time I had finished arguing and paid for two weeks and walked away so he had no choice but to keep them it was four minutes after the train departure time and needless to say it was the first train ever in the history of rail transport to leave New Street on time.

So I missed it. I caught the next one (same time next day) and managed to bluff the ticket.

Which is not in itself interesting. But when I arrived after my night in a coffin of a sleeper and my change of train to a small sit-up-and-beg Scotrail through brochure-type scenery (stags, mountains, heather etc.) and finally the sea, I discovered that the ferries had been cancelled for the past 24 hours due to gales at sea. They had even closed the toll-bridge in the night.

Everything at Kyle was very still, and a lot of things were smashed. Signs hung crooked and splintered on their posts. A shop awning had been sucked out and half ripped off. Along the narrow shore-line was flotsam and jetsam in heaps, branches with the leaves still on them, a shattered canoe, broken plastic chairs. The still gleaming streets were littered with the contents of wind-scoured bins. A bus shelter had fallen into the road.

It was very quiet, almost stunned. The odd lorry or car drove cautiously over the bridge. The ferry started chugging over from the other side. The water was still as milk.

I walked across the bridge and the sky was pale empty blue; not so much as a seagull moved. A motorbike lay sprawled on its side near the jetty, and when I went into the town the pavement was spattered with shattered fragments of tile. I had to catch a bus to the next ferry, and the whole island lay still as death around me, like a spell.

I tried to plan. The island (by Patsy's old Phillips school atlas) was small. Maybe a couple of miles wide, ten or eleven miles long. There wouldn't be many people. Her address was Tigh Na Mara, Main Road, Ruanish. That was the only village of any size on the island. It was late September, end of the tourist season; maybe hard to find a place to stay.

How long would it take?

I wouldn't just find her and kill her, that wouldn't be right. First I would investigate her. Get her story out of her and put her in suspense. I would kill her when I was ready and when I had figured out a way of covering my tracks. No point spending the rest of my life in jail.

I considered my murder weapon: knife, or heavy blunt object? Considered that it would be necessary to have a story; why should I be on the island? How could I justify the length of time I might need to stay?

Island

This is what I came up with: I would be a student doing research on the island. A woman in Patsy's house was doing an OU course for years. From time to time she would whine about her project – how the deadline was on Wednesday and she still hadn't done it. Her project was the usual pointless academic exercise. She had to ask people from specified areas about their shopping habits and correlate them with their income and home address. Is there any form of so-called education more tedious than gathering and analysing facts to prove something you already know? Rich people from big houses use posh shops. Unemployed people on estates get ripped off by the local corner shop. *Wow*. That's interesting.

I invented myself a project. The study of an island population and recent demographic shifts, to cover my mother's life. Giving me licence to pry into all the cobwebby corners and stay there as long as I liked.

From the ferry the island looks dark and steep, half forested rising to a naked mountain. It's wild and uninhabited. Primitive, a place for primeval actions, perfect for a matricide.

Then when the ferry brings you in, spluttering black exhaust, you come to this neat wooden jetty. Which turns into a road, which trundles off across grassy wasteland towards a village. There's a yellow plastic salt and grit container at the bend in the road. It is blindingly ordinary. There's a field (unfenced) with a handful of scruffy sheep then the road grows a pavement and a terrace of grey houses. A post office shop, a dwarfish bus stop and a dingy pub.

I went up the road into the grim little village. A few cars from the ferry drove past me. I felt OK, as if I knew what to do. I liked the calm brightness in the air. There were a couple of old bids outside the post office in large stiff coats (brown and green respectively, one with grey woolly hat). I went into the post office for something to eat and the back of the door was covered in small ads. BICYCLE FOR SALE, ORGANIC POTATOES, ROOM TO LET.

ROOM TO LET. £45 PER WEEK. MRS MACLEOD, TIGH NA MARA. TEL. 5763.

Who wrote the plot? Who wrote the plot? *Me*. I made all this happen. Like magic. I am in control.

I got directions to the phone box from the ancient post office hag, and I dialled her number. As before, the distant voice, posh accent, no trace of Scots. I could come and see the room now. And that is how I walked out of the village of Ruanish along the main road past fields of sheep and cows until I came to a house on the left standing alone with a fenced front garden and a white gate. My mother's house.

I had some preconceptions, obviously. Which had been influenced by the phone voice. Partly I imagined her already dead, since that was without doubt coming to her. Chalk-faced with staring eyes. But also – you know, *mother*. Like in the books. Soft curly brown hair and comfortable clothes, hands floury from baking. Maybe even an apron. Tallish and thinnish like me, definitely she would be like me.

I broke into a sweat because I was in sight of the house and couldn't turn back and I was suddenly convinced she would recognise me. I hadn't worked out what to do. If she said for example, 'It's already let' or 'I've changed my mind' or even, 'You're my long-lost daughter', what the hell on earth would I do?

The door came lurching towards me in hot slow motion, I was on a fairground ride that wouldn't stop and I did not want to be there.

Then it opened and it wasn't her. It was an old woman with a bun and a pleated skirt and cardigan so I was able to get my breath. 'Hello, I've come about the room – I phoned Mrs–'

'That's right, come in.' She spoke with the voice from the phone.

'Are you–?'

'Phyllis MacLeod. Your first time on the island, is it? It's just along the hallway here.'

I was walking through a dark panelled hall behind a woman whose head I could see over, her hair was white her back was stooped she was sliding her sheepskin moccasins along the floor as if there was something wrong with her legs, she was supposedly my mother. Supposedly fifty. She looked about seventy. Her eyes were brown and she wasn't fat but those were the only two things we had in common in the entire universe.

The place smelt of plants, not flowers but old leafy smells, soggy boiled leaves, musty dried herbs, strange kinds of tea maybe. There was an underlying compost odour, a strange complicated smell filling up the whole still atmosphere of the house.

We did the stuff – deposit, keys, heating, sheets. The room was big and light, it had an internal door and my own external door, both lockable from inside. It was possible to be private. I avoided looking at her. She asked me nothing – not how long I'd stay or why, just a week's rent in advance and the firewood's in the shed. Then she pointed to the shelves above the bed. 'Will you be wanting to use the shelves?' They were full of stones, rocks and bits of driftwood.

'I don't think so.'

'I can get my son to clear them. He should have taken all that away with him. Let me know if you change your mind.'

Thus I discovered my brother.

I had an ancient and unrecognisable mother, and a brother I never dreamt of. But I was in my mother's house. My *mother's* house. There she was, just down the hall, shuffling around in her weird-smelling kitchen. With no more idea than fly in the air, who the fuck I was. I was as unknown to her as the babe unborn. As I had once been in her power to dump, trash – so she was now in mine to shatter.

I unpacked the rucksack. The wardrobe and drawers were anonymously empty; my brother had cleared out very thoroughly. My unlooked-for unnecessary usurping bastard of a brother. *Never were two children so happy . . .* I filled the kettle and boiled it, there was a jar of tea bags and box of long life milk in the tiny yellowed fridge. Under the sink a cupboard with crockery and a couple of pans and a wooden felt-lined tray of heavy old cutlery. No TV but there was a decent radio. Also electric ring and toaster. With food supplies and a bucket you could hole up in that room for days. Barricade yourself in. But there was nothing personal there. I went through everything, sniffing, turning stuff over. Nothing in the table drawer. Nothing under the bed. No clues, nothing.

I was lying on the bed idly stabbing the side of the mattress with my biro when there was a knock at the door. The outside door. I unlocked and opened it. There was a man – a kind of rural shambolic farm-idiot-type man, with a wall eye. He was blinking too much and there was a hesitation – nearly a stammer – in his speech. Pale blue eyes. Island inbreeding, I diagnosed. 'M-my mother asked me to sh-show you the woodshed.'

Whoa. Something nasty in the. 'My name's Nikki. Are you–?'

'Calum. I live here. There. Up – up the road.'

He was wearing a long coat although it wasn't cold, a long dirt-coloured coat with a ragged hem and holes in the elbows, and an old sagging rucksack on his back. Calum. My brother. The child my mother kept in preference to me.

First impression of Calum: a fool. Too tall, too thin, slightly stooped, and his clothes hang off him like someone's dressed a stick. He's nervy – jittery – standing still, his legs pulsing, his fingers drumming to some internal beat. What he made me think of was something that's been grown in the dark, forced, like rhubarb under a flowerpot – tall and pale and spindly.

I've spent a lot of time with rejects. Q. Why are there so many weirdos in children's homes? A. (1) Kids people don't want are by definition weird. (2) Being in care makes us weird. Not that Calum had been in care. No. He was weird without benefit of care. Not a good advert for twenty-odd years of mother-love. He stood there like a dolt staring at his boots.

'OK. Where is the woodshed?'

He turned around without speaking or looking at me and set off towards the garage. I followed. When he got to the edge of the scraggy lawn he stooped down so suddenly that I nearly fell over him. I swore but he didn't even look at me. He was delving with his long dirty fingers in the soil, separating something out, brushing the earth off it. Completely absorbed, as if I wasn't there.

'What are you doing?'

He turned it over in his palm then held it out to me. A dull fragment of pottery; as he kept rubbing it with his thumb you could make out intertwined blue flowers on a muddy white background. Two inches of the rim of someone's old cereal bowl. I looked at it and then at him – he was beaming from ear to ear. He was a fucking nutter. He stood up slowly and took the rucksack off his back. It was drooping and clanking with weight. He ceremoniously undid the straps and put the shard inside. Slowly did them up again and hoisted it onto his back. I had been standing waiting for about ten minutes. He set off again like it was nothing.

The woodshed's like a garage, with double doors. He pulled one open and I could see stacks of dark wood, near the door there was a chopping block and axe and pile of sawdust. It was dark at the back, no windows. 'I g-get the wood,' he said, not looking at me. 'I fetch it all.' He seemed pleased with himself.

'Good.'

'From the sea.'

'Isn't it wet?'

'Wet on this side. Dry on that.' He indicated.

There was a sudden movement in the darkness at the far end of the shed, a scrabbling. 'Are there rats?'

He turned his head, one eye was on me one on the roof of the house behind me how could she? Was even this preferable to me? 'It's my father.'

I stared into the darkness at the end of the shed. I could make out the dark silhouette of the woodpiles against the end wall. I couldn't see a person, I couldn't see the paleness of a face. How has he got a father? 'Is he coming out?'

Calum shook his head quickly. He moved on into the darkness of the shed and I followed him out of the daylight; as my eyes adjusted I could see heaps of wood, some chopped, some in logs and planks and splintered packing cases, it smelt damp and briny and hotter than outside. But I couldn't see the father. Tall scare-crow Calum was coming back out of the darkness the light beamed on his potato face. Then he suddenly took a lunging step and was right next to me, reaching out for my neck. I jumped out of his way and banged into the doorframe – crashed out and ran across the garden to my open door. A lunatic a sex maniac a fucking dangerous nutter hanging about, grabbing at me – *what?* He shouldn't be there he should be locked up. It was beyond belief. There was a gentle knock on the outer door. I shouted 'What?'

'S-sorry if I scared you.' Sorry if he scared me. The Addams family. Oh I'm not scared when a lunatic makes a grab for my throat in a pitch dark woodshed on a lonely island where no one knows me, it's just fine. I wonder what happened to her last lodger.

'Go away.' I stood listening behind the door and after a bit I heard his heavy boots plodding away down the garden. I opened the door a crack to check he'd gone then sat on the doorstep and rolled a fag. It's not overlooked – there's a scrubby open garden and then over a fence and a broken wall, the sea.

So. Free gift. Surprise in every packet. A brother. And not just any old brother, but a sex-offending retard. A special half-wit of a brother; was there no end to my mother's generosity? Why would you get rid of a baby that seemed to be all there and keep a defective?

OK. I would kill him too. The sun was shining on the stubbly grass and the flat wrinkling sea. It was a bald ugly place, she was mad they were both mad I was going to put an end to it. Brother. Father. Nuclear family invented after the disposal of item one, the unwanted child. Of, presumably, a different father. An absentee, unavailable for marriage. Too old. Too young. Married to someone else. In prison. Incarcerated. Dead. Related. The children of incest are meant to be peculiar. Like Calum.

Suddenly he was coming back, head down, fast, why is it you can always tell if they're odd from a person's walk? Clutching a big dirty plastic bag. He was a matchstick man, if I blew he would fall over he'd never bloody frighten me again. I stood up. He stopped in the middle of the lawn. 'I b-brought you some veg.'

'What?'

'Potatoes. Carrots and stuff.' He came towards me slowly, set the bag down in front of me then backed off again. I poked it open with my foot – I could see dirty yellow onions and orange carrots, a big earthy heap of vegetables.

'Where d'you get them?'

'Grow 'em.' He was staring at me again gawping like a three-year-old.

'What d'you want?'

He raised his hand and touched his earlobe. 'Pretty.'

I felt my ear. I was wearing the starfish earrings. Little dangly silver starfish with a green stone in the middle I got them from a crystal shop in Hebden Bridge the stone was – opal? Jade? Something with calming properties. Believe that and you'll believe anything. 'Is that what you wanted to look at?'

'Mustn't grab.'

I unhooked it and passed it to him and he dangled it from his skeleton's thumb and forefinger and peered at it without speaking. Eventually he nodded and held it out to me.

'Glad you like it.'

Sarcasm was wasted on him. He squatted down on his haunches like some famine-struck African peasant and began to comb through the grass with his fingers. I didn't want his crappy veg his nutter's occupational therapy veg and I didn't want him sitting outside my door. Maybe he thought it was still his door. She kicked him out – but only just down the road. Couldn't she get rid of him? She was good at getting rid of people.

'I like s-smoking.' He was watching me roll one. I held it towards him and he took it and sucked on it greedily. 'She doesn't let me.'

'Smoke? Your mother?'

He nodded. Of course. She'd be worried about his health I suppose. About the lung-purity of a shambling gibbering mental defective. That makes sense.

'This was my room.'

Very good. 'Why did you move out?'

'She doesn't l-like my treasure.'

'What treasure?'

He waved his cigarette in the air. 'Take it away. On Gerry's trailer, p-pull it with the tractor.'

'Where to?'

'My house.'

I wanted to go in and start a conversation with the old witch, I wanted to get on with what I'd come for not be sidetracked by this ape.

'It's good. I'll show you.'

I felt in my pocket my penknife was there if I needed it. I could already tell he wasn't in fact dangerous – not like I thought in the woodshed; he wasn't going to leap on me, he was just going to hang around and bore me to death like some thick snotty-nosed kid. 'At your house?'

'In the garden. Come on.' He got up and dropped his stub. Ground it carefully into the grass with his heel then picked it up and put it in his pocket. I stood up and followed him, across the garden and along the narrow footpath that ran from there parallel with the shore, in the direction opposite to the village.

There was a little grey prefabricated bungalow ahead of us, surrounded by huge mounds of swedes or something. I thought winter feed for the cattle. As we got closer I realised the mounds weren't swedes.

61

'I get it from the sea.' Around his house were hillocks of junk, separated according to type. There was a mountain of footwear – shoes, boots, trainers; one of driftwood; one of plastic – bottles, food containers, floats, crates, broken toys, polystyrene. There was a smaller one of iron and metal, mostly orange with rust. There was a predominantly black rubber mountain (mainly tyres but some diving equipment, hosepipes, bits of dinghies, lifebelts). There were four hillocks of glass, clear, green, brown and blue. There was a stinking fly-buzzing mound of clothes and sacking, and a reddish pile of broken bricks and tile. There was a hill of bones and fossils. Like EC food mountains. He was grinning from ear to ear.

'What d'you do with it?'

'Collect it.' He seemed to think this was a reasonable answer.

'But do you use it for anything? Can you sell it?'

He shook his head, uninterested by the question, picked up a couple of shoes which had slipped down and wedged them back in their mountain. 'W-one thousand and seventy-six shoes.'

'Are they all odd?'

'Twenty-six pairs.'

I walked over and looked in the window of his cottage. It was a tip.

'Why? Why d'you collect them?'

'The sea brought them here.' His garden was behind, it was neat with straight rows, cabbages, onions, stuff like that – big as a small field. He was busy checking his treasure, in the sun it stank of rotting fabric, the sea-soaked leather of sandals and boots was cracked and curling it was nothing but junk, bloody great mountains of junk. He pulled out a boot and inspected it minutely, turning it to pore over the sole.

'I'll see you.' He didn't even look up as I went back to my room. A brother was not necessary I did not need a fucking idiot brother breathing down my neck.

8 · Seals

Fly soar swoop *fly*. Fly soar swoop fly. I had to keep myself up. I had to concentrate on her. The house was silent but I was sure she was at home. I went into the hall and listened. The stairs led away up to my right, and a dark passage beside them ended in a door which stood open a crack. Daylight shone through. The bathroom was opposite me; to the left, at the far end of the hall, the front door and before it one other closed door. I went down that end and listened – nothing. Was the man still in the wood-shed? Were the pair of them sitting in silence somewhere listening to me creeping about? I went down the dark passage alongside the stairs, listened at the door (nothing) then pushed it wider open. I was expecting emptiness but she was frozen at her kitchen table with an eye-dropper in her hand squeezing drips into a small brown bottle. When she saw me she gave a tiny shake of the head and started whispering aloud, finishing counting off the drops. 'Thirteen, fourteen, *fifteen*.' She carefully screwed the lid on the bottle and emptied what was left in the dropper into a white bowl.

'What is it?' she asked impatiently, as if I was interrupting something vital.

'I wondered if you could tell me where to get supplies – eggs, milk – is there a farm nearby?'

There was a handwritten book on the table in front of her, she kept glancing down at it. Instructions? A recipe? She had blue pouches under her eyes and loose creased skin, never in a million years would I have picked her out. She didn't look at me but concentrated on shaking the tiny bottle then emptying a saucer full of brittle dead leaves onto the table in front of her and mashing them with a miniature rolling pin.

'Get everything at the post office. Where you saw my card.' She didn't even glance up.

'What about fresh fish? Can I buy that any–'

'You'll have to excuse me,' she said. 'I'm just in the middle of–' She turned quickly to take the kettle off the stove behind her and pour a little boiling water into the white bowl. I stepped back into the hall and pulled the door to. Rude cow. 'You'll have to excuse me. I haven't seen you for twenty-nine years and I'm a bit busy mixing witches' brew right now, come back in another twenty-nine why don't you?' You deserve what's coming to you lady.

She was skinny and fragile she would be easy to beat but where was the father lurking? Not with her in the kitchen. Upstairs? Gone out?

I got my bag and set out the back way to go to the store – I noticed the woodshed door was closed so there was nobody left in there. A skinny grey cat ran past me and in through a cat flap in the kitchen door. Right at the back behind the kitchen there was a wild-looking garden plot without a single flower, with things in pots stuffed between things that were planted – scrawny straggling plants that looked diseased. Bunches of shrivelled leaves hung outside the kitchen door, and strings of old seaweed and a branch of withered berries.

I bought tea, milk, bread, butter, eggs, beans and biscuits. When I got back the house was just as deathly quiet as before. I went across the hall to the toilet – not a peep. I didn't even know if they were upstairs or downstairs; the kitchen door was shut. Listening for them to move was like listening in an empty house and I made myself go out again, to walk and plan.

It was five o' clock. The sky had clouded over but it wasn't cold. I went up the lane past Calum's dump, heading for the island's north. Then there was a path to the left so I took it down to the sea and tried to walk along the shore. It was low black rock – no beach – but it ended in a sheer cliff that jutted out into the sea, and I had to scramble up to a field. I kept going but there was no path. It was horrible walking – inlets and soggy streams and barbed wire fences and patches of gorse and brambles, you couldn't stick to a direction at all. Eventually I cut back across to the lane and just walked up that.

Planning. Next time I saw her – tonight probably, or else tomorrow – I'd ask for her help with my project. Invite her for a cup of tea, since she was clearly incapable of basic social skills like friendly chatter in passing. I'd do a bit of probing into the man's comings and goings. I needed to know when she would be home alone. A car crept up behind me and I had to stand in the ditch so it could pass. The driver was a hundred years old, minimum; the whole island was an old folks' home. After the car I heard footsteps on the lane; Calum was hurrying after me, foolish grin on face, ancient rucksack on back. Like a big eager dim dog. 'Going for a w-walk?'

No I'm painting my toenails what does it look like you thick git? I didn't want him near me. Was it congenital, what he'd got? Had I got some of the same crap genes? Might I one day have a kid and find it a grinning shambling Calum-idiot? Another great legacy from Mama.

The lane forked and he led off to the right. Then stopped and waited for me.

'What's up there?'

'Y-you can see the mountains. On the mainland.'

Fascinating. Riveting. Where did he think I'd just come from? The island looked a dump to me. There were no trees here, just bare lumpy pasture and stupid sheep that stood staring with their yellow eyes until you got close then clattered off in a panic. The lane was going vaguely uphill, there were no houses no cars no people. Wow! There was a tractor! Yes a red tractor parked in a gateway, exciting stuff here Nikki, and Calum pointed it out and said something incomprehensible (Macpherson? Macintosh? MacBurger?) referring to the owner no doubt so I nodded and he grinned to show how brill he thought it was and we toiled on up the grey lane. The light was a sodden grey and even the green of the fields was greyed. He was walking fast, swinging crooked like a broken gate.

'What does your father do?'

'He's drowned.'

'Drowned?'

He nodded.

'But – when did he drown?'

'S-seven years ago.' I caught up with him. He was entirely unconcerned, walking along as if he owned the place.

'But you said it was him. In the woodshed.'

He turned his head and his good eye looked into mine. 'He comes there sometimes. There're some planks from his b-boat.'

'He's dead?'

'Yes, in the sea.'

We walked quite a long way in silence. Mentally I went through the contents of the hall and bathroom. No male things in the bathroom; no big shoes or coats in the hall; no sound of heavy footsteps upstairs. She hadn't mentioned a husband, only a son. Perhaps there had never been a father, perhaps he was entirely fictitious. I hadn't *seen* the guy in the woodshed, all I'd heard was a noise. I had no way of measuring how cracked Calum was.

'What did he do?'

'Fisherman.' He stopped abruptly and stepped into the shallow ditch at the side of the lane. Bent down and started scrabbling through the brambles and ferns. 'Shiny,' he said. Then triumphantly pulled out a whole wing mirror on a twisted metal stem and placed it reverently in his rucksack.

'What're you going to do with that?'

'Keep it.' He straightened up and set off again. We went through a gateway and across a rough field, it was curving away down to the sea now, the sea on the eastern side. It wasn't any different to the sea on the western side; just as brown and flat and sloppy, no waves no foam no golden beaches. Thick low grey cloud squatting on the mainland hills in the distance – a thoroughly dismal sight.

'Why aren't there any waves?'

He looked at me as if I was the thick one. 'Big waves.' He chanted a verse like a nursery rhyme. 'The Blue Men are breast high/with f-foam grey faces./When billows toss,/oh who would cross/the Blue Men's kyles.'

I knew he wasn't capable of trying to impress me but I was deeply irritated all the same: I hate the way people who know things act as if it's incredible that you don't. Why assume there are certain god-given bloody things everybody's born knowing? 'What's kyles?'

'The c-crossing.' He waved his arm at the channel between the island and the mainland.

'OK.'

'B-big waves–' He put his hand up above his head. 'This high.'

In his dreams. The channel looked like a puddle in a ditch. He led the way on over the uneven ground, past exciting events like a rock sticking through the soil or a boggy bit we had to skirt. I thought the shoreline was crap. A pebbly shelf, narrower or wider according to the tide – and nothing there. We didn't even see any gulls, it was like after the end of the world. 'Look.' He stood like a post.

I looked. Nothing. Flat sea with low brown rocks. 'What?'

He muttered something I didn't catch and a hump of rock detached itself and plopped into the sea. 'Seals,' said my genius brother. Half-brother. More brown lumps shifted themselves and slid into the water. He grinned at me as if it was some major pyrotechnical display he'd arranged especially for my benefit. I gave him a thumbs-up. Fantastic! And we carried on down towards the water. If that was the high spot – a brown blob falling into the water at 300 yards – I was ready to turn back. We went slithering down the muddy rocks to sea level and then he perched on a boulder and carefully took off his rucksack. He extricated a big old check-patterned thermos and with great concentration poured a cup.

'Does your mum make that for you?'

He shook his head and passed me the cup. It was sweet tea but I drank it anyway, then I rolled us both a cig.

'Did your dad catch them?'

He looked gormless.

'The seals. Did he catch them?'

'He took – he took people out to see them. In his boat. The tourists.' He had the crookedest teeth I've ever seen.

'Very good.'

'He told them the story and they l-liked it.'

Come on then, might as well have the full entertainment package since I've paid my fare and I'm sat here with an idiot staring at a puddle of brown sea and sipping lukewarm tea. 'What story?'

'The seal girl.' He was staring out to the rocks, his mouth a bit open; you'd think if his mother cared an iota for him she'd have taken the poor sod to a dentist.

'Go on.'

'Some crofters, they were thrown out of their c-croft. They went in their boat going up the kyle and in a storm it was, their boat overturned. Right near Seal Rock.' He stopped and looked at me.

'That it?'

He shook his head perfectly seriously. 'They all d-drowned but the baby. The baby was taken up by the seals.'

Of course it was, taken up by lovely cuddly furry bewhiskered seals and fed and tickled and cuddled and cared for and the mummy seal knitted it booties and the daddy seal caught a fishy-wishy for its diddums tea. Calum had stopped to try and remember what he was talking about. It was like waiting for paint to dry.

'She sucked milk from a mother with pups. She learned to squeak and bark like a seal. Sh-she learned diving and swimming instead of walking.'

'Yeah and how did she get on in winter in the ice?'

His good eye widened in surprise. 'No ice here. She caught fish and ate them raw, p-people saw her on the rocks playing with the seals. Her hair was long like a mermaid. The fishermen tried but no one could ever get near her.'

'And it all ended badly.'

He stared at me stupidly for a minute then started snapping a twig of heather into fragments. It was enough to make me grateful for what I'd got – at least I *could* fly and fall, instead of creeping on my belly through the dirt.

'Well? What happened?'

'Sh-she's still there.'

Sure. Like his father in the woodshed. He packed up his thermos and we set off again. He wasn't going to tell me the end of the story. I didn't even want to hear the stupid thing in the first place but now he was offended and not speaking. He was making me feel bad, unkind to a dumb animal. Why should I feel sorry for him? Why the hell should *I* feel sorry for *him*?

We plodded along in silence again. Clearly he was *capable* of talking. I asked about his mumsy and dadsy and their idyllic island life. It was like dealing with a child; once he started he couldn't stop. Turned out Daddy MacLeod kept a lot of lobsterpots. Sometimes he took men with big rods out deep-sea fishing; he had sheep too which had passed on to Calum.

'Did you get his boat? Do *you* take tourists out?'

He looked at me with a strange face. 'It sank. It broke up. I'm not allowed–'

'On the sea?'

'Near the water. No Calum.'

Well what a nice protective mother caring so deeply for her son's well-being.

'He was ang-angry.'

I realised then that I could pump him all I liked. 'Why?'

'They were fighting and he j-just – he went out and banged the door.'

'What happened?'

He shrugged. 'Bits of the boat washed up around the shore.'

When I let myself back into my room there were lights on in the house. I opened my door to the hall a crack and I could hear the quiet burble of a TV. She was shut up somewhere watching telly. The room at the end of the hall, nearest the front door – that's where I reckoned she was.

I ate beans on toast and paced and listened and heard every move she made which was few. At 10.15 she turned off the TV and went along the hall to the kitchen; she was in there maybe a quarter of an hour then I heard her shuffling back along the hall. There was a bitter herby smell. She drew the bolt on the front door and turned off the downstairs lights then went slowly up the stairs, a couple of them creaked. I could hear her moving about upstairs also the sound of running water and toilet flush, she had another bathroom up there. There was definitely only her in the place. The last noise I heard was about 10.45; after that she was quiet, sleeping the sleep of the ignorant who don't yet know what's coming to them. I noted down the times. A murderer would need to know all her moves; know her little routine. I imagined going upstairs when she was out, I would look in her room for traces of me. The fact that she didn't know I was here, the fact that I had her in my power – it was a physical pleasure. It swelled me, making me tingle with pleasurable anticipation.

Island

About an hour after she'd gone to bed I crept out into the dark hall in my socks. The floor was tiled it was cold. I stood at the bottom of the stairs listening then went to the TV room. After I'd turned the handle the door swung open on its own. The floor was wooden and warmer as soon as I stepped on to it. There was a little glowing ash in the fireplace. My mother's sitting room. I closed the door and waited. But my eyes couldn't make sense of the inky blackness and after a minute I turned on the light. Sod it. If she found me I'd deal with her.

The room was full of old stuff. Not the sort of room I've ever lived in. I've seen it – in films, on telly – but I've never been in it. The walls were full of books, old hardback books with plain cloth covers, dull blues and reds and dusty black. In the gaps between the bookcases were prints, crummy old maps and pictures of old sailing boats, a big star-map, and drawings of plants and leaves and cross-sections of flowers with spidery writing on them. The furniture was old and none of it matched, there was a faded red velvet covered chair with a very straight back, rounded like a coin. Two tall black wooden tables with twisted carved legs. One of those sofas with one arm missing, in a dingy floral print. The mantelpiece was crammed: candlesticks, a china shepherdess, bits of paper, stones, dried leaves and twigs in a jar, squat brown bottles of liquid with labels in Latin, a mug with pipes and spills in it, photographs in silver frames. Photographs.

Her about twenty years younger next to a big solid man, staring calmly out of the picture. She was holding a bouquet, it looked like a wedding photo although she was wearing a dark dress. Her with a kid in a garden. Calum. Her with a kid on a bicycle. The man in the middle of a huddle of posed and grinning people on the deck of a boat. The man holding up a big fish.

Seals

Family snaps.

Fucking cow. I sat on the red velvet chair facing the blank grey telly. The room was full of old junk like an antique shop or one of those rooms they have in a museum, *typical interior from the 1930s*. Where'd she got it? It was like a lifetime's stuff. Parents' and grandparents' stuff. The rectangle of carpet on the polished wood floor was thin, it was worn and frayed under my feet where I sat on the red chair. But it didn't feel poor it felt classy. There was a glass-fronted cabinet with stuff on display: thin old china painted midnight blue and orange; old pinkish wine glasses and a cut glass decanter, little crystal tumblers, all crammed in together probably worth hundreds.

Was it hers or the man's, MacLeod's? I pulled a book off the shelf. Culpeper's *Complete Herbal*. Inside the front cover was handwritten 'Phyllis Lovage'. I looked in another further along – it was in Italian – then one from the opposite bookcase, a book about identifying medicinal plants. Her name was in all of them. It was her stuff. As I closed the plant book I noticed something brown poking out from between its pages; I let it fall open at the centre and there was a squashed brown rose. I picked it up by its flattened stem, it was brittle and dry and impossibly flat. She was keeping a dead rose.

I pulled open one of the drawers under the display cabinet. It was overflowing with papers. Bills, letters, receipts. I started to read a letter from someone called Anita thanking her for the lotion and saying her skin had cleared up completely now. There were receipts for the sale of lambs; bills for sheep dip, mortgage information. The bottom drawer was full of knitting patterns, absolutely stuffed so it wouldn't open properly. Mixed in with the patterns were more photos, of a fat-faced rather odd-looking toddler. Calum.

I sat on the floor next to the cabinet. All this stuff. All this *life* of hers. All this past that she had that was hers and not mine all gathered together and hoarded like it *was* something, like it meant something, that had been kept hidden from me so I wouldn't know about it or have any of it. All these things she had done and people she had known all excluding me. I had one box of left luggage with nothing in it but crap, cheap paperbacks, some boots that hurt my feet and a pair of polyester sheets.

She had books she'd had since she was a kid; pictures, ornaments, photos. There are no photos of me except from school, a little face people skim over looking for their own children. To have photos, there has to be someone who wants to look at you. It was too huge to swallow it was too much.

On the ornate little table next to the red chair there were two brown prescription bottles with her name on. Good, she deserved to be ill. She deserved to have this prised off her all this accretion she'd coated herself in as if she had a right to some kind of happiness or meaning. What the hell right did she have?

When she was dead it would belong to me. All this stuff in this house. To me and dopey Calum. We were her heirs. I was shaking with fury. It would never be mine. I would never have a mantelpiece like that casually full of stuff accumulated over years. I would always be flimsy and unreal and not backed up by anything; nothing would ever stick to me.

A desire was growing in me a huge red flaming lust to pick up the poker and start smashing that room that complacent cosy lifetime of a room. Crash through the glass cabinet doors smash the china smash the glasses smash the vases and the toby jugs, rake the old prints off the walls and let them shatter in their frames, stab the poker through the thin fabric of the chaise-longue and chair, drag the drawers out spill them on the ground scuffle the papers and photos and trinkets with my feet swipe the poker along the mantelpiece hit at the pipes and shepherdess until they were in tiny fragments break it up and smash it all.

It was what she deserved.

I had to get myself up and walk stiff-legged to the door my mouth was dry my tongue was thick I was swollen with lust to lay about me and annihilate that room. I made myself switch off the light and close the door and edge down the hall to my own anonymous room. I made myself lie on the bed and I pulled the covers over me and I fell asleep immediately.

9 · Table Rock

I didn't wake till ten, a very good omen, a deep still sleep a mark of approval for my plan. I could find out what I wanted from my simple brother. I could spy on her and winkle her out. I could have power over her and relish it.

I spent the morning with a pad of lined paper and a ring binder creating my Open University project. So I could pretend to be working on it at relevant moments; so if she ever thought of spying on *me* (she wouldn't, complacent cow, she didn't even consider I might be dangerous) then she would find I had a good excuse to be there.

She was in the kitchen first thing, I heard the radio, she went along the hall a few times but didn't leave the house. I liked listening to her and her not knowing I was doing it or why. At 12.30 someone came in the front door and banged it. Calum. He called out 'Hello?' and she came past my door, I heard her saying something about the mud on his shoes and needing a new light bulb in the pantry. They both went along to the kitchen. Mother and son, how sweet.

She'd cooked him a proper dinner from the smell of it. I opened my back door and sat and had a fag to quell the pinpricks of rage I felt. Imagine someone cooking your dinner. Doing it for you, anticipating your arrival and your taste. Who ever did that for me? She did it when he was a kid and she was still doing it now. I should have gone in there and asked for fifteen years of meals. She owed me that at least.

I took myself off to the village I was managing myself like a teacher manages a rowdy last-lesson class, I was keeping myself on the straight and swooping, glide and flying line, I was going to do exactly according to plan and have no difficult or intrusive or inconvenient fall. The pub was shut at lunchtime – centre of the universe as the island was – so I bought a used-looking pie from the post office (narrowly; that was closing at 1 p.m.) and a couple of booklets with dingy old photos giving some type of history of the island. Useful for OU. The old bat who served me asked me where I was staying. She must have remembered me from yesterday.

'Mrs MacLeod's. Tigh Na Mara.'

'Oh aye. Stayed there before?'

I shook my head.

'And how're ye findin' it? All right?' She was beady; suggesting she didn't think it would be.

'Why d'you ask?'

'Och, no reason. It's just some people find her – a wee bit stand-offish. And Calum–'

'Calum's pretty strange.'

'There's no harm in the lad. But if ye were after another place to bide I've a wee room in ma cottage . . .'

'Thanks. I'm not really sure how long I'm staying.'

'Aye. Well.' The woman busied herself spreading sheets of faded brown paper over the oranges and tomatoes in the window; the sun was beating in on them.

'Is there a Mr MacLeod?' I asked.

She glanced at me. 'There was.' There was a strange silence.

'What happened?' I asked.

'Well may ye ask,' she said bitterly. She finished with the brown paper and straightened up to face me, lowering her voice. 'He fell into ma lady's clutches and that wa' tha.'

'Someone told me he drowned.'

'Aye. And would y'expect the best sailor on th'isle tae drown?' She opened the door for me, followed me out and locked up behind us. 'She hasnae a friend this side o' Glasgow and tha's god's truth.' Her voice rose to its normal pitch. 'I'll be off to ma dinner then. Gude-bye.'

I sat on the bench outside the pub to eat, and looked in the book at old photos of men with tools standing in front of a huge unidentifiable machine, and two men with guns guarding them. The caption said they were German prisoners of war working in the iron mine. Did they ever get home or were they still here, little old men behind grey net curtains, still imprisoned from their homeland? I thought it would be a bad place to be kept against your will, this.

When I got back to the house it was very quiet. Calum had gone. She was in the kitchen. I could hear the odd clink of dishes and scraping noises. I had been there 24 hours. OK. I had discovered she spent long periods of time on her own making witchy potions. It would be easy enough to pick a time to do it when nobody would find her for hours. Night. Night would be the best. But before I did it I wanted to make her talk. I wanted to know what the fuck she'd done with her life that was so vital I couldn't have been in it.

The kitchen door opened and she came along the hall and started creaking up the stairs. Going for a pee; she seemed to be leaving the downstairs bathroom for my sole use. I stood inside my door waiting to bump into her accidentally when she came back downstairs. But everything went quiet; I kept my eyes on my watch and ten minutes passed. I went out into the hall and halfway up the stairs – the bathroom door was open up there. The bloody woman'd gone to bed.

I stood on the stairs waiting for another five minutes. Not exactly easy to engage her in casual conversation when she's taking an afternoon nap. I stood in a wave of heat with my nails making white dents in the heels of my palms, torn over whether to go for it there and then or wait for a chance to talk to her first. Once she was dead there'd be no chance of finding anything out.

The house was throbbing with quietness. At last I went out again, there was nothing else to do; I set out along the lane and just walked, in the opposite direction to the village. Passed the place where Calum and I had turned right yesterday and carried straight on. To my left the sea curved in towards the road. It was a shallow pebbled bay. I could see a figure standing on an outcrop of black rock. Calum again. Manky Calum. Catatonic Calum. With his rucksack on his back like a hunchbacked stork. I climbed down to the bay. He was staring out to sea. When I got closer I could hear he was muttering to himself. I got close before he turned and even then he just kind of nodded in recognition then went back to his staring and muttering. I sat on a rock. The sea was completely flat with a few black rocks sticking up. Some of those black birds, cormorants, standing on the most distant one. Nothing moving. The sky was grey and the sea was grey and right out in the distance was the grey silhouette of another island. It was a dreary view. At last Calum turned to me.

'OK?' I said.

He nodded. I thought of asking him who he'd been talking to but that would make me as mad as him.

'I can't find a coastal path. Is there one?'

'No. You can walk, but n-not always along the shore.'

I already knew that much. I wondered if he spent the whole time wandering about. He obviously had no employment. If his father was an islander . . . 'Have you got many relatives here?'

'I had a sis-sister, she died.'

It was a minute before I could speak. 'When?'

'Before I was born. She was c-called Susan.'

Well. So she was. I stared at the cormorants thinking one of them might go for a dip or do a tap dance or anything that might give me a slight diversion.

'It's her birthday next week.'

I looked at him but he was perfectly oblivious. Yes. It is. My birthday. October the 2nd. 'What d'you do on her birthday?'

'We have a cake for her, and sing.'

You evil cow Phyllis MacLeod, you monstrous evil cow. I have to remember to breathe.

'People shouldn't forget. Even b-babies who die.'

Excellent. Now I realise the root of my problems. All these years here's me been struggling along imagining I'm alive. Silly me. I'm dead. That explains it all. That explains why I haven't got a mother or a father or a home or a life because people who're dead don't have those things. Silly silly me. I get up and go over the rocks to the narrow pebbly shoreline. Just to be moving. He comes after. He's got a stick like a blind man.

'What's the matter?'

'Nothing.'

'D'you want a d-drink of tea?'

'No.'

He starts to take his rucksack off. 'Look what I found this morn–'

'Fuck off! Fuck off you moron and leave me alone!' I scramble away across the stones leaving him standing there gawping. Catching flies in his gormless gob. There's nothing but my feet crunching angrily and the slurge and suck on stones of the sea. What the hell is this about? I am quickly up to the lane again.

If he knows about his sister, did his father know? Does that make his father my father?

I walked fast and blind along the lane – thinking about going into her sitting room. I'd often imagined revealing myself to her, but now with the real woman, her real room in my mind's eye I could see how it would be. Well not exactly because she could do a number of things, she had a variety of options like believing me or not believing me or pretending to believe or not believe me; but I'd burst in there without knocking. (Why throw me away then pretend to be sad? If she regretted leaving me why not look for me?)

She would jerk her head up from her book as if she was blind and take off her glasses to rub her eyes. She might even have been asleep.

'I want to talk to you.'

'I see.' She would fold her glasses carefully, set them on the little table at her elbow. I would sit on the rounded red velvet chair, straight backed, facing her. Like on a stage.

'I have something to tell you.'

Her hand would dart nervously to her glasses then fall back, she would peer at me closely. 'Calum?'

'No.' She would be relieved. Ha, she would have no idea.

I've rehearsed it in my dreams and in my wakings a thousand times and a thousand ways but the rehearsal and the repetition don't matter because whatever I say – whatever predetermined sentence I let out into her stuffy cluttered room will have the same effect; the fingernail under the corner of the mask, the start of the unpeeling. And once it starts it won't stop, it will go on to the same result no matter what and how we do it, it will rip or slip or jolt or tear or slide off easily but whichever course, the result will be the same: she'll be unmasked. Whether she denies me or admits me whether she constructs an elaborate castle of lies or falls open at the truth with a single blow.

I was walking fast but suddenly aware of being cold. It wasn't a wind it was a wedge of cold air like when you're swimming in the sea and you move into an area of water that's suddenly much colder. Looking up I noticed the sea and rocks had disappeared behind a bank of mist.

She says I'm dead. So she can have the virtuousness of remembering me without the inconvenience of keeping me. *Why?* The lane in front of me disappeared. Literally. The mist – fog, cloud, whatever – was white and thick enough to touch; it smeared coldly against my face, it stuck in my throat and made me cough. It was right up against my eyes, everything around me blocked out. I stopped. The coldness flowing all around me made me shiver. I took one step forward, but I couldn't see my foot. I couldn't see my own legs. The vanishing of everything made me dizzy. It was absolutely quiet.

She makes a cake!

I couldn't remember how close to the edge of the lane I was. I shuffled sideways a couple of steps then realised I wasn't even sure if there was a hedge – or a ditch – or even a straight drop over a cliff to the sea. I hadn't been looking. I turned around slowly on the spot, nearly overbalancing. Nothing but thick white fog. A feature of the island presumably. A delightful characteristic; fog rolls in from the sea. Cloud falls down from the sky. Hooray for nature.

I assumed it was temporary, like interference on TV. That it would clear or lift. But the minutes crawled past and nothing happened. My eyes began to ache from peering. My legs began to ache from standing. I turned round again. Nothing. I took a few steps but it was completely pointless. I had no idea where the lane began or ended; where it curved; which way I was facing; whether I was close or far from the shore. The only thing to do was sit it out. I sat down carefully and felt the road surface around me. A rough pebbly lane. The fog seemed if possible to be thickening – not that it blotted out more (it couldn't, it already blocked the lot) but that it was less white, it let less light through. I strained to hear the sea but there was nothing.

Suddenly I heard or felt a sound. A tapping. Felt it in the surface of the road and heard it muffled in my ears. Almost immediately something invisible hit me and the tapping stopped. I screamed.

'N-Nikki?'

'Calum!' I scrambled to my feet. He was a dark shape. His arm grasped mine. 'How did you know the way?'

His disembodied voice came out of the fog, he was tapping the ground with his stick. 'You turned up the lane.'

He was watching me. Now I was alone in zero visibility with a mental retard I'd just told to fuck off. 'Where are you going?'

'Home. You hold m-my arm.'

'But you can't see–'

'I know the way.' He linked his left arm through my right and half turned me round.

'I don't even know which way I'm facing.'

'It's OK – h-here.' He tapped with his stick feeling for the edge of the lane – and we moved off together into the invisible world.

The journey lasted hours. From time to time he'd raise his stick and slash out to either side, hitting hedgerow or clacking stone wall or sharply rapping a gate. It was as if the rest of the world had been completely removed, leaving not even a shadow of itself, not even a whisper of sound. There was nothing but solid whiteness and us toiling through it. Once he stopped and said, 'Cigarette?' I rolled a couple blind and we stood and puffed our white smoke into the thick white air.

'I was going to sit and wait for it to clear.'

'It gets cold.'

Well yes. I was already shivering. 'How long will it last?'

'Tonight. Maybe tomorrow.'

While he thrashed his stick about looking for walls or turnings I let go his arm and I was helpless. I wouldn't have dared to take a step. When he tap-tapped back to me and bumped his extended arm into mine (outstretched, supplicant) I felt nothing but relief. He could have been leading me to the edge of a cliff; mummy's boy could have been taking me to the sharks.

'You c-cold?'

'A bit.'

He stopped and let go my arm. His rucksack bumped against my shoulder as he took it off. 'I've got a spare jumper.' He passed it to me, it felt rough and loose and it smelt of seaweed as I pulled it over my head, but it added a layer of warmth. He held out his arm and we moved off again. 'You were angry–'

'Nothing. It doesn't matter.' There was a silence.

'D-did you see Table Rock?'

'What?'

'Table Rock.'

'I didn't notice much at all, to be honest.' Dense fog in your eyes upsets your balance. You want to pitch forwards into it. You think you'll fall and fall. I tried to concentrate on his voice. The fog was definitely darkening. It was turning blue. It would be night.

'It's a flat rock, level with the sea. You can walk out to it at low tide.'

'That's nice.' It was so easy to crush him. I felt bad clinging to his arm and ploughing through the opaque air in stupid silence. I made an effort. 'You like going there?'

'There's a story. B-belonging to Table Rock. My father told me.' Anything was better than concentrating on the deepening blue thickness, the dizzying loss of vision and of the world. His voice was something to hold onto just as much as his arm was. A thread to lead us out.

'Tell me.'

'It seems to float on the water at high tide. L-like a raft. But in a storm the waves crash over it – it's awash.' I tried to visualise the Table Rock. Its warm flat surface on a sunny day. 'A long time ago there lived a fisherman and his wife. In a little c-cottage at the top of the cliffs. Just above that cove.' So there were cliffs. I'd thought I was near cliffs. 'One day when the fisherman was out in his boat, the w-wife was feeling ill. She had a baby in her belly and it was time for it to be born.' His voice was explanatory, kindly, as if I might not know about such things. Then I realised it was perhaps the tone his father had used to tell *him* the story.

'She went down to the beach and she had the b-baby there. It didn't belong to her husband. She carried it across the shingle and laid it on Table Rock. Then she went s-slowly back up to the cottage and made her husband's tea.'

I imagined her. Staggering around the bare little cottage, heaving the black kettle onto the fire, leaning her dizzy weight against the table as she sliced the bread. Sitting to gut the fish before she put it in the pan; staring frozen at its milky eye as if she'd never seen a fish in her life.

'After his supper, it's a fine c-calm evening – the fisherman goes down to spread out his nets. He hears a kind of mewing. Is it the cry of the gulls? Is it a bleating calf? Or is it the wind m-moaning over the rocks? Then he spots a little naked thing out on Table Rock. The tide's coming in by now but he doesn't stop to take off his boots and trousers. He wades out to the rock and gathers up the child. He carries it up the cliff path and into the little cottage, all dripping wet. He holds out the ch-child to his wife.

'"See what I found on Table Rock. A gift from the sea! We must look after her, wife, as if she were our own." And the woman takes the child from her husband and nods. She puts her to the breast.'

'Is that the end?' I didn't want it to end.

'Yes.'

The fog was black now, it had been midnight blue but then it went black. Not like normal darkness though because it was smothering, cold to your face. Like being under thick cold blankets and someone sits on the bed. I thought about Table Rock. I was in blind darkness being led along a lane which might have been cliff edge or skirting mine shafts, god knows what or where it was, I listened to the story and I turned it in my mind. As you turn a penny in your pocket, as you fiddle with a matchstick and use it to pick under your dirty nails. I retold it to myself.

Maybe the husband is a stupid man, brutal and dangerous. Maybe he beats his wife. And the man she loved, who would have taken her away, is drowned. When she has given birth she leaves the child on Table Rock because she cannot bear to kill it. When the tide comes in she thinks the waves will carry it away, carry it to its true father. Although she has concealed everything, her morning sickness by going out early to fetch him fresh water from the spring, her belly and breasts under tight swaddling bands, although she has even rinsed and hung out to dry her woman's rags each month for him to see: something has made her forgetful. She forgets that Table Rock is not covered at high tide.

When he goes out after supper she clears away his plate but has to lean against the doorframe, with the stabbing pains in her womb. Standing there, panting a little, she looks down over the cliff edge to the sea. There is Table Rock. There is a tiny dot, no bigger than a seagull, in the middle of the rock. And a man wading through the water, reaching out his arms to snatch up the child.

For a giddy moment she thinks she will die. Fall down here on the floor where she stands, let the darkness into her head.

But she sits at the table and prays, and hears his heavy boots crunching up the cliff path, his breath coming short with speed and effort.

When she sees his face she realises. Relief floods her and the sudden milk gushes from her breasts so she has to cross her arms and squeeze herself, to keep from dripping on the floor. He does not imagine. It does not enter his head to imagine, either that she could have been so disobedient, or that another could have wanted her. It does not enter his head that the child is hers. The child is *his*, by right of finding, and she, his slave, will tend his child. She takes it from him without a word, bowing her head to hide her scalding tears. She knows she has more than she deserves. A man, a home, a child.

After another hour or so Calum began swiping his stick out to the right and after a bit it clack-clack-clacked against a fence. He let go of me to undo the gate and I stood there thinking I still would have no idea how to reach the house without him, even though we must be no more than twenty feet away. The gate creaked and he took my hand again and I heard the dull bang of a door yanked wide open.

'Calum! Calum!' Her voice was distanced and muffled by fog but you could tell she was shrieking. He pulled me towards the noise and a yellowish light pierced the blackness. We moved in towards the door; she was a blurry outline on the step haloed in misty light. She plunged towards us out of the light and threw her arms around him.

'I've been phoning the cottage, Mudie's hadn't seen you. Where did you get to?' I think she noticed then that I was there because she stopped and ushered both of us into the house and shut the door. The fog had even poured into the hall, making the light cloudy and dim, filling the place like steam. It was only then I registered we'd come back to her house, that we must have walked right past his. 'It's half-past ten,' she scolded. 'I've been going out of my mind with–'

'It came on s-suddenly.'

'Where were you? What were you doing?'

He took off his coat and I realised how wet we were. 'At the Neck.'

'The Neck? Why?'

Calum didn't reply and the silence seemed long. 'I was walking,' I said, 'and bumped into Calum there. Which is lucky for me because I'd never have found my way back alone . . .' She wasn't listening to me.

'Why were you up at the Neck?' she asked Calum. 'I told you to go to Mudie's for the eggs. What were you doing at the Neck?'

He shrugged. 'I was g-going on to Mudie's.'

She didn't seem able to take it in. 'Why didn't you say where you were going? I knew the fog was coming, I could have told you–'

We went into the kitchen and Calum sat down so I did the same, I was ready to drop. She fussed with the kettle. 'In future you tell me where you're going, Calum. Every time. You hear? Or I won't let you out. It's not safe – and we've got no eggs for breakfast.'

'It was lucky for me,' I said slowly. I felt in a dream, heavy with it. 'Calum rescued me.' She knew the fog was coming.

She glanced round as if she'd forgotten my existence (again). 'Oh yes. Lucky for you. Tea? Shall I put a drop of whisky in?'

We both said yes.

'Food. You haven't had any food. There's some soup on the stove.' A big black pot with something thick and dark in it, steaming dully. She went on nagging him and it was as if I wasn't there. I was hardly there, the fog had filled my head with thick drifts and Table Rock lay there flat and firm in the horrid insubstantiality, a place of safety I couldn't quite grasp because it was also floating, floating like a raft.

My mother made supper and bedtime drinks for me and my brother, and sent us off to bed. She even made hot-water bottles. She told him to sleep in the spare room upstairs and he didn't make any objection.

10 · A daughter

I slept deeply. When I woke sunlight was pouring in the window because I'd never drawn the curtains and the room with its white walls and blue carpet glowed with light. I considered the previous day and how Calum had saved me and I knew that I would fly and glide on that day too.

I made tea and toast and sat on my doorstep in the warm sunshine. I thought about being in the kitchen with my brother and my mother. How she hovered around him like a wasp around something sweet, how even when her hands were busy filling a kettle or stirring a pan she was glancing across to him. When she'd served us both she sat at the end of the table with a little glass of whisky, she seemed pathetic and frail. She was upset because he hadn't done what she told him to. She was ill. Her face was pale as if she never went outside, with big dark pouches under the eyes. She moved slowly, her hands shook, she was skinny and brittle and dried up. She was horrible, like the Old Man of the Sea, she was clinging on to Calum with her bony claws.

Calum kept his good eye on his food and drink, he never raised his face to look at her. I could feel her willing him to, like she was a child who needed attention.

Right on cue she came out with a basket of washing.

'Good morning!' I called. Cheerily. To my mother. She just nodded and slowly started pegging things out (trousers, Calum's). So I went over.

'Can I help? I love hanging out washing.' I once lived in a house where they hung out washing. I was only there three months over the summer but they had a garden and a washing line. I hung the washing on the line when I was there and I thought, one day I'll do this, I'll have my own garden and my own washing line and I'll stand in the sun and peg it out, not go to the launderette or use someone else's drier with the knob falling off and the mat of fluff under the filter and I'll go back into my house and look out my window and my washing will be dancing in the sun. They said I had to leave because of the phone bills I ran up. In fact they wanted me to leave because they were splitting up and it was embarrassing to have me around when they wanted to fight. But anyway once they'd said it it was a week before another place was found for me so I *did* run up phone bills then, I phoned New York central library and a museum in Australia and I phoned the speaking clock and left it on for the eight hours they were at work.

She didn't say yes or no so I took a few pegs and did a jumper. She was moving very slowly, slowly shaking out each garment, reaching slowly for the pegs. She was ill.

'I wanted to ask you if you could give me a bit of advice – or help. You see, I'm doing this Open University course.' She didn't speak or stop pegging so I explained how I needed to find out some island history.

'I can't really help you.'

'But you must know an awful lot. You've been here – how many years?'

'They keep themselves to themselves round here.' She took the peg-bag off the line and put it in the empty washing basket. She headed back towards the house. 'They've a booklet on the history of the island, for sale at the post office. For the tourists.' She went in and shut the door.

She didn't bother to smile. Wouldn't you think it was normal if a person's living in your house, to show a flicker of interest? To say, 'An Open University course, what's made you think of doing that?' or to offer a crumb of friendliness in the way of an anecdote? She didn't have the generosity in her head to deal with me *even when she thought I was a stranger*. There was something in me that repelled her. The same thing that had made her dump me in a box twenty-nine years ago. And she didn't even recognise *that*, let alone me.

Or was she a snob? Did she think anyone who needed to do a course, who wasn't brought up with a nice roomful of books and all the trappings must be a loser? How right she was. *Why* wasn't I brought up with a nice roomful of books? What system of discrimination was at work when she decided my super-intelligent brother would and I wouldn't be?

I went back into my room and made the bed. If she wouldn't

speak to me I would do it soon. Not hang around to be insulted by the bitch. She was *nothing*. History. I would speak to Calum one more time. Pump him, be sure of her routines – then sock it to her.

When I opened my back door she was leaning against the shed. She wasn't moving or doing anything, just leaning there, stooped, staring at her feet. I opened the door wider and she stayed in the same position. For a moment I thought she's died, she's gone and bloody died before I could kill her, then I realised she would have fallen over. I went out, close up her face was white and sweaty. 'Are you alright?'

'Can you help me back to the house?' I gave her my arm and we limped in through the nearest door (mine). I sat her down.

'What is it?'

Her voice was weak and breathy. 'I get a pain. It's alright.'

'D'you want anything?'

She shook her head.

'A cup of tea?' I put the kettle on anyway, gradually she straightened her back and relaxed. She was nothing but skin and bone. 'Shall I call the doctor?'

'No. There's – in the kitchen – a bottle above the sink.'

I went along the hall to her kitchen. Something dark red and aniseedy was boiling on the cooker, the place was full of steam. I turned it off and grabbed the medicine bottle from the shelf over the sink. The label was handwritten in Latin. She took the bottle from my hand and while I was looking for a spoon, she swigged a couple of mouthfuls.

'Thank you.'

I made us tea and sat at the other side of the little table.

'I'm sorry. Calum forgot the wood. He went out early . . .'

Oh we're sorry now are we. Realised the piece of trash we didn't have time to talk to has some use after all. Fine. She had fallen into my hands and now I would be oily with charm, I would insinuate myself so slimily so oleaginously into her notice that she would start to reveal herself to me without knowing what she was doing. Fate was on my side.

'Calum was a great guide last night. He knows every step of the way.'

'Angus taught him all the pathways and hidey-holes.'

'He was Calum's dad?'

'Calum thinks of Angus as his father.' She put her hand on the table as if to lever herself out of her chair, then gave up. 'He's a good boy but he lives in a dream.'

'D'you want me to help you to bed?' Why the hell should I help her? It would be funny if I made her like me, wouldn't it. If I were friendly and helpful and she found me delightful; it would be funny then when I told her what I was going to do.

'I'll wait till Calum gets back, he can make me a fire.' It was warm, there was no need for a fire. 'Were you going out? I don't want to keep you.'

No you didn't, did you. 'I'm not in a hurry.'

Being stuck there was good for her, it made her politer, almost human. 'Calum could tell you as much as anyone. About the island. Except he can't tell fact from fiction.'

'Calum?'

'Angus filled his head with it. Vikings. Fairies. The clearances – it's all in there somewhere.'

'And recent history, you must know that. When did you come to the island?'

She looked at me and there was an unpleasant kind of smile behind her expression, in the depths of her face. She was ill, she was *white*, but in her eyes I could see something horrible, wicked, that she was laughing and gloating and triumphing to herself. Her white sick old lady face was a mask that she was holding over something strong and rampant.

I realised in that instant that she knew. My stomach convulsed and I nearly vomited. She was watching me, I couldn't hide it. She knew. She knew who I was. And for reasons of her own she wasn't letting on.

I went to the sink and got a glass of water. I wanted to keep my back to her. I didn't want her to see my face. I realised there was a logic – a clunk, clunk, clunk of logical results which come tumbling like coins out of a fruit machine when you hit the jackpot. I needed time to understand the meaning of her knowing, *her* being in control when I had thought that I was . . . But she wouldn't let me think. 'I rented a holiday cottage. I wanted Calum to have a nice summer. Then I met Angus.'

'But wasn't Calum's father–?'

'Calum's father was married. He lived in Italy.'

My head was bursting with realisations, with sudden shafts of illumination. If she had known since I landed on the island, since I rang her from the call box; if she had intended when I set off to walk and the fog was coming in, that Calum should be far away from any spot where he could help me . . . But she was there and talking (for whatever reason and that I couldn't analyse here and now, whether it was because I could get no good of it at all I didn't know) so I plunged on – 'Were you living with your family then?'

'I lost contact with my family.'

What is she saying? There should be no contact between parent and child? Is she warning me off? 'Why?' I blurted at last.

'They wouldn't have approved of Calum.'

I could see the evil gleam in her eye again, she was up to something she was playing with me she knew things I didn't know, I had to gasp for breath to ask my question. 'Wouldn't have approved of an illegitimate baby?'

'No.' She stared at me. I started to blush, my face was like a furnace, impossible to hide. She would know that I knew. She kept staring. 'They didn't approve. I had a little girl before I had Calum.'

My heart jumped under my ribs, it winded me. 'A little girl?'

'My mother was very strict. She didn't believe in sex before marriage.' She said this with a kind of wincing sneer I didn't know if it was directed at me. She seemed to be waiting for me to speak.

'I see.' Why didn't she come out with it? Very carefully because my lips and tongue had gone thick and unmanageable, mumbly, I said, 'Does your daughter live on the island too?' Let's have it out in the open. You know who I am – OK, let's have the conversation now, let's stop this fucking *game*.

'No,' she said. 'She died.'

11 · A sharp knife

Someone rang the doorbell. It sounded in the hall and died away, then whoever it was flapped the letterbox in and out.

'Shall I go?'

My mother nodded. I could see two heads through the stained glass panel; when I opened the door they were unlikely – two women in their thirties, a fat one and a thin one. The fat one had very baggy trousers and Doc Martens. The thin one was all in black.

'Hello,' said the fat one. Carefully neutral accent. 'We're looking for Calum MacLeod.'

Well, the boy has dark secrets. 'He's out. D'you want to speak to his mother?'

They glanced at each other and nodded and I invited them in.

They followed me down the hall to my room, where Phyllis still sat at the table. I had assumed she would know them but they stood awkwardly in the doorway trying to introduce themselves. I had to make them go in so I could get in.

'I'm Sally and this is Ruby.' The plump one had the friendly-sensible style that goes with being a prefect and knowing first aid, the kind of middle-class voice where the intonation's been taken out so it's flat and undramatic. There is a certain kind of person isn't there who speaks terribly evenly, as if drama itself was a crime and everything must be flattened out to some baseline, perhaps in the interests of democracy.

She died is what she said. She – I – died.

The plump one did all the talking. They were opening a vegetarian café in the village. They wanted organic veg. Someone had told them that Calum MacLeod–

'Yes,' said Phyllis. 'He could supply you with vegetables. He takes them down to the post office but he could sell them to you direct.'

'That would be good,' said Sally. 'Would he be able to deliver?'

Phyllis nodded. The skinny one looked at her partner. When she spoke each word seemed to have a careful space around it. As if really she was saying something terrifying – screaming obscenities – and a sound engineer had carefully synched these innocent-seeming words to her lip movements. She was completely insane. 'Does he grow any herbs?'

'I grow herbs,' said Phyllis. 'Out the back.' She indicated through the window.

'That's great,' said Sally.

103

Island

'May we look?' asked Ruby carefully.

Phyllis levered herself up. Her face was less pasty than it had been. She led them slowly through to the hall and I was left alone.

Why tell me I was dead? She was manipulating things towards some conclusion I couldn't fathom. Showing me she was still one step ahead. I thought I had come to the island to wrest control of my life back from the woman who had sabotaged it. But I was wrong. She was still writing my plot.

It dawned on me that I had *never* been in control. I had thought I'd made a decision to find her, to come to the island. But hadn't that idea been – like every other idea in my life – in reaction to her? She had built a maze and I blundered round it, each time I took a new turning I thought I was choosing my path; but she had made the whole fucking sealed system, she had me trapped like a rat. I couldn't choose anything outside what she'd laid down for me because I couldn't even *imagine* it.

I remembered my journey to the island. My pre-booked rail ticket, the train I'd missed. The storm which had stopped the ferries. She wasn't infallible, then.

I sat on my doorstep and chain-smoked. I could hear snatches of their conversation over the herb garden – the virtues of black-currant leaf tea and oil of evening primrose, the reassuring solid tones of the plump one, the high-wire control of the skinny one. What would she have said if they hadn't turned up? They were ridiculous, as if someone had suddenly pressed the channel changer, they were from another programme. The sun still shone brightly, like full lighting on a stage set. Bright and false. The thing about the storm was complicated, you could see it either way. Either she *hadn't* wanted me to find her, she hadn't put that into my head, but still she knew of it (down to the finest detail, the day on my ticket) so she summoned up a storm to coincide with my arrival in the hope that it would deter or drown me. My missing the train and being a day late was the one detail she didn't foresee.

Or she *did* put the search into my head, she did want me to find her, so she could continue to torment me close up instead of at a distance as in earlier years of my life; and knowing me as she did, as her creation, she *knew* I would miss my train; and the storm was there simply to point out to me who was boss, a threat which of course I was too blind and ignorant and *pleased with myself* to observe at all for the first few days while I still gloried in the delusion that I had chosen what I was doing.

Either way she was in control. She was in control and telling me I was dead. Which was a threat or a promise or, most likely, both.

OK. Just one thing to do. Kill her. Get it over and done with now – tonight – just get it done. Nothing more corny than films when the villain catches the hero then stands around explaining his plans, his life history and his philosophy while the captive figures out a way to escape. Just do it.

I went through the cutlery tray. Stabbing was what I had always imagined but there wasn't a particularly good knife. One new serrated bread knife with a rounded end – useless; and one wooden-handled vegetable knife that was about as sharp as my toothbrush. I opened my Swiss army knife but I knew it was no good; the blade's only five centimetres long, it might not go deep enough. It would be OK in the neck but anywhere else it wouldn't reach a vital organ. Where's the best place to stab someone? Is that why stabbings are always *frenzied attacks* – the poor murderer's punching holes all over desperately looking for a fatal spot? The penknife was no good anyway because it was mine. It had to be something anyone could've picked up in the house. Something from her kitchen.

I went to the internal door and listened. Total silence. The vegetable seekers had gone, I'd heard Calum's voice at one point but now it seemed like he'd gone too. She was ill – she wasn't able to walk unaided when I brought her into my room. Her blue-eyed boy must have put her to bed. But what if she was sitting in her TV room, just about to creep along the hall to make herself a cup of tea? Foul old witch.

Suffocate her. Tonight. Once she was asleep it'd be simple. Put a pillow over her head and lean with all my weight. She might thrash about a bit but I had more strength. Look how easily the Chief suffocated Jack Nicholson in *One Flew over the Cuckoo's Nest*. Nothing to it.

I didn't like the element of waiting, though. Just standing there leaning on the cushion. Wouldn't it be shit if you did it for five minutes then took the cushion off and found her lying there grinning at you none the worse for it? At least with a knife you're doing obvious damage – make a few holes, get the blood flowing, and you're on your way.

Strangling? But I'd have to get something round her neck before I could do it. What if she woke up while I was sliding a scarf under her neck?

I could push her downstairs.

Hopeless. And she'd know I'd done it. She'd crawl away with a broken ankle accusing me.

A sharp knife

This is why they have guns. So you can do the job properly.

I come back to knife. Has to be. She deserves it – I don't want her whole I want her ripped and slashed, I want her hurt. Stabbing gives her time to realise what's going on but not enough to defend herself. Why should I smother her sweetly in her sleep? She needs to feel me puncturing her.

OK. I opened my door. Nothing. I took off my trainers and went quietly to the TV room. The door was open a crack. It was completely silent. I pushed it open a bit more – the room was empty. Fine. She was in bed. I went back past my door to the kitchen. The fucking door was shut wasn't it. Closed tight. Either she was in there or she was in bed. OK. If she was there I'd come to borrow something. What? A knife.

Sure. A sharp knife. Suddenly I was *in* it. Calm, smooth, I know what I'm doing, I'm not scared of her I'm swooping soaring gliding. I want to borrow a sharp knife to gut a fish. My hand slipped on the round handle and it wouldn't turn. I wiped it on my T-shirt and tried again. The kitchen was empty.

There was a theatrical drip-drip-drip going on; on the table an upside-down stool with a muslin cloth tied to its legs, bulging with the wet weight of some foul green slime that looked like boiled privet – dripping into a glass bowl underneath. The liquid in the bowl was a clear poisonous bright green.

I went quickly to the dresser; on its surface was a pestle and mortar and one of those precision weighing scales like chemists have. There was a row of unlabelled brown medicine bottles, I picked one up – it had white powder inside. Maybe she was a drug baron. Suddenly there was a clatter behind me. I nearly screamed. I swung round in time to see the tail of the grey cat disappearing through the cat flap. I hadn't noticed it was there. I made myself turn back slowly to the drawer, clenching my fists to stop the shaking. In the right drawer, matches, candles, seed packets, thermometers, syringes, an eye dropper, surgical blades and wipes. In the left, cutlery. OK. I pulled out a couple of kitchen knives. One was old and heavy with a stained blade, it had been worn sickle-shaped with sharpening. I pressed the blade with my thumb and it left a rust-coloured dent. The other was little and sharp but again had a curved end. Modern knife designers just aren't on the side of stabbers are they? Gap in the market I'd say, nice pointy-ended knives. There was a knife sharpener in the drawer – I picked it up. OK. Take the old knife and sharpener. Do it tonight.

What if she got up to make tea and missed them?

Tough. Calum could have borrowed them. If she got round to thinking I'd taken them, that would give her something to worry about. Good. I closed the drawer and went back to my room. The first time I drew the knife through the sharpener was very loud; I put the radio on and finished sharpening to Pulp, 'Common People'. Like me.

It was very sharp when I finished. I touched my thumb with it and the skin just opened and flowered. Beautiful. It *looked* like a murder weapon, it was big and black handled and stained, maybe it had done a job like this before. I put it under the edge of the rug beneath my bed.

The evening was long and slow. The sky was leaden grey, I watched it getting dark. I would've gone out but I wanted to hear her movements. She went to the bathroom twice and at 8.15 she came down to the kitchen and faffed around in there for about an hour. I smelt toast and stronger whiffs of the privet juice. There was the clink of china. Her cat came and perched on my outside windowsill and I banged against the glass to get it away. Bloody thing, spying on me. At last she went creaking back up the stairs. I dipped into a couple of the books I'd brought with me but I couldn't read, I didn't want to let go enough to slide into a story, I needed to keep my attention on her.

It would be simple. Wait till 11.30, she's in her first deep sleep; creep up, creep in, locate the neck, stab. Repeatedly.

What if it was too dark to see? I didn't have a torch. I didn't know how thick her curtains were, whether they would totally block whatever natural light there was.

OK. I'd put the upstairs bathroom light on. There was nothing to it. She was skinny and frail, a puff of wind'd knock her over. It was *simple*.

Afterwards, wipe my fingerprints off the handle with the bed-clothes, leave the knife with the body, go to the bathroom, wash my hands, turn off the light, run downstairs. Unlock the front door and wipe off my fingerprints then go to bed.

Free and light-hearted. Sleep the sleep of the avenged – wake up not too early to the dismal sounds of clever Calum discovering his mumsy's corpse. Help him work out what's happened – door left open, murderer comes in – step by step – murderer goes through kitchen drawer and finds knife – murderer creeps upstairs – etc. to: murderer vanishes. That reminded me I had to put the sharpener back in the kitchen.

Motive? I wanted to steal some stuff to fake a motive but I couldn't think where the fuck to put it. Outside? Just chuck it out as if he'd got scared and dropped it? I decided to leave it to the spur of the moment. I didn't even know what she had up there. If there was a jewellery box on a dressing table I could sweep it into a pillowcase and take it down to the garden. Maybe dump it in the ditch by the road.

11.09   I was pacing my room and taking deep breaths; I was an athlete before a race. Losing sight of any whys or wherefores now, just the thing of doing it, getting it right, hitting her in the neck. What if the knife got stuck? If I hit a bone – it could. Or even worse, snapped. What if it was so old and thin with sharpening that it got into one of her tough stringy sinews and snapped? I put the Swiss army knife in my jeans pocket just in case.

11.15   It's a job. A job you have to do. You don't know the reason any more, just you have to get it done before the next thing can happen, you have to get it out of the way.

What if she's awake?

Tough. She's flat on her back in bed, you've got the element of surprise. Just jump at her.

11.17   What if she's got a weapon?

Unlikely.

What if she's got an alarm?

You can still do it and be out of her room before anyone gets near the house.

11.23   What if she's not dead?

Make sure she is. Keep at it. Chop her fucking head right off if necessary.

A sharp knife

11.29   Why 11.30? Why not 12? Or between three and four in the morning when everyone's energy is at its lowest ebb. She'd never fight back at 3.30.

Yeah but my energy'll be at its lowest ebb too, then. And I'm not staying up all night for the bitch. No way.

OK. Let's go. Knife in right hand – practise stabbing downwards. Both hands on the handle for steadiness and force. OK. Open the door – bare feet cross the hall – footprints! Back into the room, close door, put on bedside lamp, put on socks. Open door, kneel, wipe footprints with towel. Try again. Cross the hall and up the stairs, slowly, slowly, one around here creaks – the fifth. No, the sixth. Step step step step and on up to the top. OK. It's dark up here. Turn back along the landing. First door on the right's half open. Bathroom. Need to switch on the light? I'm flapping around with my left hand looking for the string to pull when there's a noise. Rustling and creaking. A slight thump. A step. She's up. She's approaching her bedroom door. Fuck fuck fuck fuck fuck. I pull back deeper into the bathroom doorway. She'll be getting up for a pee. OK. Do it as she comes in the door. Jump at her. Knock her–

She's coming along the landing. *Past* the door. Down the stairs. *Shit.* I've left my bedroom door open. I wait paralysed in the dark doorway, hear her slow steps finish the stairs and pad down the corridor to the kitchen. 11.30 at night and she's going to the kitchen. What now? My door's open. She'll know I'm not in my room. So she'll be on the lookout for me. My heart's beating clanging foully my hands are shaking. Get back downstairs now, while she's in the kitchen. Get back out of here. I force myself on to the dark landing – there's some light coming up from the hall light

111

she's switched on. Force myself to start down the stairs – the sixth one up creaks – force myself to slow and count. Sound of the kitchen door opening. I slide the knife up my sleeve and grasp the cuff tight. Get to the bottom before she – I meet her on the bottom step. She's carrying a glass of dirt-coloured liquid. She looks at me and doesn't speak.

'I – I heard a noise . . . I think something woke me up.' She moves aside so I can step down. Then she simply goes on up, ignoring me totally. I'm standing in my dark doorway with the knife blade tickling my wrist and she's plodding slowly up the stairs with her back to me. *Daring* me. I slide into my room. Shut and lock the door. Collapse quietly down to the floor. Unclasp my cuff and let the knife slither out onto the carpet. There is a stinging line on my wrist where it has nicked me.

She knew exactly what I was going to do.

I hid the knife again. The fucking sharpener was still on the table. I put it in a sock under my clothes in the wardrobe. It could go back to the kitchen another time. The house was totally silent; of course. And so it would be until I decided to go upstairs again, when she'd be sitting up waiting for me. Might as well give her a yell and tell her when I'm coming.

I wrapped myself in my duvet and sat on the bed. OK, it's a duel. Me against her. That was a warning shot.

12 · Bull Rock

I only slept for an hour or two, then I lay thinking and watching it get light. When I got up it was sunny and clear, with a new-washed feel to the air and pale sky. The sky was huge and the land was small; to the south I could see the mountains of Skye with a gauzy scarf of purple cloud about their tops. It was a purposeful, optimistic morning, reinforced almost immediately by a short V of five geese flying south. A tick of birds. Good luck. I hadn't plumbed the depths of Calum's knowledge yet. I went up to his house.

He was outside digging his garden. When he saw me he grinned like a pumpkin lantern. 'Look what I f-found last night.' His rucksack was sitting at the edge of the veggy patch. He opened it and pulled out a small grubby flat object about four inches long.

'What is it?' It was striped with ridges of dirt.

'A comb. A Viking comb.' He took it from me again and rubbed

the top with his thumb. Under the dirt the comb was yellow-grey.
Some of the teeth were broken.

'Viking? How d'you know?'

He nodded, pleased as punch with himself. 'My d-dad.'

'You should wash it, then you'll be able to see–'

He took no notice, just slid it back into the rucksack and put the
rucksack on. 'Treasure,' he said. His bad eye was pointing right at
the sky but his good one looked at me directly. 'Going picking
rowan for my mother. W-want to come?'

'Where?'

'Durris. The tide's out, we can get across.'

'OK.' How was I going to outwit her? How could I catch her by
surprise?

He put away his fork and fetched his stick and we went on along the
lane. We discussed the fact that a Viking comb – if it was, which I
doubted – was a very old thing and he could maybe take it to a
museum. Turned out he didn't know what a museum was. So much
for his cultured mother. When I explained he became very excited.

'But how come you've never been to a museum? Isn't there one on
Skye?'

'I can't go off the island.'

'Why?'

'It's d-dangerous.'

'Why?'

He didn't have an answer.

'Does *she* go?'

'To the hospital. Sometimes.'

'So when did you last go to the mainland?'

He pondered in silence for a while. 'Big school when I was eleven, f-for a week.'

'A week! What happened then?'

'My mother – she taught me.'

'Why did she stop you going?'

He grinned. 'Head in the clouds Calum. Head in the clouds.' He started scuffing at something in the path with his boot. Then he knelt down and opened the rucksack and took out a rusty trowel. He chipped at something in the path for a bit then got his trowel blade under it and levered out a fist-sized rock.

'What's that?'

He turned it over and inspected it. 'Thought it was a fossil.' He stood and flung it out towards the sea.

At last we had passed the Neck, the narrow point of the island, and Calum pointed out Table Rock. It seemed a low small thing, I couldn't believe a full tide wouldn't cover it. We walked on and the path took us nearer to sea level again. The land to our left was flat and bare. It was a weird bald place, with pale rock in big flat slabs stretching the length of a football pitch or more before it came to the sea. Out at sea I could make out a distant rocky island, very steep and sheer.

'Prayer ground,' said Calum. He struck off from the lane, walking across the short-cropped grass until he came to the bare rock. It was like a pavement. 'They came here for prayers. Before there was a church.'

It was fucking bleak.

'Out there was the m-monastery.'

'Out *there?*'

He was pointing to the distant rocks. 'Y-you can see the ruined wall–'

It was true. What I had taken to be the sheer steepness of the rocks was in fact a high black stone wall. They had built upon the rock as it reared out of the sea, the monastery had perched there like a cormorant. 'And they came over to convert the islanders?'

He shook his head. 'You can't get on or off. Only at high tide. Sometimes n-not for weeks. That's why they built it there.'

So they couldn't get on or off. Sure. We walked to the edge of the flat stones. The sea was calm but there was white spray around the base of the monastery crag.

'People came to hear mass on Sundays.' He knelt on the rock facing out to sea, a ridiculous sight with his rucksack still on his back. The monastery was half a mile away.

'They wouldn't have been able to hear.'

He didn't move.

'The monks couldn't see the islanders and the islanders couldn't hear the monks and they sang mass together?'

The great Fount of Island History nodded. You can see it can't you: pious natives muttering their prayers while on the other side of the water stark-bollock-naked monks yell bawdy songs and piss themselves laughing. True son of the isle Calum appeared to be praying so I left him to it and wandered on along the natural pavement. Wouldn't it be nice to be Calum. Able to believe in the people all sweetly gathered here at the last stroke of the bell, their brains filled with the chanting of the monks drifting across the waves. They couldn't see their faces and couldn't hear their voices but still they all kept time. What a pleasure it would be to be so simple.

When he joined me we walked on in silence, heading north. It became much more bleak, just rock barely scattered with tufts of grass, no trees or bushes. The rock was black now, it was poking out of the sea wet and slimy and plastered with strips of weed like slicked-down strands of hair on a baldy. It must all be under water when the tide was in. We weren't on a track any more we were picking our way across slippery black rocks with puddles in their hollows and disgusting little red blobs of what looked like raw liver. I nearly lost my footing twice, it was stupidly dangerous.

'The ch-children had to cross this to go to school.'

'People lived here?' There didn't look much to recommend it unless you were a bird. Or a lump of raw liver.

'Six families. They asked for a bridge but . . . If school ended when the t-tide was high they just had to wait.'

The track climbed steeply up onto the end island, up a grassy ridge. From the top of it you looked down into a wide basin, where the ruins of some cottages stood, and three trees laden with bright red berries. The cottage roofs had gone but walls and lintels and doorways were still there.

'See?' He stood next to me looking down. Nobody would've known you were there till they climbed the outer ridge.

'It's like a fort.' He ran down the slope to the nearest ruin, then walked around it patting the top of the wall. I watched him and he went on to the next one and did the same, like a superstitious kid walking home from school has a routine of tapping lucky fences or pulling leaves off the hedges. He went round them all, with that air of complete conviction mad people always have. Then he bent down, took off his rucksack and began chipping at something on the ground. I went down to join him.

'What have you got?'

'Part of a b-bowl. Look.' He held it up like it was the crown jewels. It was another blue bit of pottery. He carefully brushed the dirt off with his fingers and put it in his rucksack. Then he started on something that had been under it.

'How long till the tide covers the path?'

'We're OK for an hour or two.' He got his trowel under the edge of it and prised up an old bit of metal, looked like the back of an alarm clock. He put it in his rucksack and stood up. 'C-come and see Bull Rock.'

We crossed the basin and climbed the rim on the far side. When we reached the top the wind hit us. The sky had clouded over but it was still bright, almost as if the sea was shining. Ahead was reedy grass and bare rock spreading down to the sea. On the horizon cloudy outlines of two other long low islands. There was a sudden real sense of space. 'Bull Rock!' He pointed to a humped black rock in the silvery grey water, very close to shore. There were two smaller ones beside it.

Calum sat down and patted the grass, taking his thermos out of his rucksack. I rolled us both a fag. I was going to find out every single thing about her. I was going to find her weak spot. 'Your mother was very worried about you last night.'

He glared at Bull Rock. 'She's always worried.'

'What d'you mean?'

He carefully poured the tea and passed it to me. 'She wants me at the house. Sh-she said paint the woodwork and it doesn't even need it.'

'You go there every day, don't you?'

'For dinner. I g-go there every day.' He had a stone in his hand and he began to pound a tuft of grass with it, bang bang bang. 'Once when it was foggy she took away my boots.'

'Your *boots?*'

'I went back to my house in my socks and I took two boots off the pile. They were stiff with salt, I got t-terrible blisters.' He went on bashing at the pulverised grass, grinning happily to himself.

Well, Calum the teenage rebel. Calum the wild tearaway. The wind blowing in our faces off the sea was warm and sweet, it riffled the reedy grass like a hair-drier. I sipped my plastic-tasting tea and the foulness of her knowing receded. OK she knew I was her daughter. OK she was playing games with me. But she wasn't *god,*

119

if Calum could annoy her. There was no reason I shouldn't regain the upper hand, and pretty quickly too.

'You know about Bull Rock?'

Sure, everyone's born with that knowledge. 'No, Calum.'

'Next to it is Cow. And Calf.'

'How sweet.'

This was received in silence. The rock did look a bit like a bull, it had heavy hunched shoulders and a tapering rear end.

'Go on Calum, tell me.'

'It was a bull once. It belonged to a hag who lived here.' Long silence; around the black Bull the sluggish sea heaved and swelled at its surface tension, failing to break it, a lazy sea of mercury.

'Go on.'

'On the m-mainland there was a king and he fathered twins but they were – Their mother was his sister. It was bad. There were storms, the crops all failed and there were no f-fish to be caught. The people of his country got thin and poor and hungry. Then his advisers met and they called for the sinful twins to be k-killed.'

Incest again. No. There hasn't been any incest yet. There was adultery at Table Rock, not incest. And a baby extra to requirements. Now there were two. If Angus had been my father he would've told *me* stories. I like it when you know a story's shape, when the first few sentences seem to sketch a shape in the air, that gradually gets filled in. I worried that Calum might miss something out.

'The twins' mother was hiding with them, she put them in her bed to keep them safe. But the advisers came banging on the door and ripping everything up trying to find the babies, and they grabbed the first one and chucked him right in the fire. Then they came after the other one but a good man . . .' Calum paused, 'who was a – a–'

'Wizard?'

'Druid. Said he would take the baby away to another land and then the curse would be lifted. So he did. He brought him here. Right here to this beach and he gave him to an old hag who had nothing on this earth but her patch of potatoes and her three white cattle, the bull, the cow and the calf.' He'd stumbled into a few sentences of his dad's, like someone who's battling across rough ground and they suddenly get onto the worn familiar path. You could hear the other voice coming through him. 'And she promised to care for the boy as if he were her own. So next day she put him on the back of her great white bull and led the bull into the sea to w-wash the boy. And every day for a year she did that, put the baby on the bull's back and bathed him in the sea. And when the year was up exactly to the day the bull turned black – completely black – and he rushed alone into the sea. And there he is, he stands there night and day, letting the sea wash him clean. And the boy grew up big and strong and clever, with no stain or spot at all, so that one day they sent for him from the mainland, to go over there and be king.'

'That's a terrible story. Terri-bull.'

Calum wasn't quick on puns. He said, 'What?'

'Why should the bull get the dirt?'

'It's an animal.' He screwed the lid back on the thermos and stood up. 'The rowan.'

121

I'd forgotten. 'Is there time?'

'It's quick to pick.' He headed down to the ruined houses again. All three of the trees were stunted and misshapen, with their branches pointing towards the mainland. Calum handed me a plastic bag out of his rucksack and began stripping clusters of the red berries from a tree.

'What're they for? They look poisonous.' I began to pick them anyway.

'She makes jelly. Good for you.'

'How does she know?'

'Sh-she knows all the plants. She can make anything.'

'Medicine, you mean?'

'Good and b-bad.'

Sure, Calum. 'What use is bad medicine?'

He shook his head mysteriously. 'N-never touch it Calum it can kill you.'

'She's just trying to frighten you.'

'N-no.' He was so indignant he stopped picking and stood facing me, his bag dangling from his left hand. 'She made me s-special medicine for my fits.'

'Fits?'

He nodded. 'I had f-fits nearly every month, she made me this special medicine out of h-hemlock.'

'Really? Did it cure you?'

He nodded importantly and returned to his picking. 'If you drink too much it makes you die.'

I remembered the eye dropper and saucer of dead leaves. 'Does she make medicine for other people?'

'Yeah. She knows everything.'

Sadly true. But might poison be less predictable than me crouched behind the bathroom door with my knife? I remembered what I'd been meaning to ask him before. 'Calum, does your mother have many visitors?'

'No.'

'Never?'

He snorted. 'Only me.' Only him. All the rest of the time, she was alone. So even if it took me a while to polish her off – she couldn't expect any help.

The berries came off in clusters. 'Don't the stems matter?'

'She s-sieves them.' We worked in silence for a space then he said triumphantly, 'See? She knows the good and the b-bad.'

'What're you on about?'

'The poison's in the seeds. See? She told me.' He came to me with a cluster in his hands, squashed a berry between grubby thumb and finger to reveal the little yellow seed inside. 'She cooks it then she s-sieves it and all the seeds go in the sieve.'

'The seeds are poisonous?'

'Yeah. It's t-time to go.'

How could I get her to eat a load of rowan seeds? Not exactly easy to disguise.

We got our feet wet going back to Aysaar, the tide was already coming in. I was thinking about poison. 'Does she keep it in the kitchen?'

'What?'

'Your special medicine. Hemlock.'

'On the t-top shelf in the pantry.'

'How much does she give you?'

'A little goes a long way,' he recited like a parrot.

'How much, Calum?'

'One half-teaspoon every week.'

Probably he grew out of his fits anyway. Herbal remedies – crap. But it wouldn't take much to polish her off. She looked half-dead yesterday when I brought her in from the shed. I had a sudden memory of her taking her medicine bottle from me; unscrewing the lid without even looking – putting it to her lips and tilting her head back. Glugging it like an alky.

What to do was as obvious as a gift. I was getting back on course.

Calum took the rowan berries to her. I sat in my room and read. I started *One Thousand Acres* by Jane Smiley, I got completely wrapped up in it until I noticed I was trembling with hunger. I made sandwiches and cocked an ear to the old cow's movements. She was in the kitchen, her radio was on – and when I opened the outer door to have a fag her cat was stretched out on my doorstep as if it owned the place. I kicked it off and sat there for a couple of hours until it got too dark to read. I finished the book at ten, and spent a while pacing and listening out for her. At 10.20 she crept to the kitchen, at 10.31 she turned off the hall light and went creaking up the stairs.

Best to get in the kitchen straight away – maybe she was about to make a habit of rising at 11.30 p.m. I waited till she'd finished in the bathroom upstairs and I'd heard her bedroom door click shut, then I nipped along to the kitchen. Turned on the light and shut the door. Her medicine bottle was in its place over the sink, and the pantry door was a couple of inches open. There were rows of bottles on the top two shelves; I carried a chair into the pantry and climbed on it to see them properly. Calum was perfectly right. Four bottles in the corner on the top shelf labelled CONIUM MACU-LATUM HEMLOCK/WITH CARE. I took the back one, and went over to the sink. Don't stop, don't think, just do it. Her own medicine bottle was half full. I emptied it straight down the plughole and filled it to just over the same level from the hemlock bottle. I put her medicine bottle back in its place and the hemlock bottle behind the others in the pantry. Put the chair away and closed the pantry door. The medicine I'd poured down the sink smelt nasty – I went to turn on the tap and remembered just in time how noisy her plumbing was. Poured the contents of the kettle down the drain to swill the medicine away, and got myself back to my room all in under ten minutes.

Good.

I stood by my door listening for a while but it was perfectly quiet. She would have to be clairvoyant to know what I'd done. Which quite probably she was, but on the other hand – if she didn't think about her medicine until she needed it – if she didn't need it till she was as desperate as she was yesterday – then there was no reason on earth why she shouldn't glug half a bottle of hemlock before she even noticed.

I felt good. I put myself to bed.

13 · Enthusiasts

I fell asleep easily then woke with a start at two. I had a sudden premonition she would come into my room and kill me. She would have spare keys – of course – to both my doors. There was a bolt on the outside one, which I drew. I left the keys in both locks, half turned so you couldn't push a key in from the other side. And I pushed the big armchair in front of the door to the hall. Blocking doors and listening for footsteps in the middle of the night was like having Fear, but Fear is about the unknown. Whereas I was simply defending myself against her. I knew who she was and what she looked like, her skinny arms and legs, her wrinkled hands, her glittering knowing eyes. A fight would be easy as long as I was prepared; all I had to guard against was her creeping up on me. (And part of me knew she wouldn't attack me *herself*, that would be far too simple – she would have a way of making something else happen, something that made it seem my fault, like I'd accidentally walk off a cliff or get run over by the island tractor.) But still it felt purposeful to barricade myself in my room. When I was done I fell asleep again, I didn't lie awake listening for anything.

In the morning it was raining hard. I lay in bed in the gloom for a long time listening to it pelting against the window, listening out for her. I didn't hear the stairs creak. Eventually I got up and ran a bath, which gave me the excuse to prowl up and down the hall a few times. She wasn't up. It was cold and dark as if the night had forgotten to end, but it was nine o' clock in the morning. Why wasn't she up? Was it possible – already – that she'd woken in the night feeling ill, fumbled her way downstairs to the kitchen, picked up her medicine bottle and poured it down her throat? I went to the kitchen door and listened. Nothing.

I had to be patient until Calum came. It would be too easy for her to be dead already. Far too easy. I locked myself in the bathroom.

It's an old-fashioned white enamelled bath, very deep and stained yellow where the taps drip. Imagine always bathing in the same bath. Imagine growing up and knowing the shape of one bath. The wooden towel rail a bit wobbly on its feet, painted dark green; the washstand with the old-fashioned bowl and jug, the toothbrush mug made of that cloudy brittle early plastic. The big white towel, scratchy with washing and drying on the line, fraying at one end where it's come unhemmed. A curly PM embroidered in the corner in pink. Imagine *wearing things out*. Or having things from new. Imagine the life span of a possession like a towel. Would she have had them as a set for her wedding? Thick initialled white bath towels? All the bottles and jars and tubes on the shelf were hers or Calum's, they weren't the leftovers of people who'd moved out last month and already been lost track of. No one else would use her perfume (I used it), she could leave the pretty bottle of bubble bath on display (a Christmas present from Calum?). Imagine cleaning a bathroom and saying to yourself, 'My bathroom looks nice and sparkling.'

After my bath I lit a fire. The house felt deserted. It began to seem possible that she really might be dead. I paced around my room waiting for Calum to come for his dinner. There was nothing I could do until he found her. The minutes crawled.

At twelve he came in and went to the kitchen; after a while he plodded upstairs. And then I heard her voice – she was alive. A drone which very quickly got louder until she was screaming at him. His replies were low and rumbly. I put my ear to the wall, to the pipe – opened the door and stuck my head out – the words were still indistinct. Had she discovered the hemlock? Was she blaming him for it? There was a long low outburst from Calum and then a hearty slam. I heard him stomping down the stairs. I pulled open my door and waved him in.

'What's going on?'

He shrugged. 'She's cross.'

Der, yes. 'What about?'

But he'd spotted my earrings on the mantelpiece and was picking them up and peering and turning them over to inspect. He dropped one and spent a while feeling around in the fireplace for it.

'*Calum.*'

'She just gets cross.'

'Has she taken anything – anything she shouldn't?'

He looked at me strangely.

'What's wrong with her, for god's sake?'

He glanced at the internal door as if he thought she'd catch us talking. 'Cancer.' I wasn't expecting him to say that. He waited a few seconds then he went on, 'And she's always had – sh-she–'

'Yes?'

He glanced at the door again. 'Nothing.'

'She's in bed.'

'We have to g-go out.'

'It's pissing down.'

He didn't reply, just moved back towards the doorway.

'I don't want to go out.'

'Can't talk here.' He thought it was possible to escape her influence by putting distance between himself and her. I was tempted to tell him how far away I'd spent my life, and how her claw marks were all over it. I put on my jacket and went after him but he stopped as I was locking the door.

'Mac?'

'This is all I've got.'

'I've got an-nother in the cottage.' He led the way; at the corner of the garden something made me look back. There was a movement at the upstairs window. She was watching us from her bedroom. Watching to see where we went.

I followed Calum. His hair was tangled with a flat patch at the back where he'd slept, like a three-year-old. 'The rain's stopping, look.'

'What's she cross about?'

'Sh-she didn't like it when I moved out.'

'So?'

'I – I – it was my fault. I didn't tell her.' I followed him into his cottage. It was full. Food, clothes, piles of junk from the sea, sacks of potatoes and onions, mud, dirty dishes, old rags; on the table a heap of rocks like the ones on the shelf over my bed, and a packet of fish-hooks and a load of line and a trowel and a scattering of dirty mugs. He knew exactly where the mac was: he picked a cardboard box full of old fertiliser bags off a chair in the corner, rooted under a couple of blanket-type things that were over the chair, and pulled it out from underneath. It was green and blue with a STORM label, it was in good nick.

'I found it last s-summer. Too short. You have it.' There was a huge bucketful of ashes one side of the fire and a pile of driftwood the other. Not chopped into nice manageable logs like at his mother's house, but in big lumps that you'd have to wrestle into the fireplace. A bundle of scrumpled up bloody newspaper resting on the cold ashes in the grate. He saw me looking at that and grinned.

'F-five fish this morning.' Next to the chair by the fire was an upturned tea chest and on it, dirty cup plate knife fork, half a loaf of bread and a tub of Flora, a jar with knives and metal things in it, to do with fishing I assumed. There was an open tin of metal polish and a heap of that pink wadding that comes in it, a saucer full of buttons, a dirty comb, a little pile of sea-smoothed pebbles and shells, matches, two lighters, an apple core and a seed catalogue.

He was ready to go, he went to the door. I had this sudden wave of complete nostalgia for my room, my first proper room, the room I made a tip of when I was seventeen. I remembered the smell of it and the way it looked so dense and crammed and layered with my stuff like it was my nest my outer coating. I've never done that to a room since. Since that cow cleared it up. I've never *seen* a room like it since; sure, I've lived in all sorts of filthy untidy dumps but they were like that through vandalism or wanting to fuck over someone's property or the room not belonging to anyone (sitting rooms in shared houses, filthy soulless tips); not through one person living in them night and day and gradually building up layers of nice or useful things all around them precisely they know where and no one else comes in or makes you change it and you can lay your finger on the cigarette lighter or the pen or the knife and you are as at home in it as in your own skin your own head your own round furnished world.

'I like your room.'

He glanced around. 'She doesn't come here. She – she used to make me tidy up.'

I could imagine. Everything stuffed in drawers. The vacuum cleaner booming in the chilly hall outside my door. 'Let's go.'

'I'll show you where the b-boat came in to take them away.'

'Them?'

'The crofters. To clear the land for sheep and deer.'

I wasn't there for a history lesson. Any direction would do. We set off northwards then turned right along an unsurfaced track that rose and skirted the bottom of the mountain; its top was hidden in cloud.

'I'll take you up there when it c-clears.'

The path was already steep enough and rough enough for me. I was having trouble keeping pace with him. 'You were saying. You didn't tell her when you moved out?'

'I knew she'd try to stop me and I just – I just–'

'What did she say?'

'She tried to kill herself.'

I stopped and he stopped and looked at me with his good eye. We sat on a broken-down stone wall, and I rolled us cigs. The rain had petered out but it was windy. 'Why?'

'Sh-she didn't want me to move out.'

I was impressed by his heartlessness. But it didn't make sense. Why would she try to kill herself? Of course, if she had succeeded she would have foiled my plan, but it seemed an extreme length to go to just to spite me. It would have been quite amusing, I suppose, imagining me putting time and effort into chasing her to the island, only to find she'd topped herself. She could have had a good laugh about that. If she hadn't been dead. But she wasn't dead. Which meant she probably never intended to be.

'What happened?'

'She thought I was just getting rid of the – the stuff she said was junk. But I cleared my room. She started crying and I j-just – I left.'

The lower edge of the cloud was rising slightly around the mountain, just clearing the top of a tree, revealing a jutting-out rock, revealing a higher band of solid stuff behind the mist. 'I hadn't got any sheets so I went back after tea. I thought she'll be watching the news and she won't know if I go in. Take the sheets off my bed.'

'You found her?'

'A-all the doors were open. It was quiet, no TV. I looked in the sitting room and she was—'

'What had she taken?'

'Something she made. One of her brown bottles. They had to take it to the chemist to test.'

'She must have known you'd come back.' What was wrong with waiting till night and poisoning herself at bedtime, if she was *interested* in dying? What was wrong with assuming poison might take a few hours to work? She wanted to be found alive, to make him feel like shit.

'What did you do?'

'Phoned the d-doctor. The helicopter took sixteen minutes.'

'So they took her to hospital and pumped her out and sent her home again.' We sat in silence staring at the mist inching up the mountain like a magician very very slowly pulling a cloth off a something he has magicked out of emptiness. A girl in the secure unit killed herself when they locked her in solitary. She tried to hang herself from the window bar with her knickers, she looped them through one leg to attach them to the bar then stuck her head through the other leg hole, but they ripped they wouldn't hold her weight. So then when someone forgot to collect her plate after supper she smashed it and rubbed her wrists with the broken pottery. She wedged a shard between her feet and sawed away until she got through to the artery. She was more or less dead when they found her in the morning. They couldn't resuscitate her. She *meant* to kill herself. What the old witch did was designed to bring Calum round, not to kill herself. 'A cry for help.'

'Now she has these tablets – anti-d-depressants. But she makes her own medicine, she says it's better–'

'Is she going to die?'

He looked at me gormlessly.

'The cancer. Will it kill her?'

Calum's good eye swivelled towards me then away. He set off along the path again. Was it unimaginable to him? We followed a track through a plantation of fir trees, they were huge and dark, their boughs flailing in the wind and showering us with drips. A baby dumped up there wouldn't have stood a chance. You could see down the straight lines between them past trunk after trunk spinning away to darkness. The field in the light at the end of the track was luridly green, when we came out into it it seemed unreal.

'Twenty-three families lived here,' said Calum. It was empty, full of lumps and hummocks sloping down towards the sea and facing the steep blank hills of the mainland. He squatted down and began to probe with his fingers in the long wet grass.

'Right.'

He examined a few stones and shards and slipped a couple of them into his rucksack. 'The grass grows different, over the ruins.'

It was empty, emptier than empty. I didn't much care about his twenty-three families but I was beginning to be impressed by his enthusiasm. People with enthusiasms are glamorous. How do they get them?

I mean, I can see the world is a fascinating place full of all sorts of things and I could be obsessive about say Indian miniatures or jazz. But I'm not. It's a lack (another). Either they're groupy enthusiasts and they belong to a gaggle of birdwatchers/bikers/born again Christians – or they're lone enthusiasts like Calum. The lone ones are best because they're pure, they're not doing it to be one of the gang, they're doing it out of genuine insanity. Genuine love for seventeenth-century snuffboxes. I would like to be passionate about something, have a hobby, an obsession: cake decorating, tap dancing, topiary. But I don't. Which makes us Rejects excellent fodder for all the groupy enthusiasts. We'll join things because we want to belong. We'll fake enthusiasm, we'll swear black is white to be allowed *in* to some charmed circle. From my peer group at the Underwood home Cathy G. joined the scientologists when she was seventeen and Billy Josephs struck up with a bunch of evangelicals who after a couple of months took him to live in their retreat in north Virginia. He was never seen again. I haven't fallen into the religious slime (despite the best efforts of the Hare Krishnas who pursue me for miles down the street – like dogs'll follow a bitch on heat, they *know* if you're susceptible) but I did join a kind of farm. It never had a name we could agree on until in the last weeks Peter began calling it Stalingrad and that stuck because they needed it to, it wasn't true but they needed it to be. Stupid to join something. Yeah. Idealistic people working together and sharing the proceeds and not exploiting each other or the land. In your *dreams*.

Gerald was the only one who wasn't a nutter or inadequate; in fact, he was probably the only real enthusiast. Certainly if it hadn't been for his enthusiasm we wouldn't have reached that point, of being on a real farm. There was a lot of money tied up in it and most of that must have been Gerald's because I didn't put any in and I can't imagine many of the others did. And it wasn't just the money. At weekly meeting Gerald would have the ideas and make the suggestions, and the rest of us would try to look intelligent and kick them around for a while and say OK. Then Gerald would implement them.

Needless to say it didn't work. Because of people like me? I fancied Gerald. I knew it wouldn't happen because he was too classy for me, also he cared more about making the farm work and he didn't want people to screw everything up with personal relationships, he wanted us to 'make the big picture work to begin with'. Which was saintly but still people like to have an intrigue and fuck from time to time and he seemed to rather frown on all that which made it thrive the more. It was great for the summer, there were loads of people around, we grew veg and hay and we mowed the hay and dried it and we kept goats and milked them and made cheese and we kept hens and in the autumn we harvested the apples. A week of picking and packing and lugging the crates to the road, rich with them, laughing, getting drunk on our own achievement.

Then in the autumn people started to drift back to other places, other work, and it got smaller and tighter and grimmer and the jobs Gerald was putting up on the week's list were things like *Clean out and disinfect hen houses, creosote exteriors* and *repair fencing and replace rotten posts in field bordering main road* and *chop firewood.* And they'd still be there on the list the next week. I always did stuff, I didn't not do stuff, but I didn't choose things like that because it was too cold and would have taken all day. He started making us take jobs then, dividing them up between us but there were rows. 'The thing's got to work because people want to make it work' was the main bone of contention. And Gerald became the taskmaster. Then the guilt-Meister. We'd sit in the kitchen and he'd be striding off across the yard with a coil of barbed wire over his shoulder and the clippers. He wouldn't be in till after evening meal and he'd eat on his own and fall asleep at table.

By New Year it was feeling bad. I knew I'd leave quite soon. People living together and respecting each other and respecting the land and sharing the proceeds was coming down to: you can't sit near the fire tonight unless you've chopped some wood, and only people who can pay in extra for wine can have it because the apple money's all spent now and there's a red electric bill. We were supposed to have pooled all our resources. Why were some people still able to *pay* for wine?

And then Gerald said we all had to come out and help prune the orchard. Now, in January, we couldn't leave it till spring. Everyone had to come and help because each tree took about an hour and there was no way one person could cover them all – also while they were dormant they needed spraying for aphids. And Liz said the cold set off her asthma so she'd cook for the rest of us and Rich said he'd promised his agent he'd write four more songs before Easter and he was sorry but that had to come first and Geri said she was scared of heights and couldn't go up a ladder and did Gerald want her to break her neck and Si said he was fucked if he was working outside all day in this weather and Peter said fine he'd do it but then he never got up till three in the afternoon and Sandy and Karen said they had to go visit her mum because her angina was bad and they'd promised to go before Christmas. And Gillie said who the hell was going to look after the kids or must two- and three-year-olds go and prune trees in sub-zero temperatures too? And I didn't say anything (why the fuck should I?) and in the morning Gerald came into my room begging.

'Please Nikki, come and help me – you know how good the apples were this year, you know how much we need that crop and that cash – *please*' and because he guilted me I went (although I know he tried the same thing with Sandy and Sandy told him to fuck off this life was meant to be about contributing what you could not being hassled night and day) and the two of us spent a bitter freezing day holding the ladder for each other in a tearing gale and snipping away at apple twigs and we did a row and a half, which left about 400 still to do. And on the way back to the house (I was so cold when I dropped the secateurs my fingers wouldn't bend to pick them up again) I said 'Those bastards'd better help us tomorrow or I'll kill them.'

Gerald said, 'I've worked it out. It's my fault – it's because I assume responsibility. We have to leave the apples and let the crop fail. Then everyone'll realise next winter that pruning is important. They've got to *want* to make it work.'

And I said (I was really angry. I was frozen to the marrow) 'How can you be so fucking stupid? They won't still be *here* next January if the apples fail – they'll all fuck off and not give it a second thought' and he didn't reply and I looked at him and there were tears running down his face.

When I woke up next morning I saw him through my window

walking across to the orchard carrying the ladder all on his own in the driving rain. And I got up and packed my rucksack and left. It wasn't ever my bloody enthusiasm so why should I have to feel guilty about it failing? I would have pruned the apples. I would have pruned the apples all day and night if it'd been just for Gerald and me. But I was fucked if I was pruning them so that those idle wankers could get the benefit next autumn.

Gerald went to India after that. When the farm was repossessed. That's what happens to political enthusiasts. They attract people like me and we shit on them. It's better to be like Calum. With an enthusiasm that's just your own. His mother could complain about his junk but she couldn't destroy his obsession. The treasure and the stories they were real to him and the reality didn't depend on anyone else's contribution.

Calum paced about over and round the hummocks like an animal, making sure it was still his territory. When he was ready he came back to me and spread his mac on a mound. It wasn't raining at all anymore but it was damp, low skied and dingy. I was worried she might die before I could kill her. I perched myself beside him. 'When does she go to hospital?'

His good eye moved from my face down to my neck and he stretched out his hand.

'What?' It was unnerving the way he did that.

'Neck-lace?' I'd forgotten I was wearing it – cheap Indian beads. I undid it and let the string slither into a green coil on his grubby palm. He held it close to his eyes for inspection.

'Calum. Does she go for treatment often?'

'She's making herself better. She knows how to.' He passed me back my necklace.

Sure. The first herbal cure for cancer. It was good she was ill I was glad she was suffering but I had to get in there before nature wiped her out. I couldn't wait for her to get around to a sip of hemlock. OK. I'd definitely do it that night; whether she knew about it or not. Even if she was awake and trotting round the house I was still stronger than her. That first night I should have stabbed her going up the stairs – it was just the thought that she knew that fazed me.

Calum wanted to talk about the ruins. 'This was the village. Twenty-three houses here, you see?'

'I see.'

'They grew all their food, oats and barley and greens my dad said. And the men went fishing and they kept sheep that were more like little goats. Th-the women had to spin and weave the wool, then the men took it to the mainland to sell.'

Just what I needed now, a history lesson.

'You know they cleared them off?' he said.

'Go on. Why?'

'The landlord wanted all the land for grazing. He wanted as many sheep as he c-could get – not little sheep but those b-big ones, the ones as big as cows that can't get up when they fall over. They don't come from here.'

'Why?'

'More profit.'

I let him carry on. But I wanted to interrupt all the way through. I like stories but not those bleeding heart ones you've heard a thousand times before. Not the ones where things simply go from bad to worse. What's the point of a story like that? Oh the wicked landowner and oh the poor peasant. Why isn't there a story about the poor oppressed landowner who's struggling to do his best for his tenants? Trying to get them to modernise and stop all this stupid spinning and weaving lark because the cloth they weave is lumpy itchy shit and no one wants to buy it. He wants them to breed up some good hefty sheep with a bit of meat on them to sell as mutton at the market. And the peasants haven't got the wit to do anything different than their parents and grandparents ever did. If the land can't be made more profitable the landlord can't afford to keep it because his income from it's still only the same as what his grandfather was getting but he's just had to pay his grandfather's death duties. He's had to sell half his land and the roof of his house (alright, mansion) is leaking and last year's harvest was crap and he simply can't afford to keep the island if it won't yield a bit more. The peasants are a dozy bunch and they can't be doing with these big sheep or with not having the wife busy over her loom so they carry on as usual and the extra dosh the landlord's invested in fifty big sheep for them to fatten is wasted because they don't fence off the cliffs and don't bring the big sheep under shelter in the gales and object to giving them extra feed in winter.

'It's worth it,' pleads the landowner. 'If you give them hay over the winter they'll fetch an extra florin each at the spring markets.'

But that's too hard for the dim old peasants. So the landowner makes a year's spectacular loss on the island and his roof falls in. He has to sell the island and it's bought by evil landlord X. Who knows the profitable thing to do is to clear off the fucking useless peasants and put in four competent shepherds to look after an island full of big sheep.

There. What's wrong with that? Whose fault was that?

Calum was intent on the pathos of his tale. Roof beams. These innocent crofters owned little or nothing. Not the land they farmed nor the earth their homes stood on nor even the stones and roofs of their own houses. *However*, they did own the roof beams.

How? Why?

Calum didn't know – but he knew it was tradition that the crofters had no rights to fell trees on the island (being as every scrap of it was the landowner's). They (or their parents, or their parents' parents, or some old and scabby Viking thirty generations back) imported, stole or bought the roof beam, without which the building of a croft was impossible, from somewhere the other side of the sea, in all probability Norway. So when the factor and his men came (as we all knew they would from the beginning of this story) to the village this used to be and told the villagers to leave, a number of men said they wouldn't leave without their roof beams. So there were stricken women weeping and tearing their hair, bewildered children running about screaming, brave men dashing back into their burning homes to drag out the looms with the cloth still in them, and the factor and his men demolishing the crofts. And when the roof beams crashed to the ground the crofters dragged them charred and splintered from the burning rubble and hauled them over the rocks to the sea.

This lot didn't all get on a leaky ship for Australia or Canada, they got in their own little fishing boats with their roof beams tied up with ropes, bobbing along behind them in the water, and they rowed across to Durris which is the little rocky crag island to the north; to that very settlement Calum and I had walked around only the day before. The landlord had no designs there because you couldn't run cattle or sheep on it or grow oats or anything useful because it was just a lousy barren windswept little crag. And there these poor indomitable crofters rebuilt their homes in the only sheltered spot available using the ancient charred roof beams and lumps of rock which were plentiful nearby. They planted three rowan trees for the magic, and went fishing and ate fish and stayed alive and from time to time traded fish for other kinds of food. Or from time to time (when the shepherds were busy) raided the north of Aysaar and poached a rabbit, a deer, a big meaty sheep.

Then came the Great War, and the men of rocky Durris, whose government had done nothing for them, not provided healthcare or street lights or even a street, let alone a bridge to the big island, were called upon to fight for king and country. Which they did.

And when they came back from the Great War (some of them did come back from the fields of mud and blood to the barren rocky island) they'd had enough. And they got in their boats and rowed to the south of Aysaar, where the land is most fertile and where the outlines of their ancestors' strip fields were still visible under the surface and they dug the earth and planted crops: oats, barley, potatoes, greens. They built a little hut and each night two of them would stay there to guard their crops while the others rowed back to the crag they called home. They didn't hide anything or steal anything, they simply grew fodder on the fertile land which had been cleared and farmed by their ancestors.

I knew of course that the story would end badly because these tales of heroic working folk always do. Calum the Brain *honoured* them for being victims. If I'd survived the trenches I would've gone straight back to my old home on the big island and I would've rounded up those giant sheep and had a barbecue. And I would've chopped down the landlord's trees for new roof beams and built a load of new houses, a Barratt estate. I would've tied the arms and legs of the scab shepherds and set them off in a boat with no oars. And when anyone came to get me I would've said I was a shell-shocked war hero and refused to take orders from anyone but my General.

Why were they so creepily God-fearingly decent and humble? Why didn't they raise hell?

Calum proceeded to the end of his pathetic tale. The police came from the mainland and asked them to leave. A party of crofting men came over from Skye to support them against the police. The men *refused* to leave (non-violently) and the police removed them by force and took them in boats to the mainland, and charged them with trespass and resisting arrest.

The end was completely unsatisfactory. When the thing came to court they were let off on a technicality so they were found neither innocent nor guilty. And when they came back they carried on exactly as before, farming on Aysaar and rowing home to their rocky crag to sleep, and the police couldn't be bothered with them any more and neither could the landlord because he died and eventually the island came into the possession of the Ministry of Agriculture and Fisheries and the *next* generation, the children of the Great War soldiers, were told they could buy crofts on Aysaar again if they liked. But as most of them were sick of crags and sea and fish and bored to death with the whole bloody saga they went to the mainland to seek their fortunes, leaving the ancestral roof beams to fall into decay on the rocky island where not even holidaymakers would want to stay.

'Very sad,' I told Calum. He looked at me completely gone out.

'Sad. They were a bunch of losers. Why didn't they fight? What were they doing killing honest German peasants in the trenches and leaving evil bastard landlords alive?'

My clever brother sat with his mouth half open and his eyes looking east and west. What the fuck was I doing, sitting in a dripping field having history lessons? I was way off course. I got up and ran back into the forest.

I could hear him calling after me. 'Nikki! Ni-ikki!'

'Fuck off. Just fucking well fuck off!'

I hurt his feelings. Why not? It's what I'm good at. Trashing things. Trash trashes things.

14 · Mother's
weak spot

I looked back down to the abandoned village once I had gone through the forest and gained some height. I could make him out, crouched over, digging at something I suppose. Looking for treasures. That was what he did, I thought – he had so bloody little life of his own that all he could do was collect the detritus of other lives and pore over the stories of ghosts.

When I got back the Life Source was audible in her kitchen. The Fat Controller (only she was skinny); the arch manipulator. I went straight to the kitchen, knocked and asked to borrow some milk. She was making pastry – she really was, her hands were all floury and she told me to help myself from the fridge. She was making steak and kidney pie for Calum.

'D'you make his dinner every day?'

'If he was left to his own devices he'd live on bread and cheese.'

She gave a little laugh. Did she imagine it would amuse me? She went on rolling and cutting while I stood there. I noticed there was a nice row of jars of red jelly on the dresser. So those poisonous rowan seeds would be waiting in the compost in a squishy mass. I should go and find them later.

'What exactly's wrong with him?'

'Nothing. Nothing. He's just a bit different.'

'Can't he get a job?'

'There's not much on the island.'

'It's nice for swimming here in the summer isn't it?' I wanted to make her lose her temper. She poured a saucepan-ful of meat and gravy into the pastry shell. She was concentrating as if she hadn't heard me. 'Does he enjoy swimming?' I needled.

'Oh Calum can't swim.' She began brushing the edges of the pastry with water then spread the pie lid over it and crimped the edges. She was giving the pie 99 per cent of her attention.

'Why not?'

'It's not a good idea.' She broke an egg into a cup, beat it with a fork and began brushing the top of the pie with it.

'But he fishes.'

'Not from a boat.'

'Why can't he go in a boat?'

She didn't reply.

'Don't you think his life's a bit restricted?'

She put down the pastry brush. 'He comes and goes as he pleases. He has his food cooked and the run of the place.' She picked up the pie ready to put it in the oven.

'That's not much more than you'd give a dog.'

There was a little silence while she stared at me and I waited for her to crack.

'I'm glad you popped in,' she said. 'I wanted a word with you about your room.'

'My room?'

'Yes. I'm going to be needing it. I'd like you to find somewhere else.'

'Needing it for what?'

She opened the oven, slid the pie in and closed the door. 'I'm giving you notice.'

'Why?'

'I don't think I have to answer that question.' She started scraping up the pastry scraps with the side of a knife.

'What have I done? What have I done wrong?'

'It's unsettling for Calum to have someone in his old room.'

'He's enjoyed talking to me—'

'I'd be grateful if you'd leave him alone from now on. He's not used to young women.'

She turned to the sink and started running the water. I felt as if my head was going to burst. I ran to my room before I started screaming and swearing at the bitch.

149

She wanted me away from Calum. She knew Calum was her weak spot. Calum was the only person who could hurt her or fool her, so Calum and I had to be separated. It was so obvious. And I had been playing into her hands (again) by falling out with him. I had been too stupid to realise the only way we could beat her was together.

Calum. Calum and I had to work together. Together we had a chance.

I set off at a run from the house; jogging back the way I'd come, up the track past the iron mine and down towards the dripping forest. I was sweating and gasping for breath, get back and make it up to Calum. Get back to Calum and win him round. Persuade the poor dope I never yelled 'Fuck off!'

After a bit I had to slow down. There was a movement in the ditch beside the track – my eyes fastened to it before I realised what it was. Black. A crow, pecking away at something dead. Not a crow, please, not a crow. I turned my head away and walked on quickly and it didn't fly up past me it didn't force me to look at it, I hoped I might have got away with it.

I plunged into the still forest – when I came out Calum wasn't at the ghost village. I walked across the empty lumpy field and the sound of laughter came to me – fractured jeering laughter. It was coming from the other side – the seaward side of the field. I went to the edge and looked down. It was a drop of a hundred feet or so to a rocky shoreline and the flat sea. Calum was on the rocks and there were three men with him – sitting, sprawling on the rocks. As I watched one threw a can to another and he missed; it crashed against a rock and burst in a shower of white froth.

'Dickhead!' The one who'd missed the catch got up and went to fetch another can. He was young – they were all youngish, no more than twenty. Calum was drinking too, I watched him tilt his head back and drain the can. Calum's friends?

There was a steep narrow little path away to my left, it zigzagged down the cliff face, in places it was steps cut into the rock. I started to scramble down. Mud and rock skittered out from under my feet. One of the youths looked up at me and wolf-whistled. 'That your girlfriend?' he called to Calum. He didn't have a local accent. Calum pulled the tab off a new can and it sprayed in his face. They were braying with laughter. Now I was closer I could see they were watching him. They were nasty, full of pointless energy. I reached the bottom and called.

'Calum. It's time to go.'

'He's gonna show us 'is treasure,' said one with thin greasy brown hair. 'Have a lager.'

'No thanks. Calum?'

'Give us a chance, 'e's the first bleeder we've met since the ferry. 'E's gonna show us the sights.'

'What are you doing here?'

'Daytrip, innit.' The others laughed.

'What ya got in that bag?' the biggest one asked Calum. He was fat, with a tight black T-shirt. Calum was intent on his can. He waved his arm at the rucksack and Greasy Hair kicked it over to his mate so they could look in it. Big Tub tipped out the piece of driftwood, old brown bottle, fragment of tile and heap of stones Calum'd collected so far.

'Wow! *Antiques Roadshow!*' The one who hadn't spoken yet, shaven hair and spots around his mouth. 'Chuck us the bottle.' Obvious what was going to happen and I said *'Don't'*; Big Tub glanced at me then threw it, it smashed at Skinhead's feet.

'Oo-er, should've listened to Miss,' said Greasy Hair. Calum scrambled over and began to pick up the biggest pieces of glass.

'Calum, leave them, you'll cut yourself. Let's go.'

'You his sister?' said Skinhead. 'Wanta come for a drink with us?'

'No.' The first person in the world to take me for my brother's sister.

The other two began laughing and then they started shaking their cans and spraying each other. They threw another can to Calum who caught and opened it.

'Calum I'm going. Are you coming?'

'Aar aar!' Big Tub doubled up with laughter and Skinhead stood up and jerked his crotch at me. 'Coming Miss! I'm coming! Uh! Uh! Uh!' They weren't dangerous they were just stupid little fuckwits.

'This the best beach you got?' Greasy Hair asked. Neither Calum nor I spoke; the skinhead said, 'Island of fucking dreams this, innit?'

'Tropical paradise mate,' said Greasy. 'Lucky that wanker in Skye told us about it–'

'Yeah,' said Big Tub. 'What about them palm trees and coconuts and them big rollers on the golden sands–' He gestured to the grey stony beach and flat brownish sea.

'You like living on this shit heap?' asked Skinhead.

'I – I – it's not a–'

Big Tub shook his can and sprayed Calum's face. 'Sh-sh-shut it you.' The others laughed.

'Not a sh-shit heap,' persisted Calum, wiping his face.

'Is too,' said Skinhead. 'There's fuck all here. What's there to do?'

'Shag,' muttered Big Tub and they glanced at each other.

'Sat what you do?' Skinhead asked Calum. 'Shag yer sister?' He turned to the others: 'That's 'ow they get divs like 'im!' All three of them laughed but Calum was getting up, his mouth was opening and closing.

'You gonna show us this treasure then?'

'You sh-shouldn't–' began Calum.

'S-S-Suck my knob, Braindeath,' said Skinhead and the other two roared with laughter and Skinhead tipped his head back to finish his can. And Calum hit him.

I knew it was coming from the minute I saw them all together, but it had happened the wrong way round. 'Calum! Calum!'

'Call fucking King Kong off!' Greasy shouted. He was scuttling away backwards over the rocks, he didn't want a fight. Skinhead was kicking and flailing at Calum and Calum was shaking him.

'Let go you shit you thick fucking ape.' Skinhead was crying and Calum's face was wide like a grin and he was holding Skinhead with one hand and pulling back with the other to punch him and Big Tub was shouting, 'Kill the bastard Gaz! Gaz! Kill 'im!' and

Calum punched him hard and he went down. Big Tub darted in to help him but Calum swiped him away and went for Gaz again. He was roaring, he honestly was, roaring like a ham in a horror film.

'Calum! Calum! No!' He was completely gone, he didn't even blink, he was just grabbing for Gaz who was scrambling on his arse over the rocks to get away. Greasy Hair was coming back in at the side of the picture with a long splintery plank. He was edging around to try and get behind Calum. Nothing would stop Calum, I could see that. I threw myself after him and grabbed his arm just as he was raising it to throw another punch. And he took no more notice of me than a fly, he simply punched with me on the end of his arm and I went sprawling at his feet. I lost it briefly then, I could hear but I couldn't see for a minute. Calum must have stood still staring at me because it gave them time to leg it. I heard their retreating voices screaming abuse and threats. I started to pull myself up, I could taste blood on my lip, my cheek was numb. Calum was just standing there panting, staring at me.

'You fucking idiot look what you've done.'

Calum sat down. 'Sorry.'

'Sorry! Sorry! You could see they were fuckwits why did you let them–'

'I lost my temper.'

That nearly made me laugh. I pulled myself up and sat down next to him, I felt giddy.

'I'm sorry. Does it h-hurt?'

'Of course it fucking hurts. Why didn't you *stop*?'

'I j-just – I just get so–' He was gulping for air, like his stammer was stuck in his throat. Suddenly he leaned over to the side and vomited. He kept coughing and choking on it for a long time and when he finally lifted his head up he was crying. It stank, it was nothing but the lager.

'Stop it. I'm more hurt than you, *I* should be crying. Come on, move away from the smell.' I took his hand and led him along the beach a bit. We both had to sit down again. 'Calum. Stop it–'

'Sh-she told me not to d-drink. And now I've hurt you . . .'

'I'm alright. Let's go home.'

Hand in hand we crawled back up the cliff path and onto the track. After a bit he stopped snuffling. 'He said I sh-shag my sis–'

'He was being stupid. He was a pillock.'

'I h-haven't sh-shagged anyone.'

'No. That's alright.'

We walked in silence for a bit longer then he said, 'I'd like to sh-shag someone.' I let go of his hand. My head was splitting I could feel my cheekbone ringing now every step I took, I had completely and utterly had enough.

'Shut up. Stop talking about it.'

He did shut up but when I glanced at him I saw he was crying again, silently. 'Stop it.'

'You d-don't like me.'

'How can anyone like you when you behave like an idiot?' I was so dizzy I could hardly put one foot in front of the other. My eye had

155

started to throb. By the time we got to the house he was leading me and the vision in my left eye was blurred. He took us in the front door and I sat on the chair by the telephone. My head was clanging. He called and his mother came shuffling out of the kitchen. There was some exchange between them I don't know I couldn't look up, the hall seemed to be filling with dark mist it got darker and darker. I could still hear her voice I was straining to get my eyes open but they *were* open, all they could see was blackness. Then I pitched into it.

When I woke up I was on my bed and there was something cold and wet pressing on my left eye and trickling down my cheek and into my ear. There was a noise – I could hear something – someone in my room. The sound of a drawer being eased out; the rustle of clothing being shuffled through. Someone going through my things. With my right eye all I could see was the wall by the bed and a mound of duvet. The drawer was gently slid shut. I closed my good eye and held still. The liquid trickling into my ear tickled maddeningly. Careful shuffling footsteps moved to the wardrobe. The door opened, there was a tiny clink of clothes-hangers as she riffled through my clothes – my pockets? – what was she looking for? What the hell was she doing? I heard her move again, closer to the bed. There was no one but me and her there. She could do *anything*–

I half turned to my right, giving a kind of cough, then ostentatiously woke up. When I opened my right eye she was leaning over me with a bottle in her hand.

'Are you awake? Good, you can have a dose of this for the bruising.' She started to measure teaspoonfuls into a glass. It was dark green.

'I don't want it.'

'It'll do you good – it'll bring down the swelling.'

'I don't want it right now. I'll take it later.'

She had the glass in her hand ready to hold it to my lips.

'Thank you. Leave it by the bed for now.'

She put it down slowly. 'That poultice needs changing as well.'

Before I could react she'd grabbed it off my eye. I opened it and got a letterbox slot of vision. The whole side of my head ached. She was fiddling with something in a bowl and told me to close my eye again.

Anything – she could be doing anything to me and who on earth would know? I knew she was dangerous and yet I'd come and casually – unthinkingly – put myself at her mercy. Got myself hurt and helpless under her care. So she could go through my stuff; snoop, steal things, do what she liked to my injuries. Call yourself intelligent, Nikki? Call yourself in control?

I tried to slow my breathing. She slapped something freezing cold and stinging on to my eye and I yelled out.

'It's all right, it'll feel cold for a minute or two, that's all.'

I didn't want her to see how scared I was. I wanted her out of the room. She shuffled towards the window, the room got darker. Her voice was apologetic. 'Calum's very upset. I've told him – it's the alcohol–'

'I'd like to go to sleep.'

'He doesn't know his own strength, that's the trouble, he doesn't know when to stop.'

'I should have kept out of it.'

There was a sudden silence, she must have frozen, then I heard her shuffle on to the table and sit down. She spoke quietly. 'One day he's going to kill someone. One day there's going to be someone who doesn't say *it's all right* and he's going to end up in jail.'

'It's all right.' The sound of my own voice sawed through my bony skull.

'But it's not, is it.' There was a long silence. 'He's like a child. While I'm alive – to pick up the pieces – to keep an eye on him – we stagger along. But when I go . . .'

I turned my head fractionally to see her better, she was just a dark hunched silhouette against the white light of the window. She was holding her head in her hands, she was sniffling. It sounded as if she was crying. I couldn't follow her convolutions, first she was trying to excuse him, then when I *said* it was my fault she wanted to tell me how seriously dangerous he was. Was she threatening me with him? Saying she couldn't be responsible for his actions, he might run amok and kill me? The whole room was fuzzy. She was sobbing, her back was to me. 'I wish he was dead and buried. Sometimes – I do. Then I'd know he was safe . . .'

Well. I suppose if everyone was dead we'd all be safe and nothing nasty would ever happen to us again.

'Please will you let me go to sleep now.' My voice squeezed up out of my sandpaper throat. I wanted her out away gone I didn't want another glimpse or squeak of her. She stood up slowly and shuffled to the door, opened it and shut it behind her with a little click. I levered myself to sitting upright, fireworks were going off in my head. I felt my way along the wall to the door. Turned the key in the lock. Then I staggered to the sink and filled a glass with water, held myself upright there and swallowed it mouthful by mouthful. My whole body was heavy and slow, she had drugged me already I could tell, she had given me something to slow me down. I wouldn't let her in again. I lay down and fell into deep blackness.

When I woke it was morning. I touched lightly at my face with my fingertips. The left side was swollen, my lip, my cheek, even my forehead on that side felt puffy. There was a squashed green mess of soggy leaves on my pillow. I crawled along the bed till I could see my reflection in the wardrobe mirror. It didn't look as bad as it felt. I was hungry and my head was clanging like a doleful bell but I was clear. Her potions hadn't deprived me of my senses yet. Unless this – being here on all fours on the bed – was a delusion.

I boiled the kettle and made some tea, I made toast and scrambled eggs. Moving my head was strange and I had to tilt and turn it like something mechanical a periscope or something, to see everything I needed to out of the right eye. I sat at the table and ate my breakfast and I felt surprisingly well.

There was one of her brown bottles on the bedside table. Latin hand-written on the label. I sniffed – it had a sweet dark syrupy smell. She was nice to me because she was afraid I might report Calum's violence to the police or someone. She worried about what would happen to him after her death. She would do *anything* for Calum – even to the point of being willing to have him die – if she thought it would protect him.

The only way I could hurt her was through Calum. It came in a stab of light as I turned my bad eye towards the window. A piercing shaft of illumination. Calum was the only thing on earth she cared about. If I took Calum *away* from her I would take away her reason for staying alive. Everything she did she did for him; without him she would be as unnecessary and unloved as she had rendered me. Taking Calum away would be the punishment she deserved; to kill her would, in comparison, be a kindness.

The sun was shining brightly. I opened the back door. On the step was a jamjar full of tiny orange flowers like stars, and purple Michaelmas daisies. There was a folded bit of lined paper nestled amongst them; I opened it up and saw that it was childishly printed in pencil.

NIKI I DINT SAY THANKYOU FOR HELPPING ME THANK YOU I HOP YOU ARE AWRITE AND I AM VERY SORY. XX CAL.

There you are. I helped my brother. What d'you think of that? A selfish bitch who can't even help herself, wading into a fight and saving her big strong brother from murdering or being murdered. Makes a change eh? I put the flowers and note on the mantel-piece. And I thought if she comes snooping I hope she's fucking jealous.

15 · Ashplant

Calum called for me after his dinner; from the smell she gave him something fried, or maybe it was chips. Hot fat pervaded the hall and I was entirely glad to be dining on water and a fag. It was a hot, glowing mid-August type day suddenly fallen into early October. I sat on my doorstep and the sun made my skin prickle.

'Your p-poor face.'

'It's OK. Where are you off to today?' I passed him a cigarette and he sat next to me on the step. He didn't have his coat on, just a shapeless T-shirt which hung limply from his thin angular shoulders. He leaned forward, elbows on his knees, right leg trembling like a dog's. He was avoiding looking at me.

'I'll take you to the s-sithein.'

He assumed I was going with him but all I wanted to do was sit and absorb the sun. I felt dopey. I don't know why but I wanted him to look at me. The dull ache around my eye was soothing and mind-numbing, it excused me from things. 'I think I'll stay here.'

'No. You come. It's – it's a special place.'

'Is it a climb?'

'No – no, it's near the woods. Beautiful, you'll like it.'

He was wretched, guilty and solicitous. I felt sorry for him, his mother had him trapped. She would have told him off for hurting me. She wouldn't like it if I went with him today . . . slowly I remembered the things I had to do, they surfaced in slow silence as things do in the fog, materialising out of nothing. I couldn't afford to waste the day. I had to act. I had to get Calum off her. This hot drowsiness that was pulling me down – I had to shake it off.

'Have you got some water in there?' He put my mineral water bottle in his rucksack and we set off. We walked in silence, the island was glassy in the heat, the lane shimmered with mirage. It was very quiet, somehow suspended – I was suspended, the day was suspended in a strange hot glassy calm. We came to the edge of the woods and had a drink and a smoke in the shade of a warped tree dotted with blue-black berries. I asked him what it was.

'Elder. The birds eat the berries.'

There was a Mother Elder in a fairy story, but my sleepy brain couldn't recall if she was good or bad. 'I'll be leaving quite soon,' I said.

He looked at me properly for the first time that day. 'Why?'

'Well, I have things to do, I have to get another job.'

'You can stay here.'

'No.' I realised that I'd stopped seeing his wandering eye. I was automatically looking at the good one.

'Because I hit you?'

'No. You can come with me if you want.'

I saw him consider the suggestion. 'But—'

'What?'

'My m-mother.'

'Other people don't stay with their mothers all their life.'

He shook his head.

'Wouldn't you like to see where I live?'

He was twisting a couple of long grass stems in and out between his fingers. 'I can't go off the island.' He moved away abruptly through the tall grass. After a hundred yards or so he stopped and crouched, cupping a growing stalk in his hand. 'Look.'

Two little snails with their shells on their backs were toiling up the grass stem. He went on slowly, stopping again for a stone which he said was a fossil, then for an old pen lid and a plastic bottle, which all went into the rucksack. I felt light and weak, my powers of concentration and persuasion were like water. How could I entice him away from her and off the island? It seemed terribly easy and simultaneously, impossible.

We skirted a wood until we came to an overgrown field. The long grass had feathery seeds, reddish and purplish against the green stalks. There were three hummocks in the field. 'More ruined crofts?'

'No.' He made for the closest. At one side there was a narrow opening; bending down I could just see into a dark stone-lined space like a small cold cave.

'It's a sithein. The Little People live here.' He moved off round the other two humps, touching and checking them in his Calum-ish way. I sat down and leaned my back against the grass-covered hummock. The sun was hot, I closed my eyes and it shone redly through my lids. My cheek was throbbing gently. I heard him come and settle down next to me, he passed me the bottle of water.

'Thanks. D'you like me, Calum?'

'Yes.'

I opened my good eye and turned to face him, he was frowning at his knees. I patted his hand on the grass. It felt rough and dry. There was a little silence filled with the buzzing of bees and the soft rustle of breeze in the grass.

'Nikki?'

'Yes?'

'You know about the Little People?'

'No.'

'They live in this field.'

'I don't believe in fairies.'

'You sh-shouldn't say that.'

'Why?'

'They can't keep sheep in this field – the Little People drive them mad.'

'Yeah?'

'If the sh-sheep graze on the sithein they start to run round in circles. Nobody can make them stop, they run in circles till they die.'

Long hot sleepy pause, the sun has drenched through to my bones, I am hot and molten and Calum's soft stammer with its note of anxiety – wanting to convince me – is pleasantly distracting, just keeping me on the surface. The heat is sexy too, I undo the top buttons of my shirt. 'Go on then. Tell me about them.'

'Don't you know?'

'Sod all. Nothing. Not a peep.'

'You know they came from h-heaven?'

'No Calum I don't.' So easy to let that sarcasm in; it curls him into himself like a snail when your shadow falls across it. Be sweet. 'Please – tell me. Why did they leave heaven?'

'They were Lucifer's angels. When he was thrown out they fell too. They were hurtled to earth and some fell in the sea. The Blue Men, they d-drowned my dad.'

'Blue men?'

'In the w-waves. Foam-grey faces, sometimes calm but always plotting . . .'

His voice drifts off; I open my eyes and squint at the woods bordering the field. The sunshine makes the leaves glint like metal. 'Some fell in the sea–?'

'The others fell on land. The Little People. Daoine Sithe. They have all s-sorts of tricks.'

'Like what?' A fly comes buzzing round my sweaty face and I flap it away.

'People who annoy them – th-they spoil everything for them. They can suck the insides out of stuff and leave it looking just the same.'

'Explain.'

'A meal, say, a feast. They suck the goodness out of everything and leave it just a h-hollow shell. It looks good but when you touch it crumbles. To dust.'

I know this, I've heard this before.

'They do that to gold and j-jewels, cattle, houses, anything. It still looks all right but they've s-sucked the insides out.'

'Can they do it to people?'

'I don't know. There are lots of things they've ruined and people don't even know.' He's hacking at a tuft of grass with a stone he's picked up. Agitated, his voice anxious. 'Some people say they've done it to the whole w-world already.'

Silence. My back itches. I wriggle against the hummock. 'Well they sound horrible, Calum. Why are we sitting here?'

'Sh-shh. You mustn't say that. If they like you they bring good luck. They can make your wish come true.'

'I'm getting too hot. Can we move into the shade?' My hurt face was smarting and stinging, I suddenly thought it would be really stupid to get it sunburnt. And I suspected I might be leaning against an ants' nest. I crossed to the edge of the field and shook myself and scratched my back then lay down in the shade of a huge beech tree. Calum was stroking the tumulus like a pet. When he came over to me his expression was lugubrious. I rolled onto my side and watched his eye register my cleavage in the open shirt. 'Go on about the Little People.'

'They d-don't want to be bad. But they haven't got a home. All they can do is prey on people.' He sat down and I rolled him a cigarette, and he told me his story about the Little People.

'It was right here in this wood. A priest was on his way to a baptism. It was hot as today, and when he came to a clearing he sat down for a rest. He stuck his crook in the ground beside him.'

There was a sharp squint of light coming in my injured eye – I lay back down and shielded my eyes with my arm. My neck and chest were tickly as if an insect was crawling over me; I brushed it off and ran my fingertip into the little hot valley of sweat between my tits.

'There were all sorts of noises. The priest could hear rustlings and sounds like whispering voices – coming from the trees.'

With my arm over my eyes I could see Calum and he couldn't see me. His face was anxious with the effort of getting the story right.

'He – he saw, suddenly, at the edge of the clearing, a c-crowd. A crowd of little people. With tiny pointed faces and raggedy clothes, like dirty little monkeys. He was shocked. He did the sign of the c-cross but they didn't disappear. One came nearer – a wizened little man with a long grey beard and eyes like raisins.'

I was so hot I felt like melting. I wondered if the black eye had somehow caused a temperature. Stupid to be wearing jeans and a shirt in such weather. I undid the cuffs and slowly rolled the sleeves up. Calum seemed to have stopped. 'Go on.'

'The little man knelt down and asked the priest to bless him. "Who are you?" said the priest. "Daoine Sithe. Little People. We want forgiveness. We want to be God's children and have our souls back. We are sorry for our sins." The priest was very angry. "Give you my blessing? When God has thrown you out?" The little man and all the fairies groaned. They had tiny hands like skinny chickens' claws, they raised them up to the priest. "Please forgive us." "Never! My walking stick here will sprout leaves before God forgives the likes of you."'

I rolled over onto my belly. My whole body was ticklish and tingling – maybe it was the after-effects of that medicine she gave me. I wanted to pull off all my clothes and rub myself against the cool green grass. There were waves of heat rolling through me. Calum shifted on the grass beside me. He's your brother, Nikki, don't be gross. Brother, *half*-brother, what the hell does it matter anyway? He's *simple*, Nikki, he's just a big kid. With a perfectly adequate male body, and sweet as can be, he'd be all hot and trembly and uncertain.

It seemed like quite a long silence. 'Have you forgotten the rest of the story?'

'Oh no.' He coughed to clear his throat but when he spoke again his voice seemed husky. 'The Little People all stood staring at him with their beady eyes. And he hitched up his cassock and ran as fast as he could and their soft wailing voices came curling after him through the trees like smoke.'

Another Angus number, obviously. I wondered how many times over Calum'd heard the stories. To remember them word for word.

'The priest visited the new baby and did the baptism. He was ready to go home but he couldn't find his walking stick. Then he remembered he must have left it in the clearing. When he was going back through the woods he could hear the Little People still crying through the trees. As if they followed him. But when he came to the clearing it looked different.'

I like it when you can see it coming. Sprouting. There's a sexy word.

'Where his crook had been – there was a great big ash tree – beautiful, with spreading branches, taller than all the other trees. Over – over . . .' he hesitated.

'Over what?'

'Overtopping. Overtopping all the trees of the wood. As God's mercy outreaches man's.' He delivered his punchline with a note of relief.

'So the priest was a bit gobsmacked?' I rolled over again so I could see his face. He was nodding and grinning. I sat up to undo my trainers so I could feel the grass with my toes.

'He knelt down – even his teeth were chattering!' Calum said delightedly. 'And he was staring madly everywhere in the trees staring and staring to find their little pointy faces. And he called to them, "Please forgive me! Little People! Forgive me!" but all he could hear was the noise of wailing far away in the trees.'

'Too late,' I said. 'He was way too late.'

'Yes, he went up and down—'

'This way and that—'

'In and out—'

'Through the trees—'

Calum stopped, looking at me worriedly.

'It's OK. Just joining in. He never found them did he? There's no happy ending?'

Calum's face dropped. 'No, no happy ending.' He peered at his fingers combing through a tuft of grass, as if they didn't belong to him. Then looked up at me. I rolled onto my side again.

'Calum, why don't you come away with me? It'll be fun – we can do all sorts of things . . .'

He was sitting with his legs drawn up in front of him. I raised my foot and pressed it gently against his shin. I could make him do anything.

'I like you,' he said.

Of course he liked me.

'Nikki?'

'Yes?'

'Can I marry you?'

Bull's-eye in one! 'When we go to the mainland – maybe we could talk about it . . .'

Ashplant

'I do like you.'

'I know.'

He moved suddenly onto his knees and he was kneeling over me, blocking out the light. I struggled to sit up. 'Nikki do you like me?' His voice was uncertain but his face loomed in very close. Right next to mine his sweet hay-breath on my face I could see his lips and they were as soft and dry as a whisper. He'll come away with me oh yes he'll follow me wherever I go she's lost him now the fucking bitch has lost him.

It was slow as a ballet each move inevitable but not dangerous each move hypnotically sweet. He grazed my upper arm with his fingertips just brushed the skin I felt the ripples in my belly. He raised his fingers to my bruised face and gently cupped the air around it he whispered 'Kiss it better kiss it better.' I put my hands on his shoulders to steady myself I shifted my weight so I was kneeling up to bring my face level with his and I could feel the heat of his flesh I could feel his shoulders trembling. He dropped his arms to his sides. Our bodies were facing one another the three or four inches of space between was thick like water it slowed us it pressed us it held us apart but through it each felt the other's heat. He leaned into it fractionally and my throat tightened so I had to gasp the air in he was close he was so close he was coming closer. Then I drew in breath his chest just touched my nipples and it was still slow-motion, slow and teasingly sweet as creeping to the edge of the highest cliff and slowly peering over it was possible to control to choose and control to delicately move to lean in a centimetre closer and feel his weight against my tits spreading circles of heat he was trembling but he didn't move just knelt there simply arms by his sides. I put my face closer to his again it was as if there was a resistance in the air between us a little barrier a current that when we touched it dissolved and there was nothing between us but the tug of gravity.

The slow trance snapped. Our bodies collided. We fell.

It was my fault. I'm perfectly aware of that. When is it not my fault? My fault, or her fault for making me. I egged him on. I drew him in. I was the only one who knew we were related. He was innocent of that knowledge. He did nothing wrong. He attempted only what nature invented him for: to pass on his genes.

True to the hateful contradictoriness of my character, in the moment at which the outcome of our frenzied grappling became inevitable, I realised that I absolutely did not want it to happen. Which made things worse for both of us because I scratched him to bleeding and he ripped my jeans and grabbing me round the neck with one hand pressed my face into the ground and half suffocated me. It was over in a minute. Then he burst into tears and let me go.

I crawled out from under him and went and leaned against the nearest tree. I bent over to vomit I would have liked to vomit myself out – entirely – to vomit myself inside out so that the whole of me got transferred via the circle of my retching mouth into a heap of half-digested matter on the ground.

That would have been the best thing. He was crying and it was entirely my fault but I couldn't stay near him. I got my trainers and ran as best I could through the trees. Just keep moving that was all I could do but eventually I could see the sea up ahead and that was what I wanted, I got myself to the edge and took off the horrible clothes and went in, stumbling and slipping on the stones. It was cold at first it numbed my hurts and I scrubbed at myself all over I ducked my head and kept it under until I thought it would burst I scratched and clawed at the dirty skin to scrape that layer off. The salt seared my cut face and the line of the scratches on my arms and wrists, and on my hip where I'd been pressed onto something sharp. The pain brought tears to my eyes and the relief of crying. I crawled out pink and cold and peeled; took my slimy jeans back into the sea and beat them in the water. At least it was on the jeans not in me. When they were clean I put them on – started back into the trees, curled up all soaking wet as I was and fell asleep. I don't know how I could, but I did.

16 · Dislocation

When I woke I needed a fag. I didn't have my tin it must be where Calum was. It was getting dark and my throat was sore and parched. I didn't know where I could go then I thought, the pub. He won't come there, she won't come there, I have to make a plan, I have to sit down with a cigarette. I set off through the trees trying to keep my back to the sea. The trees were black and underfoot was treacherous with roots and holes and dead branches; twice I fell, each time I looked back the trees were gathering closer together in a tight dark mass behind me. At last it seemed lighter ahead and I burst out into a field and the sky was open all above me and I stopped and got my breath. Then I crossed the field and came to a road. When I looked back the trees had congealed into solid blackness. I followed the road around two bends and then ahead I could see lights. There was a moon and the clouds were moving across it so there were patches of silvery light. The bare sky was dark blue and I could see the road easily, and the lights of the village ahead.

There were half a dozen wizened old men in the bar, they all stared at me. I asked for cider and change for fags; the machine was in the dingy corridor that led to the bogs. In the Ladies I stripped off and stood with one foot against the door, washing myself all over again with a sliver of grey soap and a threadbare towel. The reflection of my face looked like a battered plum.

When I was dressed I put my money in the cig machine. Sat down on the cracked plastic chair beside it then realised I didn't have matches. I sat there for a minute, it was too hard to move. I didn't want the men looking at me. The door from the bar opened and a woman came past. She stopped.

'You alright?'

'Have you got a light?'

She produced a lighter from her pocket. She was staring at me. The first lungful of smoke was the sweetest thing.

'Yeah. Thanks. I'm fine.'

She nodded and went on her way to the toilet. There were photos stuck to the wall – snaps, rows of them. Some local festivity. Grinning faces, people in costume, men in helmets carrying a Viking boat. I sat and stared at them, gone out. The effects of the cigarette were spreading through my body like stars. When I'm dying of cancer I'll remember smoking that fag, and how I knew when I smoked it that it was bringing death closer and that knowledge was the kernel of the pleasure it gave me. The woman came back out of the bogs. 'Have you got a drink? Want to come and sit with us?'

Did I look so bad? I was feeling better. 'Thanks. In a bit.' I watched her go back into the bar. Dyke – I'd seen her before. Yes, the vegetarian café woman. Sensible. Safe. Sally. What would we talk about? Hello, I've just been fucked by my brother.

I lit another fag off the glowing butt. I couldn't make myself think. It was too hard. My concentration skittered off it like drops of water in a frying pan with hot oil. Skittered and spat and jumped off the surface.

What did it matter? He hadn't *hurt* me. A few bruises. It didn't mean anything. It wasn't as if I hadn't put up with stuff I didn't want before. I knew it was my fault I didn't even need to think about that. Then I had to get up and go to the toilet to retch again. There was nothing but yellow bile. It made my throat sore.

I'd lost the plot. Taking him off his mother . . . getting revenge on her . . . I was going to kill her but the only person getting damaged here was me. I was sitting on the cracked chair again staring at the photos. There was one of a big guy in a Viking helmet with his arm over a Red Indian's shoulder. The Red Indian was grinning from ear to ear like a turnip. He was young, about fourteen. He was Calum. On the other side of him was a woman in a long cloak with shiny moons and stars and a wizard's black hat. Laughing. Her.

I went over and knelt to look at it better. The big guy must be Angus. It was a flash, the background was dark, you could make out shadowy figures behind them. Calum was the same. A tall happy kid. The three of them together. A family. Captured in their togetherness moment. A sealed bubble I couldn't burst. Safely in the past.

Someone came down the corridor behind me – the dyke again. 'Oh, you're still here.' She stopped and looked over my shoulder. 'It's a New Year's festival they have. It's brilliant.'

'Right.'

'They burn this replica of a Viking boat they've built – loads of people come over from Skye, they dress up and get pissed for a solid week.'

'Right.' Nothing changes only you have different kinds of crap some are new and some familiar. Recognition. Re-cognition, an again-knowing of my fallen state my state of loss my hollowness. All the New Years of my life I've spent with strangers, pointlessly.

I lurched to my feet and she took my arm. 'OK? Come and sit down. What happened to you?' She didn't recognise me, well it wasn't surprising. She picked up my fags and led me into the bar. The skinny woman was sitting at a table by the wall. She pulled out a chair for me. They already had my cider on the table. I drank it and lit another fag.

'What happened to your face?' The skinny one. She was tight and intent, as if she might be able to read my mind. The plump sensible one went to get more drinks.

'I slipped on the rocks.'

'Oh.'

I drank my cider and asked her where she was from. There were more men at the bar now, some younger ones too. They were staring at us.

'London.' She started to tell me about the market stall they'd run.

177

Island

I didn't mind sitting with Sally and Ruby maybe I could even go back with them and stay in their house but it was a pain having to talk to them. There was something happening at the sides of my vision, at first I thought it was just the black eye but then I realised it was on the other side too, things moving past at speed like you're on a motorbike, I was catching glimpses of high speed movement out of the sides of my eyes.

They talked about their café it was going to attract tourists and they could do catering for outside events. They were doing a naming ceremony in Skye next weekend.

'Will you get customers here?' I was able to talk and pass for normal. I drank my cider and later Sally bought me another although I didn't want it.

'There's nowhere else to eat out on the island.'

'But vegetarian? Isn't it pretty traditional round here?'

'It'll be good for the island, it'll be an extra incentive for tourists.'

'This is a special place,' the calm one said. 'It's a spiritual place.'

God help us. I listened with a sliver of my mind. They were such caricatures. I thought what would they say if I told them what's been happening to me what sensible politically correct ideologically sound advice would they give? The skinny one had to stop and let each sentence past the censor before she could even utter it. What had she built that persona on top of? What awful fucking swamp? They kept buying drinks and I kept drinking, my aches and pains were receding. I had to go and pee and when I was sitting in the toilet I felt my eyes closing. It was all receding, I wanted to be asleep. I didn't want all those wankers' eyes flickering every time I moved. Get out of here get to your bed lock the doors and sleep.

I said goodbye to the women the sides of the room were whizzing past now faster than ever it would take me all my concentration to walk back to the house I wouldn't speak to anyone never again unless I chose to.

I walked out into the night. It was clear. Stars. Moon. Very very big. I was walking on the lane I could hear my own footsteps. Something . . . I knew it was a disaster but I had something up my sleeve . . . I couldn't remember what it was but at least thank god I wasn't like those two so scared to be the mess I was I had to construct a new personality-by-numbers. I was honest at least I wasn't nice or kind or careful or thoughtful I was a fucking horror but at least I didn't hide from it and pretend to be together at least my purple face was the truth and every dreadful thing was the truth at least I was better than those poor bitches at least I knew my worst. I was walking and there were a billion stars.

Then I lost it. From one minute to the next these transformations these assassinations are inflicted and if it was a film they'd stop shooting now and blame somebody: *Continuity for fuck's sake!*

There's no continuity. It's outside my control. First I am functioning: then I am powerless. I am something – no matter how low, *something*: then nothing.

I was walking. There were a billion stars

and then everything was moving the whole lot rather lurching–

the thing the firmament it's called was shifting its position in an unstable way and that movement was mirrored in my head (how could you hold the inside of your head still even with superhuman control, when the sky and stars started slipping about and the dark horizon tilted like a sinking ship?) and I felt it all – all–

everything I knew sliding inexorably down to the right into a crashing tinkling heap and my lungs constricting and my pupils dilating and my lenses shifting mechanically like a very expensive camera changing focus automatically and my ears peeling off their nice deadening layers of normality and it is when it happens it really is like the old horror movies when the nice guy turns into a werewolf and he looks down and the hairs are sprouting on his palms and he gasps in horror and his manly nose pops out into a snout

it's like that I can feel it physically the change I can feel myself transforming and the sky and stars around me the whole physical world dissolving and reappearing sharp

dangerous

Fearful.

I was in the middle of a dark road with blackness on either side, empty fields. Outer space roaring over my head.

I was crouching down, I don't know how long for but my legs ached. I tippled over onto my knees. It was difficult to breathe, the weight of the atmosphere was pressing on my lungs.

When it happens everything's different. Real. How it really is.

Appalling.

I twisted myself to look behind me. Blackness. The yellow street lamps of the village in the distance. Those two women in the pub sane and intelligent and blessed, organised, controlled, with one another to hold onto. I saw how the thin one glanced at the plump one as she talked, the little flicker of warmth running between them. Neither of them would ever be here. Prostrate in the road in the dark on their own. Gasping like a fucking fish on dry land.

I made myself get up. It hurt. Every bit of me ached. I had to move forward through the darkness to get to the witch's house. When I lifted up my foot I didn't think there was anything underneath, it was as long and giddy down to the ground as an astronaut spiralling on the end of a cable an umbilical cord in space. I am not even attached. I am floating I am falling I am not screwed down. There's no cord.

Lift – push forward – lower. Is the movement. Make each leg do it. When one foot is down, lift the other. Lift, push forward, set down. I am moving like a radio-controlled robot along the road. Slowly. With zigzags.

There was a moon. It's gone. I have stopped. I am looking at the appalling sky which is leaky with light with pinpricks and little gashes of light someone on the other side has been stabbing and poking to get through to get at us.

Aah. Haar. Aaah. I can hear my breaths groaning and crashing through my throat good god it's a terrible noise will no one stop me? And where's the moon? When I came out I saw a moon and now it's gone it's been taken away plucked off the sky like an apple and eaten gone away to nothing.

When I get into the room it will be rustling and breathing she may be in it lurking. She *will* be in it because she knows where I am and what I'm doing she's watching me she's a scientist with an experiment. Watching the rat go through the maze. She's watching me and she'll be waiting for me there but if I don't go back

If I turn around and go all that dark way along to the lighted pub again–

What then? It's no use. It won't be any use.

I steer myself, I am an alien vehicle, along the path of blackness to my mother's house where muffled light shines through the curtains and my hypersensitive ears distinguish the voices of the characters in the film on TV and the sound of her shifting in her chair and the rasp of pulling wool and soft clicking of her needles as she knits.

I can go round the back. But this gasping tearing noise must stop. Stop it now or she'll hear. I close my mouth the noises and breaths gulp at my throat like fish trying to leap out of deoxygenated water. The ache in my head looms so big it fills my vision and swamps my other senses quite mercifully, I unlock the door and get inside without seeing or hearing a thing. I lock it behind me, stand in the deeper dark, listening. Stand completely still. Take shallower breaths. Slow my breathing.

I am here. I can hear the TV very clearly even the words they are saying. And I think the sighs of her breathing.

I am grateful for the removal of outer space. The ceiling gives me relief. There is less to deal with. Best to stand perfectly still and listen. I am back to the door hands against it chin raised. Time passes. I am breathing shallowly and regularly. Night will pass.

She is getting up. She moves to the TV. She switches it off. I hear her moving stiffly around her room. Rattle of fire irons, scrape of fireguard. Click click as lamps go off. She shuffles to the door. I breathe. I am still breathing. She moves down the hall to the front door. Puts on the safety latch. She shuffles along the hall towards my door. She hesitates outside, my breath is caught in my throat and won't go in or out I keep my eyes fixed on the oblong of darkness with the crack of light beneath it I think I see the shadow of her feet. She shuffles on; click; the crack of light beneath the door vanishes. She is moving slowly a step at a time up the stairs. I must kill her.

But she has planted in my head every move I might make and is controlling me even now holding me pinned here with terror up against the door while she shuffles her way up the stairs. Does she know about Calum? Is he here? Or is he hiding too – from her, from me?

I break away from the door. How can you break away when someone else is controlling your mind? How can you think a single thing they don't want you to think? Does the thin lesbian in the pub know the answer? *Know* to be suspicious of anything that comes into her head quickly, spontaneously – *know* that she can only be *herself*, not manipulated, if she takes that pause to be calm and deliberate? *Know* that her first reaction to anything is not to be trusted. Is planted by a controller; a mind reader; a mother?

I have got to the bed and I am sitting on it, which gives physical relief. There are shooting pains in my legs. I can sit on the bed and by staring forward at the window (which needs to be watched anyway) also keep both doors (on opposite sides of the room) in peripheral vision. I find I will sit like this for the night, because it is possible to keep watch in this way. There is deep silence in the house, only a floorboard creaks from time to time contracting perhaps in the cold of the night, I imagine the roof beams supporting the rafters and the tiles all lying one overlapping the next I imagine the weight and structure of the house above me which is sheltering me from the sky. It is extraordinary that something holds me together in one machine as the separate bits of wood brick and tile cohere into a house it is extraordinary that things hold together and impossible to understand why they should, why they shouldn't spin off into the chaos of blackness and sparks throbbing above us, why should they cohere?

I am holding myself together. I am holding my skin around my blood to stop it all gushing out and falling in rivers on the floor. She cannot destroy me unless I *allow* it.

I must hold my head very still. A slight tilt either way takes one door out of sight. All entrances must be guarded constantly.

17 · Salt

When the shape of the window begins to lighten I am very very cold. It is quiet everywhere. The day is beginning. Nothing has come to either door. She has remained upstairs and silent. The greyness makes it, what, 5.30? Now it will get lighter. Nothing will come in daylight.

My body is so stiff it can hardly move, I let myself topple sideways on the bed and pull at the covers so they are half wrapped around me. I curve myself, facing window and door. It is getting lighter all the time. The covers create the beginnings of warmth. I close my eyes.

Knocking at the outside door. I am sweating, panicked, searchlight sun in my eyes.

Knock knock knock.

'What?' My voice cracked and dry.

No reply. The cover is folded under my weight trapping me on the bed. I struggle and crawl and stagger to the door. I am drenched in sweat. Turn the lock. Open. Calum is kneeling on the step. His face is red his eyes are swollen.

'I'm – s- I'm s-s-s-'

The bright sunlight pierces my eyes. The sun is dazzling over the sea. It must be afternoon.

'Sorry. Sorry. Sorry.' He is like someone at prayer. 'Please,' he says. 'Please.' The sun flares in my eyes and explodes inside my head the doorpost slices down my back.

A shadow shielding me from the blinding light, cool water tilts against my lips. I swallow. When I open my eyes he flinches, his crouching figure jerks back. I hold out my hand for the cup – drain it.

'I never – I never–' He is crying.

I can't speak only lie dully against the doorpost with the blessed water taste in my mouth.

'Sh-shall I get my m-mother?'

'No.' I haul myself up to sitting. I am faint with hunger. 'I'm hungry.'

'Shall I make you some toast?' My head is heavy and swollen it will not nod, I raise my hand. Carefully, giving me a wide berth, he steps into my room. I sit on the step staring at the blades of grass and the grains of dirt between. I hear the cupboard open the rustle of paper the bread slotting into the toaster the scrape as he pushes the lever down. The swish of the little fridge door as he looks for butter the smell of toasting bread wafting towards me I am drooling I am dribbling with hunger. He puts down a plate beside me the butter is melting into the toast and I cram it in my mouth. He stands outside again. His wrists dangle by his sides.

When I have chewed it all up, there is quiet.

'N-Nikki?

I am staring at his feet. His boots are soaking wet.

'Nikki?'

'What?' One of his laces has broken and been knotted together. A brown lace and a black lace knotted together.

'I didn't mean–'

'It was my fault.'

'No–' He is crying and I sit here with the sun warming me and my stomach growling and clamping on the toast. Just an animal really. A bit of warm meat that takes up this much space. What does it matter.

'I'll never – I'll never–'

'Alright. Be quiet.'

He breaks away, down to the end of the garden, he's crouching by the fence his hands clutching on to it. It looks strange, as if something's pulling him down into the earth. And he's clinging to the fence for dear life. He's jerking his head. He's banging his head against the horizontal bar of the fence. I can see the whole fence juddering as he hits it again and again.

Island

'Calum.'

My voice cracks. Louder. 'Calum.'

He stops but doesn't move. He's too far away. I can't shout. Slowly get up. All these pains. My back. My face. My legs. Slowly I can walk to him. I can speak to his back.

'It was my fault. It was a bad thing. We'll forget it.'

He doesn't move.

'I don't want to talk about it. Or think about it, *ever*.'

The effort of walking and speaking makes me dizzy. Back to the safety of my doorstep.

I sit a long time. Calum comes up the garden, edges past me into the room. There are noises of water, crockery, cutlery, the kettle. Later he slides past me out of the door again. He avoids looking at me.

'I made your breakfast.' He turns away around the corner of the house. I go in to table, sit, drink tea, eat boiled eggs and more toast. I sit at the table staring at the shapes of the eggshells. After a bit I rest my head down on my arms. Time passes.

I am disturbed by something slithering on the floor. It comes under the door from the hall. Something of her. It is white.

For a long time I watch it carefully. It is oblong and white, it pulses with radiant whiteness. It seems likely to spread and grow, maybe to flood across the floor. I could put my feet on the chair. Later it holds its shape – rectangular, flat. I pick it up, it is an envelope. Inside she has written me a letter.

Salt

Dear Miss Black, it would be better for you to find alternative accommodation. You will understand I have my son's interests at heart. Mrs McCullough at the post office might be able to help you. Please vacate by Friday 29th. P. MacLeod.

The meaning of this letter? I have to sit patiently to study it. Firstly: she is sending me away, again. Secondly: she knows what I am up to. What am I up to? Thirdly: she wants to get me away from Calum. That's too late. Fourthly: thinking is very hard. 'Alternative.' Why that word? Alternative. As if there was an. As if two things might balance equally or there might be a place where you could *choose*. 'Please vacate.' Vacate is empty. To vacate = to empty. Please empty myself from this place. Please die. Which is a threat. Calum was a threat now vacating is a threat.

Later Calum is back at the door. The same day? Another day. Standing outside the door looking in but not at me, to the side of me, even with his good eye. Wretched, grey faced. He has put my tobacco tin on the step. I pick it up.

'I've g-given her her lunch.'

I do not reply, it's nothing to do with me.

'I th-think you should go out. For a w-walk or something.'

'No.'

'You might feel better.'

'Go away.'

He stands still looking at the ground.

'Calum! Cal-lum!' His mother's voice is calling him from the front of the house. 'Cal-lum!' He remains still staring at his feet. I hear her open the front door and call again. 'Calum!' She thinks he has gone up the road. He folds his arms across his chest and stands there obstinately staring in silence at his feet. She wants him to come to her, I want him to go away.

He is not going to her he is staying with me. This is quite funny when you consider that it is what I was scheming to achieve. 'Go away Calum.'

For answer he sits down on my doorstep with his back to me and his face buried in his arms. We can both hear the half-ring the telephone makes each time she dials a number on it. Four times, a local number, she is ringing him at home. We hear her tut and the bang of the receiver going down. We hear her open the door again and the space of time it takes her to go down the path to the road. 'Calum, Cal-lum!' Her distant voice.

We sit in silence a long time. I do not go out like this. I'm afraid I won't be able to get back. When I have fear I have to wait and watch. What else is there to do?

'I won't walk near you. I-I won't talk to you.'

'Be quiet.'

'You can't just s-sit there—'

The silence yawns. He continues to wait like a dog.

I get up slowly. What difference does it make? Inside or outside, if someone else is there? What difference really? He thinks I'm scared of him. But I'm not. He's the last thing I'm scared of. 'Not far.'

'No. We'll go to Viking Bay.' He jumps up, eager to please, pitiful. 'The stones there are black and round as bowls.'

I carry my body out of the doorway. He backs away to leave the big edge of space around me that I require.

'Sh-shall I lock?' He turns the key, passes it to me at arm's length. In my pocket, heavy and cold.

He sets off across the garden I can walk behind his rucksack. He walks one two on his legs like a stork there are bands of noise near and far. The thumping and rustle of us – feet, clothes, breathing (nearer, yes, the booming of my heart). The humming of the air full of insects, bees flies midges I don't know what but the air is moving and buzzing. The zooms of distant sound; traffic? Aeroplanes? Did I speak?

'Submarines in the sound. They test torpedoes.' Submarines in the sound, sound of submarines would I hear the whoosh of torpedo under water? Hear the clunk of it hit the thud the explosion, water everywhere broken into shards and leaping fragments glassy in the air?

She is dangerous. She is it. Behind all this clear brittle sharp each layer of sight of sound like glass, each pane of double glazing I go through she is right behind it all. Calum leads the way I would not even get through without him I would have to stand still on that spot where she could target me. Torpedo.

'N-Nikki?' He waits and I can move again. We move on step step in time our legs rise and fall. He moves through the bright air nothing is cutting or hurting him. The sounds part as he steps through.

It is crystal, when I step into it it will shatter and cut me but instead I watch his legs he pushes his feet forward and it doesn't shatter it parts like water. He can walk along. We can walk along. I can walk. I want it to stop the sea is glittering like knives like razors' edges. I am afraid. I am breathing and the air is too thin no goodness in it I am breathing and breathing it trying to get it in I am trying I am gasping. I should not have come.

'S-sit down.' He sits on a grey stone grave grey stone he pats it sit here gravely. He slides away to the edge. Stopping is as dangerous as moving when you move it could shatter at any minute and lacerate you cut you to a thousand pieces but when you stop – when you stop it all stops. Suspended. Moves in. Comes to your edges, closes in around you, comes right up tight and wraps you suffocatingly close like clingfilm over your face the edge of the world comes right to your edge and clogs your mouth and nostrils and seals you tight as an unopened cellophane packet no air gets in to make it stale you will be vacuum packed and keep for ever in one spot.

'Breathe slowly. Count. One potato t-two potato three p-potato four, five potato, six potato seven potato more.' He moves he sits he moves his face, makes the sound to come out and nothing bad comes I can. I can. I can too.

We are sitting quietly, Calum says, 'You see that ruin over there? Th-that tumbledown cottage?' I see road it has little specks that glitter sharply: ditch; thistles, sharp crowns of thorns and rose brambles with their triangular thorns I see the hurting things they want to cut to puncture to slash to pierce.

'S-slowly. Breathe slowly. One potato t-two potato—'

I see a ruin two half-fallen walls the third is higher I see charred roof beams still there and blue polythene is wrapped around one. 'Yes.'

Salt

'The salt murderess lived there. Shall I t-tell you the story?'

A mother. See the flashing blades see the points?

'It's not scary. It's got a h-happy ending.' I think I am hollow I am brittle as those chocolate bunnies at Easter they have bright tinfoil they have dark smiley faces all rich and chocolatey but they have a seam down the middle and you get your fingernail in and the bunny falls in two just like an empty shell. The Little People got here first. Nothing in the middle, nothing to eat, nothing to mend. No meat.

Pressure shatters hollow things. She is willing me to break.

'C-can I have a cigarette?' Calum is looking at me I feel my pockets I give him the packet and lighter Sally's lighter he takes out two he lights them both he gives me one. It is so kind of him. He lights it for me he passes it into my fingers, it is simple kindness. Tears spring to my eyes. Everything is crystal clear, Calum, inhalations of cigarette, the circle of paper at the lighted end turning into ash, a distant tractor, sigh of wind. I hear the faraway honk of geese I hear a baby crying a woman scolding I hear sobbing I hear—

'Don't be afraid.' Calum waves his hands in the air. 'The island's f-full of voices.' We wait. We listen until silence falls like sleep.

'I'll tell you her story.'

This is the story he told me. How much can you see by lightning? Everything; one flash; everything. I was distracted (meaning mad; that's the old meaning, not just inattentive, but mad). I saw the whole story together, beginning and end like a painting the plot and outcome simultaneous, not a story plod-plodding the line from one event to the next.

Island

I can't paint you a picture. I can't show it in a flash. By now I will have forfeited most of your sympathy. Why should you listen to me? You have to be patient. I can only attempt to deliver it as it came to me, which is fragmentarily. If it was food my life would be a trail of half-chewed fragments, it would be a pile of cores and peelings and then a long stretch of saliva strands to the next item, maybe a plain bread roll a nice no-nonsense roll with butter. This is what it's like. I have not been served a menu in order. Probably you wonder why I don't tidy it up. Why should you have the regurgitations or the still lives of old leftovers?

Maybe I will. Maybe if I keep on telling it will get tidied in the telling. As Calum's stories are tidied and smoothed by telling into shapes that fit like sea-pebbles in the palm of your hand. Tided by telling, by the waves of the sea.

Maybe 'The Ancient Mariner' was once regurgitated seafood. In the meantime you should be glad because the story Calum told me of the salt murderess is a round dish that you can have all in one like a bowl of soup perhaps, a deep red bowl of bortsch with a pale swirl of soured cream and brilliant green sprinkling of chopped chives on top. At least that's how it was to me even in extremis as I was at that time. And it's how it is now, I'll tell it for you now. I call it *Salt*.

A woman lived here who murdered her children with salt. Joyce. She didn't come from here. She came from a city. She spent fifteen years in prison, before she came to the Island.

Her children were one and three, both girls. She didn't set out to murder them. She didn't think she set out to murder them. No. What happened was this.

Salt

The little one didn't sleep. She simply wouldn't sleep. In the evening Joyce started by telling her stories, as she had to the older girl. In the end she was just counting. 'Four thousand seven hundred and eighty-four. Four thousand seven hundred and eighty-five.'

When the child's breathing was even and her fluttering eyelids closed, Joyce would stop. Wait. Listen. Then infinitely slowly, put down her right hand on the floor, turn her stiff creaking body to the right, shift her weight onto her knees. She would wait, kneeling on all fours, for the rustling of her clothes and creaking of the floor to subside. Then very slowly, hand against the wall for support, haul her aching self to her feet.

Nine times out of ten, as she inched towards the door, the baby's eyes and mouth would fly open and a yell would freeze Joyce where she stood.

If the baby did fall asleep, she stayed that way for about an hour. Then she would be up again, rattling the bars of her cot, calling, babbling, crying. If Joyce tried to ignore her and remained slumped on the soggy sofa, the crying became wailing became shrieking and the crone next door began knocking on the wall with her stick and the older girl clutched Joyce's legs and shouted 'Naughty! Naughty! Naughty!' and the walls of the room throbbed in and out with every exhaling shriek and indrawn breath and the band of suffocation tightened over Joyce's chest.

When the child slept, Joyce slept; sometimes sitting propped against the wall by the cot; sometimes sprawled on the sofa; sometimes curled on the older girl's narrow bed with the bedclothes twisted into a plait beneath the pair of them.

Island

She gave salt to the older girl to punish her. It was morning and she was at the sink, quietly washing yesterday's dishes, running through in her mind what she might be able to do if the baby slept on. After the dishes she might have a bath; she would gather up the dirty clothes and put them in the machine. She would take the bin down and empty it, if the baby slept, maybe even sweep the floor. Outside there was watery sunshine, a gleam of hope on the wet black tarmac.

Then the older girl fell off a chair. She'd been standing on it, leaning forward over the table to reach a crayon that had rolled – went to set her foot back down on the seat and missed it – fell sprawling sideways, pulling the chair over on top of herself, screaming with fright and shock. Instant stereo from the bedroom.

Joyce picks the fallen girl up by the scruff of the neck, plonks her on the righted chair, bawls into her face. 'Now look what you've bloody done!'

The girl sits snivelling; from the bedroom the screams get louder. Joyce buries her face in her arms folded on the work surface; at last raises her eyes and focuses on *salt*. Before she's thought she's poured a slug through its Saxa red funnel into her daughter's mug; half-filled with water, stirred till the cloud's dispersed.

'Here.' Slamming it on the table. 'Drink that. That'll teach you.'

The girl sips and puts it down carefully.

'*Drink it!*'

'Don't like it.'

'I don't give a fuck what you bloody well like. *Drink it.*'

Salt

The little girl picks up the mug and drinks. When she is half done she starts to retch. Her mother picks her up and takes her to the bathroom, stands her in the bath.

'Puke there if you're going to puke.'

The coughing subsides.

'Now get out of my way. *Get.*'

The girl scrabbles out of the bath and runs to her bed. She gets in and pulls the covers up. Joyce stumbles to her room and grabs the screaming baby.

At first it was a punishment. Something she could make them both do, that they didn't like. Force the girl to drink it. Put it in the baby's bottle and let her gulp until she tasted it. Give her something to scream for, that would.

Then she noticed it made them sleep. That first morning, the girl stayed in her bed till noon. If they drank enough to make them vomit it exhausted them and they slept even more. Or it gave them stomach aches and they lay whimpering quietly, squirming in their beds, unable to run around or bellow.

The baby'd drink it without a fuss, mixed in juice. With the older one, she and the girl both knew it was punishment. For making a noise. For spilling something. For being clumsy or untidy or simply in the way. For *being.* And she was big enough to say no, to go without a drink. Joyce slapped her away from the taps and the fridge. When she drank her dirty bathwater Joyce started putting salt in that.

It was never intended to kill them. She didn't know it *could.* Just wanted to teach them a lesson.

Teaching them a lesson is for their own good. Joyce had been taught lessons. She'd learned I want doesn't get and nothing in this world comes free. She'd learned not to get above herself and not to ask for the moon. She'd learned money doesn't grow on trees. She'd learned life's a vale of tears. Valuable lessons, needing to be learned by young children. Joyce was helping them to learn. Helping them not to be like herself; so desperately furiously suffocatingly trapped, so caged and raging, so dissatisfied. They were born bad, like her, and she could teach them to be otherwise. Teach them – herself – a lesson.

When the older one had a fit, her body twitching and convulsing like a fish flipped out of water, Joyce watched with tearful sympathy then carried her, calm and floppy, to her bed; tucked her in and kissed her. Poor little kid. So much pain in life. She might as well get used to it now. Joyce was doing her a favour. Poor little mite; now she was beginning to understand the truth of it, life.

When they were both in bed all the time, it was easy. Poor things. It was for their own good. If they learned who was boss now it'd stand them in good stead for the rest of their lives. She mopped up the vomit lovingly. Bought fresh orange to put the salt in.

The baby died first. It had been sleeping a really long time. So long that Joyce herself was calm and refreshed, humming as she made herself a cup of tea, smiling at the TV presenter, only mildly annoyed by the car alarm that went off under the window, loud enough to wake the dead.

It didn't wake the baby.

The baby was cold to touch. In terror Joyce grabbed her up.

Thumped her on the back, tried to breathe into her mouth, ran to the phone, stabbed 999.

It was only when she was being asked her details in the hospital that they found she had another; back went the ambulance – and back again to the hospital, bearing the older child still breathing, but salted down into a coma from which she never would recover.

The salt murderess. At her trial she cried salt tears and said she was only trying to keep them quiet. Why is it on sale if it's a poison? she wanted to know. The prosecution said it was a poison so unpleasant that no one would take it unless forced by measures of extreme cruelty. That the physical sufferings it induced included painful muscle cramps and contractions, raging thirst, vomiting, diarrhoea, hallucinations and convulsions.

'But they drank it!' wailed the mother.

'You gave them no alternative.'

The salt murderess was sent to jail, judged to be of perfectly sound mind and a danger to all children.

In prison all children visited her, convulsing up and down the walls of her cell. For fifteen years she lived in a cell where children writhed around her like worms in a fisherman's bucket. For fifteen years she half lived, numb with pain, blind with too much vision.

And when they let her out of prison she came to live on the Island. A fellow prisoner had talked about it. About the emptiness, and the gleams of light on water. From the prison library Joyce borrowed books on gardening.

She found an empty cottage – that very one we sat by: semi-derelict, forgotten, owned by someone on the mainland.

Island

She lived there lightly, with planks and polythene sacks across the roof, an untidy plot of onions and potatoes at the back. Walked to the post office each Thursday to collect her giro, buy a few groceries. Never bought salt. Spoke to no one. Sat in the evening and the morning staring out to sea, the sides of her head unpeeled to the horizon, not a wall not a child in sight.

Dreamed by night of glistening saltchildren floating in white from the sea, sculpted and still as bars of soap in the moonlight; saltchildren, a million crystallised tears. They floated gently as ice in the black water, bumping and nudging in to shore. But in the morning when she looked they were gone, there was only the brown seaweed bobbing to the surface, and the occasional grey-backed gull.

Salt preserves and salt destroys. All life sprang from the salt-soup of the sea but her children are dead as rocks and hang as heavy about her heart. It was a madness, an accident, an impossibility. How can there be a thing done, which can never never be undone? How, in a botched and transitory life, can one thing become irrevocable? She sees she is only that: a saltmurderess. All the rest of her life is void. It was all, waiting to become that, and living to regret it. Clouds and sea spume are the colour of salt; sea air keeps the taste of it in her mouth: even here, there is no escape.

Then one frosty salt-grained night there's scrabbling at her propped-up door; scrabbling and snuffling and shuddering sobs. Head still full of salt-mummies she stumbles to the glassless window and leans out. A young girl is battering weakly on the door, fists upraised, hair salt-silver in the moonlight.

'Here,' Joyce calls. Her voice has scarcely worked for sixteen years.

Salt

The girl comes blindly to the window – Joyce helps her over the sill, leads her to her matted pile of bedding, wraps her in a blanket. When the girl has snuffled and burrowed herself to sleep, Joyce lies beside her, curling her body around the warm question-mark of the girl's blanketed back.

It is no mystery where she comes from. She's the younger daughter of old McCaulin. Who that night had tried with her what he'd been doing with her older sister the past five years. Only the nine-year-old did not lie sickened and still but fought like a cat, scratched him to bleeding and ran two dark miles to the safety of the nearest dwelling: Joyce's.

And there she stayed. Walking down to get the boat for school, and back in the evening to Joyce's cottage. When McCaulin was out fishing she fetched her things from his house, and two of his six geese that she said were hers. They kept them in the ruined front room and they made fine watchdogs. She showed Joyce how to collect winkles, and where the blackberries were. They ate no salt.

And when Joyce sat staring out to sea in the evening, the girl coloured in her exercise book on the flat rock beside her; or if it was wet, they sat either side of the driftwood fire, and made up spooky stories.

Joyce never spoke of her children; nor the girl, her father. This was their life. And when Joyce lay curled around her island-daughter's sleeping back, she had no more dreams of saltchildren, but dreamt instead she was at the prow of a boat, with the warm sun on her face and chest, sailing forward into the light.

18 · Birthday cake

After the story we went on down to the shore at Viking Bay where all the pebbles are black and we looked for things to go in Calum's rucksack. A child's broken plastic truck (red and yellow), some polystyrene (white), shreds of torn net (green). While we were on the beach it clouded over, the sharp sunlight was muffled, swathed in clouds. I felt safer. Calum gave me a drink of hot tea out of his thermos. I was very – small. Concentrated. I was a small compact bundle for me to carry around and although susceptible to attack I was slightly protected, I was volatile but wrapped. I was carrying me quietly, concentrating on the black pebbles and the bits of polystyrene.

And when we walked back up the beach and back to the path he told me the Viking Bay story. Which I will tell you later. And we went back to Calum's house and I was alright, I watched him add today's finds to his mounds. Then he was taking a sack of onions down to the shop to sell, he slung them over a bike and wheeled it and I went with him there as well and bought some bread and tomatoes and kippers for my tea. I bought a newspaper to read. Calum bought tobacco and papers, he was excited, it was the first time he'd bought some himself. I was holding it together and I was able to think I remember this quite clearly, thinking I am managing to get back on balance I'm doing well. This may only have been a Fear-wobble not a plunge, I'm going to be all right. It depended on the night I realised that but I was controlling things well. I was OK with Calum, there was a clear space between me and Calum, and nothing like that would ever happen again.

It was quite dark when we got back to her house, Calum didn't ride his bike, he wheeled it beside me and I was glad of that. The house seemed very dark, as if she'd forgotten to turn on any lights, Calum leaned his bike on the fence and went to the front door. 'Come this way,' he said and I followed him. It smelt smoky. And waxy. There was a candle burning in the hall. I thought there'd been a power cut. I followed Calum into the kitchen. There were candles arranged in three rows from end to end of the table, and in the middle a cake. She wasn't there. Calum was staring at the table.

'What is it?'

'I-I forgot.'

'Forgot what?'

'It's Susan's birthday. My sister who died.'

It was my birthday. October 2nd. It was on my birth certificate. Some years I have forgotten it completely; woken up in late October and thought oh, my birthday's gone. When I've been with people on my birthday I've nearly always not told them. They might wonder why I have no cards and why I haven't got anyone better to celebrate it with than them I hardly know. They might think I've told them in order to get presents off them or to make them feel sorry for me. They might even think I've made it up.

The cake was iced white, and in quavery pink letters, SUSAN.

'Does she do it every year?'

Calum nodded; he'd sat down and was staring at the candles.

'What happens?'

'We just light the c-candles and we sing. Then my mother cuts the cake. I'd better go and see if sh-she–' he pushed back his chair and went upstairs. Every year a cake is made for me and candles lit and my brother and my mother and presumably at one time my step-father too all sit down together and think pious thoughts of me.

It was draughty in the kitchen, the candle flames wavered. What was she thinking as she lit them, as she set them out each one in a jamjar lid? 'This is for you Nikki this is a death wish'? Her hand clasped around the medicine bottle. The whispering shuffle of her feet and rustling clothes snooping through my bedroom or hovering outside my door; watching me, listening upstairs for my movements. I suddenly realised she knew when I went through her sitting room. Her presence filled every room of that house. In the kitchen it was observing me calmly, I was a voodoo doll and she stuck in pin after pin.

The flames against the darkness were hypnotic. I started to blow them out. I realised I could pick one up and hold it to the curtains.

Easily. Hold it to the curtains till they were alight; put another to the thin wooden shelves of the dresser and make them burn. Put one by the table leg, one to the rag rug by the stove. In minutes the place would be blazing. The candles for poor dead Susan would make a funeral pyre for Phyllis MacLeod.

I could get rid of her as easily as that. But what I planned to do would hurt her more.

I blew out all the candles. The kitchen was dark and small, filled with black shadows. No sound from upstairs – no voices, no footsteps. It seemed like it would have been a good gesture to eat a slice of my cake but I felt sick. I went to my room.

When I take Calum away she'll be alone. No one to love and be needed by; no one to help her or turn to. No reason to cook or clean the house. No reason to be. Like I have been all these years. Alone.

My plan was a plank across the abyss. I could walk along it. I could act.

I raked out the fireplace and lit a fire. I made a pot of tea, and I read the newspaper from cover to cover, turning the pages very carefully so they didn't rustle. It was after nine when Calum's footsteps came downstairs; I let him in and he went and crouched over the fire.

'Her bedroom's cold. She won't put on the f-fire. Just the electric blanket.' I passed him a cigarette. 'She's very upset,' he said, as if I'd asked. 'I can't get her to eat anything. She-she's just lying there crying.'

'What're you going to do?'

He stood up then shrugged as if he couldn't be bothered to talk about it anymore. 'She's had two sleeping tablets. She should go off s-soon.'

'What's she so upset about?'

'She gets depressed about Susan.'

'What did Susan die of?' I might as well know, since it was public fact number one. But Calum shook his head. We sat in silence.

'You know she's asked me to leave.'

'What?'

'She's asked me to move out.'

He stood up slowly, shaking his head, he looked dazed. 'B-but this room is – is – mine. It's not, no one else is–'

'It's because she doesn't want me near you.' I realised as I said it that maybe she had known – or planned? – what happened yesterday.

He flinched and turned his back to me, looking down into the spitting flames. The driftwood was still damp.

'Did you tell–'

'No.' It wasn't possible. How could it serve her ends in any way? And it was my fault. Yes, it's you she controls, Nikki.

No.

Calum raised his hands to his face and held them there, like a child hiding. 'She can't make you go away.'

'I can't stay in her house if she doesn't want me to.' She didn't make that happen. She couldn't have known how I would react – even she.

Silence. Something burned through and collapsed in the fire.

'What are you going to do?'

'Go back to the mainland.'

Another silence. Different. A drawing, growing, circling silence. He crouched down by the fire again, folding his knees like a grasshopper. 'She shouldn't do that. She shouldn't send you away.'

True enough, dear brother; that she should compound her original crime by repeating it is almost beyond belief.

'It's not fair,' he said.

'No.'

He was shaking his head as if he couldn't get rid of flies buzzing around him. 'She never asked me. She just – acts as if I'm stupid.' He looked up at me. 'She treats me like a baby.'

'Yes.'

He got up again and began to pace from the fireplace to the door with fast jerky steps. 'She kicks you out. She treats me like a baby.' His voice rose. 'It's not fair. She's not fair.'

I sat and watched while he walked and talked himself to the point.

'I'm coming with you.'

'Tomorrow?'

He didn't even hesitate. 'Yes.'

'We'll get the seven o'clock ferry. Before she's up.'

'Right.'

'We'll pack our bags tonight then. We'll just go, without telling her.'

'Yes.'

'Alright then Calum. I'll see you in the morning.' He picked up one of my earrings from the mantelpiece and peered at it, then put it down and went to the door. 'See how she likes that,' he muttered to himself. 'Just see how she likes that.'

When he was gone I locked the doors and switched off the light; pulled the chair up close to the fire. I could see quite clearly what she hoped for: either that I would simply creep away and vanish, terrified by the death-wish of Susan's funereal birthday cake; or I would be tipped by that into rage, grab the last flaring candle and incinerate her where she lay, delivering her to the death she craved and blighting my own life (even those years in the future, supposedly beyond her reach) by my culpability for her murder.

I cleaned my teeth and got into bed. The firelight made dancing light like the candles in the kitchen had done. I had no Fear.

19 · Tempest

The day of our departure. Nikki and Calum cross the water. Nikki tests the length and strength of Calum's chain. Nikki pits her strength against her mother.

We were getting the early ferry; he tapped quietly on the outer door at 6.15, I was up but not ready, I let him in. The light was murky and a gust of wind came in with him.

'I – I've got to tell her we're going.' He crossed to the inner door.

'Calum – why? You don't have to tell her any–'

His feet went up the stairs. I drank my tea and put my coat on, there was the sound of their voices rising – indistinct but both of them agitated. Then the quick sound of heavy footsteps on the stairs. 'Come on. L-let's go.' He ran to the outer door as if she was chasing him.

I shouldered my rucksack and followed him out, he was hovering at the edge of the garden. 'Come on–' We literally ran away from the house.

The weather had changed overnight. Wind was coming in from the sea in great big swoops, great buffeting gobbets that pushed you and sucked away your breath. Strong but not cold. We half ran down the lane to the village, breathless and exhilarated. Huge clouds were shifting across the sky, back lit, everything was on the move – like a theatre when it goes nearly dark and they bundle all the scenery around, it was suddenly *all change*. And the thought of me and Calum, me and my brother going over the sea and back the way I had come on my own, filled me up with laughter. Calum grinned his big turnip grin and we hurried past all the sleeping houses and out of the village and down to the jetty. That was the first time I looked at the sea. The sea was excited too. It was standing up on end in spiky rows like punk hair; except the spiky rows were running across from right to left and flinging themselves over each other in their hurry.

'Look!' The waves were smashing against the jetty and the ferry was bobbing up and down on its moorings like a cork. 'Look at the sea!' I shouted at Calum, spray was hurtling into the air above the jetty and raining down on us, everything was in motion like us, swooping, soaring, flying. It was alive.

Calum had a funny look on his face. Last time he told her he was going somewhere she tried to kill herself. Why does he care? Why care about the bitch? She's *nothing*. There was a car with two men sitting in it, staring across the sound. Calum went over to the driver and he opened his window. The wind snatched their words away but I saw the man look at his watch and shake his head. The two men conferred then the driver spoke to Calum again. Calum stepped back, the driver reversed the car then drove off towards the village.

'What is it?'

Calum shrugged, coming towards me. 'It's not going.'

'What?'

'The ferry. Sea's too rough.'

'Not going?'

He nodded.

'But it has to go. People're stranded here.'

'The forecast's bad. D-Davy said.'

'Is he the driver? The captain?'

Calum had turned back to face the teeming sea.

'But – but when will it go?'

He shrugged.

'In an hour? At dinnertime?'

'S-sometimes it can't go for days.'

'*Days?*' I could see the opposite shore. It was a ten-minute boat ride away. You could *swim* it. It was completely and utterly ridiculous.

Calum turned his back on the sea. 'Come on.'

'But they must sail later. What about the farmers? What about bread and milk?' Calum started to walk back towards the lane and I had to go after him.

'You c-can always get cut off.'

Ah no. This weather was for us; it was saying *yes! Yes! You can do it, you and your brother together yes!* It wasn't so we could go meekly back to the old witch's house and sit there listening to weather forecasts.

'Calum! Isn't there another boat we could get? Couldn't we pay someone to take us over? What about the fishermen?'

He looked puzzled.

'We can still go. We *can* go, we'll be alright, I know we will.' I couldn't bear the idea of losing all our momentum. How long before he changed his mind? 'Calum! Calum! Don't you know someone we can borrow a boat off?'

He stared at me then grinned. He turned his back on the village and began to scramble up a narrow path that ran on along the coast – it would have been an extension of the lane, if the lane hadn't turned down towards the jetty and run into the sea. I hurried after him, the wind was tearing at my clothes and flipping my hair in my eyes. I wanted to shout out loud. He was running up in front of me then he suddenly disappeared; I got to the top and the path went straight down into the next little cove. There were three wooden sheds like garages there, on the edge of the stony beach. Calum was running down to them. At the first one he reached up and felt along the ledge above the double doors – found a key, unlocked the door and began to drag it open. It had dropped on its hinges and stuck against the ground, I ran down and helped him to heave it open. There was a little boat in the dark shed. I couldn't stop laughing. 'Is it yours?'

'N-no. I'm not allowed–' Of course. His mother didn't let him go out in boats.

'How d'you–'

'Gerry sometimes takes me out in it. J-just for an hour in the evening, when my mother's watching telly.'

'Gerry?'

'He knew my dad.' We went into the dark shed, it felt warm after the wind. There was an outboard motor on the boat and a pair of oars in the bottom, it was quite new. It would be over that sound in minutes.

'Jackets.' Calum pulled two orange lifejackets off a shelf and threw one at me.

'We don't need–'

'I c-can't swim.'

'OK, you wear one but I–'

'Nikki you m-m-' I put it on to humour him, no point wasting time in argument. Then we began to drag the boat out and over the pebbles. It was white and red. Its name was *Iris*.

'It's brilliant! You weren't going to tell me, were you?'

'I'm not supposed–' I couldn't hear the rest because he turned to look over his shoulder at the sea. There were waves but it was per-fectly OK. 'You get in–' He held it while I stepped in then he pushed it deeper while I started to row.

'Come on, get in, it's afloat.' He clambered in making it rock like crazy, his feet were wet up to the knee. 'OK?' The wind made my throat laugh. I heaved on the oars and dug us away from the beach. 'Aren't you starting the engine?'

'I don't know how—'

'Haven't you seen Gerry do it?' Calum clambered over to the motor and peered at it dumbly. I thought OK, fine, we can row if necessary. 'Come and do the oars while I have a look at it.' He came clumsily back towards me, he was too thin to be really heavy but the boat tilted madly and I nearly lost an oar. 'Calum! You great fool – sit down!' I could hardly get my breath for laughing. I edged along the seat to make room for him. 'Now swap over to this seat. Careful – don't upset us—'

He moved slowly and as soon as he was seated I got him to take the right oar and slide his left arm round behind me to take the left. Then I shifted across and over the next seat to the motor. It was one of those where you pull a string. The waves were hitting us sideways on with a slap and great spray of water, I knelt down to pull the string and my knees were in a puddle.

'Row Calum! Get the boat turned round a bit.' I yanked on the string and it made a clucking noise but nothing else. There would be a place to switch the fuel on, I felt around the side and underneath. The boat was rocking from side to side as if a lunatic'd got hold of a hammock – 'Calum! Aren't you rowing?' I glanced round at him; he was sitting with the oars up like wings, frowning at me. 'Put the oars in the water! Row!'

He shrugged. We swung round a bit and the wind was full on my face, pouring into my mouth and nose, rushing into my lungs. It was alright he couldn't row. I would take us. It would be me – I was soaring, I was in my element, I could do *anything*. I flicked the switch and yanked the cord again and the motor choked out a cloud of blue smoke. Again – and it was going. I knew it. I knew it would. The boat started pushing through the water, there was a primitive handle for steering. I turned us so we were heading into the waves – sat facing Calum as we went crashing through them, rearing and plunging like a horse. He was still holding the oars.

'Isn't it great! Put them in the boat! Put the oars in the boat!' Spray from the prow was cascading over him – he lifted the right oar out of the rowlock then turned up his collar and while he was doing it a wave caught the left oar, jerked it up and out of place and sucked it into the sea. He grabbed for it and missed.

'It doesn't matter. We don't need it.' I was bellowing to be heard over the motor and the wind – we were moving away from the shore now, you could see the distance opening up, we were moving away and the motor was chugging and I'd never managed a boat before but it was perfectly obvious and easy, nothing to it. I was flying, I could do anything.

Suddenly the waves got bigger – not just bigger but more random, they started coming at us on the slant as well as from ahead – suddenly we started tipping down them like something chucked down a lift shaft.

'N-Nikki!' I couldn't hear what else he said. I swung the steering handle round to try and get on a better line with the waves, we were being slapped by them and juddered, we were suddenly falling into big troughs between them. I looked up and saw the end of the rocky promontory dividing us from the jetty's bay – OK, we were out of shelter, we were in the sound, it was OK – then we went down and up again and something seemed to swivel us round and the air was so full of torrential spray there weren't any gaps in it and I couldn't see which way we were going. I tried to stand to see over the top of the waves and spray but the land had disappeared. It was darker everywhere, the sky was darker and lower, it had all closed in.

'Calum! Calum! Can you see–' we were rolled sideways and the propeller came right out of the water whirring madly then we were crashed down again and a whole wave poured itself into the boat. It just crested and broke, like a bath being tipped onto us. The boat was full of water to our knees.

'Bail! Calum, bail it out!' There were a couple of plastic jugs floating around; I started scooping and hurling the water out. The noise of crashing and howling was louder and louder, we were right *in* the water, it was taller than us on all sides.

'Calum, bail!' I'd let go of the rudder – when I grabbed it again I realised the motor'd cut out. I just kept bailing. We got it down to ankle level before we stopped, the waves were hitting us and spinning us round and dropping us over their edges but they were keeping out of the boat. As we slid up one and I lifted my head I could see the promontory off behind Calum.

'Keep bailing–' I pulled the cord for the engine. Nothing. Again. Nothing.

'Nikki!' His shout came swooping in with the wave that seemed to swell up directly underneath us and suddenly shrug us off sideways so deftly that we were upside down while I was still yanking on the cord. I went right under and my clothes dragged me down like hands pulling me, the lifejacket a weight not a help and my lungs were bursting. I scrabbled to get to the surface I was impossibly deep it was pitch dark – then my head popped through the surface into air and it *was* dark, it was black with a kind of thumping crashing echo all around me. My lungs froze in terror until I realised I'd come up under the upturned boat. I felt for the edge of it and ducked down under, keeping my fingers clenched around it. Now the jacket wouldn't go down – I had to force myself with all my strength. Outside it was light but raging – Calum *Calum*, I was looking for Calum – I couldn't breathe for water slapping in my face I was coughing and gasping and the water was going down my throat and the boat was jerking out of my hand. Then something was grabbing me and pulling me under, yanking at my shoulder but I didn't let go the boat and I gasped a lungful of air and turned my head and it was Calum lunging and spluttering. I got an arm around his neck and dragged him close.

'Hold on! Hold onto the boat!' His flailing arms hit the side of it and slid off. 'Calum, hold the edge of the boat!' I managed to get one of his hands to clasp on and his brain must have started working because he brought the other one up and then he was coughing and spluttering but his eyes opened and saw me. Our heads weren't really out of the water because the waves were slapping and cresting and spraying against the boat and the sea was so churned up that air and water weren't separate it was one choppy mess we were trying to breathe, the boat was moving and dodging with the waves slapping against its other side, showering spray onto us, jerking our arms out of their sockets.

'Hang on! Just hang on!' I couldn't – it wasn't possible – to see. It crossed my mind to try and turn the boat over but with no oars – at least if it was upside down it couldn't fill with water and sink.

Island

We hung on there. I don't know how long for. It wasn't cold, I didn't think about that. It was just the thing of keeping breathing, every time you gasped water came in too, or it slapped right over your face – it was just trying to keep your nostrils clear of water – and the arms beginning to ache – and mind still racing over what to do whether to try and hand-over-hand to the prow and then swim toward land tugging the boat after? Utterly unfeasible since we were too low to *see* land and neither of us could have tugged the boat – the water slapped and pushed it where the water wanted it to go, we were powerless.

I tried to shout to Calum but either he couldn't hear or was too terrified to respond and water was plunging down my throat too frequently for me to finish a phrase anyway.

Something suddenly hit my feet jarring my ankles nearly breaking my legs. It was hard as iron, I pushed my foot against it – rock. The waves slapped the other side of the boat and it came on into our faces and we found ourselves knocked backwards onto rocks that were climbing out of the water. The boat was pinning us against them, we had to hold it off and wriggle our legs out and crawl half-slither up the rocks out of the water like things that'd been born in the sea. We crawled up out of the reach of the waves and the battering boat then sprawled on the cold hard rock pulling on the air pulling it into our lungs gasping and grasping it in like drunks swigging on an empty bottle. My stomach clenched and my throat went into spasm. Frothy sea water came out, long strings of it mixed with bile, a long watery trickle of vomit.

Calum was retching too. He tried to breathe in on it and made it worse, couldn't get his breath. I scrabbled over to him and hit him on the back and he went down face first onto the rock. Blood came out of his nose and a stream of water gushed out of his mouth, then his eyes opened and he lifted his head. We put our arms around each other's huge jacketed bodies and gasped in unison. Eventually we crawled and staggered along the rocks (the rocks dividing our bay from the jetty bay) to the stony beach and up to the cave of the boat house. It was so quiet out of the wind that it boomed. All I wanted to do was lie down and sleep but Calum was badgering me, pulling on my arm, grunting at me to do something. Blankets. There were some blankets on a shelf at the end of the shed, blankets and a sleeping bag.

'T-take off your j-j-'

My fingertips were numb my fingers couldn't bend or do anything I got something off, the jacket, I rolled the blanket round me and curled up I went down to the bottom.

When I woke I was very cold and aching all over. I remembered where I was from the beginning. From dragging the boat out of the boat house – *Iris* – dragging it across the pebbles to the water's edge. I realised.

It was her. Our mother.

She had done it. Made the storm. She had done it to stop us leaving. To keep Calum on the island.

He was lying behind me – I checked, but I could hear him snuffling anyway. I turned my head back and rested it on a bunched up bit of blanket so I was facing out of the shed towards the sea. It was raining now and the wind seemed to have dropped, but I could still see lumps of foam blowing off the tops of the waves. The Blue Men. Her storm. It was obvious.

It was the first time since I'd been there that they'd had a storm. A sudden storm that shows up just before the ferry leaves. To stop me taking him away. And when I get round that by demanding a boat – she lets us get far enough out to drown then swamps the boat. We could have drowned. We could both be dead.

No. *I* could be dead. Despite what she said, Calum wasn't intended to die. Calum was intended to remain captive.

My teeth were chattering and my whole body was shaking. Cold, yes, but also shock. She deliberately set out to kill me. When it came down to it and Calum actually made a run for it – she would stop him. With force.

With a fucking tempest.

We needed to get warm. My watch was full of water, I had no idea what time it was. I crawled to Calum and poked him awake, his skin was grey. 'Come on.' He staggered and stared around him as if he couldn't believe it. Then–

'G-Gerry's boat.'

'Fuck Gerry's boat. We'll have to pay for a new one. Your mother can pay. Come on.' We got to the top of the little path and cut across the field to avoid going through the village – staggered in our blankets up to Calum's place without seeing a soul. It was raining so hard the blankets were as wet as our clothes.

He found me a T-shirt, sweater and jeans that I could hold up by tying a scarf through the belt loops, and a big pair of socks. I took them into his squalid bathroom and locked the door before I changed. The clothes were clean but they made my cold flesh shudder. Calum lit the fire and I made cups of tea. I emptied my poor soggy tobacco tin into the fire and Calum ferreted about on his table and passed me his new packet of tobacco to put in it. I rolled us both a fag and we sat in front of the fire and gradually the heat crept through and we began to thaw, he put more wood on till the whole hearth was alight and we both must've drifted into sleep again. When I woke up it was dark. The fire was glowing and my body ached in every limb and muscle. My throat was raw and my eyes stung. I felt as if I'd been turned inside out.

I listened for the wind but it had dropped. She'd called it up for exactly when she wanted – and having prevented us from leaving, she let it blow itself out. Calum was asleep, his head tilted down, his breathing harsh. His face was as blank as a child's. She'd tried to drown him. To stop him getting away from her. Or so she would know he was dead before she was. There was nothing she wouldn't do . . . the storm before I arrived. That was my welcome from her.

The trickle in my belly was a kind of fear. But I knew its dimensions. It was containable. She made us choke and crawl for our lives. I got up quietly and found my shoes. OK. Anything I might do to her ran the risk of being what she *wanted* me to do anyway. It didn't matter anymore. It was time to give myself the satisfaction of action.

I couldn't stop shaking, everything I touched I seemed to drop or knock over. But Calum slept like a baby. I put another lump of wood on the fire and pulled the old fireguard in front, and quietly let myself out. His key was in the lock – I took it and locked the door after me then pushed the key back in under the ill-fitting door. He was safe for the night. I was going to confront her now. Now while I was angry enough to slit her gizzard and laugh as she bled away to nothing.

20 · Susan's father

I was stumbling as I walked along the lane, I couldn't work out what was wrong then I realised it was the clothes, Calum's trousers were too long for me. But I was ravenous as well, once I began to move. I was clear. It would happen now, no point in going softly or attempting to control it. It would happen now and I would deal with the consequences afterwards. She had to be finished before any other life could take place.

I went in my own back door and crammed some biscuits into my mouth, standing there in the dark chewing and gulping them down as fast as I could, unable to think about her or anything that was happening until I had something in my belly. Like putting petrol in a car.

Then I went through to her hall. The TV was chattering softly in her sitting room. I knocked on the door and went in. She was in her chair in front of the TV, when she saw me she scrabbled to get up and her paper fell off her lap.

'Where's Calum? What's happened to Calum?'

'Did you think you'd drowned him?'

'Drowned?'

'You nearly did.'

'Is he alright?' She came close to me and clutched at my clothes. 'These are his – where is he?'

'He's at home. At his home.' I didn't want her near me. I moved away.

'Did he go–?'

'How could he go? How could we go? In that storm.'

'But he didn't come for his dinner–' She seemed completely stumped by this. She let herself down slowly onto the edge of a chair, took off her glasses and dropped them. Then she stared at me as if it was a deep mystery only I could solve.

'Well no he didn't. Surprise surprise. And you know damn well why.'

'Why?'

What a performance. What a poor, vague, confused, incomprehending innocent. All her massive power carefully shrunk down into this harmless-looking fragile vessel. But I don't want to play this game. It's making me shake with anger and there are things to be said before I do it. I make myself sit down. Her remote is on the chair arm. I turn the sound down to nothing. 'What is the point in pretending?'

'What?'

'Fuck it I *know*.' I kicked the side of her chair. 'Forget the four-star acting I fucking *know*. I know what you are I know you tried to drown us there's no point in all this bullshit anymore.'

She opens her mouth then closes it. I go over to the other side of the room and look out the window at the dark. I am breathless with anger. 'Admit it.'

'I don't know what you mean.'

'I know who you are. You're my mother and you just tried to drown me.'

She stares at me without replying then she starts to get up.

'I've traced you. I've been to your parents' house. You can stop pretending now.'

She is going past the fireplace. The fire is burning, it is too hot in this room.

'Where are you going?'

'I want to phone Calum.'

I am across the room before she can get the door half open. I slam it shut. 'No.'

'I want to hear him say he's all right.'

'If I was you I wouldn't call up a storm unless I was damn sure who it would and wouldn't drown.'

She is edging away from me, feeling her way along the wall backwards.

'Stand still!'

She stops. I suddenly feel like laughing. She is trying to get away from me and she can't, after all that. She is my victim. I sit back across the arm of her wing chair. 'Those magical powers always backfire, don't they? You know the one where he wishes everything he touches will turn to gold? Then dies of starvation?'

'What d'you want?'

'I want you to admit it.'

'Admit what?'

'Who you are.'

'I don't know what you're talking about.'

I rest my head back against the chair and let my eyes close for a minute. Why won't she give up?

'Have you found somewhere else to stay?'

'*What?*'

'I asked you to move out by the end of the week. Have you found somewhere else?'

'OK. Listen to me. I am Susan Lovage. I was born October 2 1968. I was wrapped in a white towel and left on the steps of Camden post office. OK? I was found by a cleaner at 6.30 a.m. and taken to hospital and my mother's name is Phyllis Lovage and her address was on the birth certificate. So there's no point in you pretending anymore.'

There's a short silence. I can hear the rain dashing against the window.

'What d'you want?' She is polite as ice. 'Money?'

225

'Sure. Money would be nice. I'll have money. But I want to know why, OK. For a start, why?'

She comes away from the wall and moves slowly to her usual chair. She sits. 'Whoever told you this. They should have told you Susan died.'

'I'm not dead.'

'Susan died when she was ten months old.'

'What of?'

'I don't know.'

'You don't know what your own daughter died of.'

'Get out.'

'You what?'

'Get out.'

'Well, no. That's not the plan.'

She's shuffling to her feet again. 'I'm going to call the police.'

'Are you? What're you going to say to them?'

She doesn't reply. I let her get close enough to reach for the handle then I slam my foot against it.

'Let me out.'

'No.'

'Let me out!' She raises her arm to strike my leg but doesn't. After a bit she goes and sits down again.

'Why don't you know what your daughter died of?'

'I wasn't there. I was in Italy.'

'So how d'you know she died?'

'My mother told me.'

I open my mouth but nothing comes out.

'This is none of your business.'

'Where did she die? In care?'

She speaks with slightly exaggerated patience as if to an idiot. 'It is none of your business.'

'You're going to get tired of this before I am.'

She shakes her head.

'D'you want more proof? I've got my birth certificate. School reports. Social workers' assessments.'

No reaction.

'You *know*. You've known since the day I got here – before. You *know*. You can't play games with me anymore because I know you know.'

She doesn't even flicker. Just sits there in her chair staring at her hands clasped in her lap.

'You hear? I *know*.'

Out of the weariness and the aches and pains from the buffeting water and the weight of the boat and the sharp stinging grazing of the rocks and the choked expanded half-drowned lungs and gasped raw throat, anger is coming. A big strong hot slow wave of anger builds. That woman sits there looking away from me.

'Who was my father?'

She looks up briefly. 'Susan's father was my father.' She looks at her hands again.

Anger is red. A hot flood of red across the eyeball. A warm waterfall of blood.

21 · Seven swans

I woke up sweating in a panic my hands were lost I couldn't touch my face. I was in bed. I sat up. My hands were covered in Calum's long sleeves which had unrolled, I still had all my clothes on, all *his* clothes on. There was a bottle of milk gone sour by the cooker, I could smell it from my bed. The light was murky, around dawn I'd say. My throat was sore and dry.

I ran some water and drank. My tin was in the trouser pocket, I rolled myself a cig. Leaning on the sink, I remembered her sitting there. Completely composed in her chair. Staring politely at her hands like she was in a waiting room. Denying me.

I unlocked my door and went into the hall. Her sitting-room door was still open. The light was still on. I saw her glasses and the remote on the floor by her chair. Then I saw her feet.

She was hidden from me by the coffee table. After a bit I moved into the room. My eyes were drawn to the TV, the picture was moving but there was no sound. She was lying on the floor between the coffee table and the fireplace, she was stretched out with one hand by her face.

I pulled Calum's long sleeve down over my finger and used the covered finger to press the TV button. The screen went black.

Very slowly and quietly I moved round till I was standing over her. Her clothes still covered her neatly, her hand was stretched on the carpet in front of her. It looked quite normal, there was her wedding ring, there was her wristwatch.

I knew I had to look at her face. Because everything else was quite normal.

Her head lies in a dark circle which must be blood. Her mouth is pushed half open against the carpet. I am looking. I can't take my eyes off her. Her face is bluish. Her hair is red and wet and matted. Her eye is half open, looking at the carpet. She looks like a police photograph of a murder victim.

Enough. I go back to the hall doorway and listen. Nothing. The house is perfectly still. I go back and crouch beside her, put my fingertips against her wrist. It is cold. Nothing moving. She's dead.

I get up again and walk round the chair and round her. She looks like a murder victim. She looks quite small, curled there. Almost like a girl. I crouch again. Under the coffee table I see a dark shape – I reach for it. An old flat-iron. She keeps one either side of the hearth. I do not look at it closely. It has a wooden handle. I carry it to the fireplace. Its partner sits quietly beside the coal scuttle. There is still a little red glow of embers in the grate. I put the used flat-iron on top of the embers and stir with the poker. I add kindling from the basket. There is a bit of a hiss and a crackle. I wipe my hand on Calum's sweatshirt.

Then I go to the hall again. The phone is not ringing but it attracts my attention. I stand staring at it for a while. I don't pick it up. The front door is closed but not locked. The cat is sitting by the closed kitchen door. I open the door to the kitchen, it slips through and clatters out through the flap. I go back to my room and wash my hands, take off Calum's clothes and put on a T-shirt and jeans of my own, transfer my tin to my own pocket. I put Calum's clothes in a bag, lock my door behind me and set off for his house.

He's not there. It's just after 7.30. Peering through the window I see the chairs we sat in yesterday, pulled close to the fire, and the heap of wet blankets on the floor. The door is locked. I leave the bag of clothes on the doorstep.

I took the lane north, towards Durris. The morning was bright grey and watery, sky and sea shining at each other, all calm and pearly after the storm.

I came to the narrowing of the island where the sea bites into the land on either side; the part Calum called the Neck. I stopped to look down at the bare surface of Table Rock, then went on to the flat pavement of the prayer stones. I climbed the ditch, walked out into the middle of the prayer stones and stared across to the monks' island. If you stood there and thought you heard mass when it wasn't being sung, how would it be different to standing there when it *was* being sung? Would the mass in your head be any less real?

I had not expected anything she said to help me. I had expected her death to help me. The finishing of her should free me, like a diver cut free of the wreckage. When he's cut free he can power away through the water, surge up to the surface.

But I was not free. I still didn't know the truth.

I was on the bare stones looking over the flat sea. At the end of a run, a foray, a raid. The meeting with my mother behind me. My mother *dead* behind me. And nowhere else to go.

When I went on towards Durris I saw that the tide was not fully out; water lapped over and around the bigger stones, it was not possible to cross without getting wet. I took off my trainers and socks and rolled up my jeans. The water was cold but no deeper than my ankles. It seemed to be coming in. Soon the little island would be cut off. OK.

I climbed the slope and looked down from the rim into the dish of land where the ruined cottages stood. No sign of Calum. I crossed the hollow, climbed the ridge at the other side; the island was empty to the sea. I didn't know what to do. There was something so desolate about that empty stony land and flat grey sea that I turned and went back down towards the ruins. I sat on a wall and tried to work out what to do.

Phyllis was dead in her sitting room. Calum was gone. Nothing had changed. I was the same as I always had been.

I had a vision of all the frenzies of activity I might enter into next, one after another. Buying and decorating a flat. Enrolling on a course. Starting a new job. I might have a child. Take in stray cats. I might hitch across America or pick up a new man. I might even reach the point where I'd go and sit in a church and talk to the Invisible Bastard. I could see them all clearly and each one would be as hollow as the next, none would contain satisfaction, each would be as unutterably futile as the pursuit of my mother had turned out to be. And each would be bounded and circumscribed by Fear. My life would be full of little projects, little attempts to discover whatever it was real people knew, to copy them hard enough to convince myself that I was real too.

The best thing would be to die. It would be less trouble.

I was very calm; all around me the little island, the last island, the island off an island off an island was still. Stillness was most natural. To go on scrabbling and running and grasping after some kind of life was aberration; stillness was lasting.

I didn't have any means of killing myself to hand, but it seemed to me it must be possible to find something on that little island. Drowning was the most obvious but it's difficult to drown when you can swim and the sea is calm as milk. Should've thought of it yesterday, eh. I got off the wall and started looking for a bit of broken glass. Inside the ruined shell of the cottage there was all sorts of crap, charred sticks and cans where someone'd made a fire, rubble, soggy scraps of an old newspaper. I turned stuff over with my foot but didn't turn up any bottles. There's a surprise. *First time ever no glass found in ruin* complains would-be-suicide. Since when has anything ever been easy, kid? I thought of Calum's glass mountain, clear and brown and green and blue, twinkling invitingly when the sun shone on it. I thought of it like that but it wasn't true. It was mostly dull either with dirt or being ground by the sea. The best bits weren't shiny at all they were an opaque pale green, worn to smooth shapes like sucked sweets. You could see light through them but nothing more, their transparency had been ground to a white frost. The cutting edges were smoothed to the roundness of pebbles, the sea had worn away their sharpness.

I came out of the broken walls and went back up the slope towards the sea. The sea was the only clean thing. She was lying there with blood seeping out of her head. The carpet would be ruined. Everything you touch becomes dirt, doesn't it? All these island people, look at them. They moved from their houses on the fertile land in the south, they came up here where they could hardly scrape a living – they built new houses and did all that work all over again – and then what happened? They got old and sick and their children left as soon as they could. And the cottages fell down and now they're here like rotten teeth and the ground is littered with lager cans and charred sticks and the smell of piss in corners. That's all that's left of people's hopes. Anybody's.

I went down to the edge of the sea, a breeze was coming off it, the water came in little laps to the stony beach and rustled through the smaller pebbles just lifting and resetting them. You couldn't believe it was the same substance as yesterday. The Blue Men with their foam-grey faces. This was silk. I walked in. It was cold when it first came into my trainers but then it warmed a little. Standing still up to my knees looking out, it was like the land didn't exist, just me and the flat water. I'm not going to be afraid any more, that's why I came here. I'm not going to have Fear any more.

The water all around me was unbroken, reflecting the grey light of the sky. There was just me and the water and the sky, it was completely quiet, I didn't want to move and break the peace at all. If I walked on and the water started to cover my head I would gasp and splash. I would swim, almost certainly, I wouldn't be able to make myself inhale the water naturally. I would choke and splutter and break up the smooth surface. The best thing to do would be to *allow* myself to swim. A nice quiet breaststroke. Swim right out until the island was out of sight. Swim for the Arctic, until I was so tired and cold that I drifted down gracefully without resistance, without brutishly struggling to stay alive. I started to push my legs through the water again.

'Nikki! N-Nikki!' I turned. He was standing on the crest of the land above the ruins. He started to run down towards me. I didn't want to go back but I certainly didn't want Calum leaping and splashing and carrying on behind me – probably falling over and drowning in two feet of water or even worse rescuing me and towing me triumphantly back to shore.

'It's OK,' I called when he got to the edge but he came in anyway. He moved splashing and thundering through the still water. His face was red and swollen, his eyelids so puffed up his eyes were slits. He stumbled towards me splashing me all over, he reached out and grabbed my arm and began pulling me towards the shore. I didn't resist; he was tugging my arm, leaning his weight away from me, almost pulling me over. When we got to shallower water he did overbalance and he pulled me down with him. The cold shocked me.

'Calum!'

He kept crawling towards the beach, dragging me after. 'You d-don't go in the sea. You d-don't go in the sea.'

'Calum, I–'

'No!' he bellowed at me; I slumped down on the edge of the sand

235

and he grabbed me by the shoulders and dragged me two yards further up the beach. 'No sea!'

'OK. OK. No sea.'

He crouched beside me and burst into tears. I lay there and cried too. As if there wasn't enough salty water in the world.

When we calmed down the quietness crept up around us. The quietness of the sea our splashing had disturbed, the quietness of the land our crying had interrupted.

'N-n-never–'

'OK. I won't.' By now I would have been out of sight. A dot, far out, like a seal's head.

He hugged his knees to his chest, staring out to the horizon. 'Sh-she said you're my sister.'

It took me a while. 'She? Your mother said?'

He nodded. She told Calum I was his sister.

'When?'

He was completely still, clenched in on himself. As he spoke tears and snot continued to stream down his face, he didn't bother to wipe them away. 'I woke up and you'd g-gone so I went to the house.'

I imagined him on the dark road. Approaching the lit window. Perhaps hearing our shouting voices. 'Calum, I–'

'She said Nikki's moving out tomorrow.'

'Last night? Are you talking about last night? Where was I?'

'Sleeping.' His right eye, the squinting one, was blinking uncontrollably, his face was twitching with exhaustion.

'But last night–'

'She said it's not up for discussion, it's decided, it's none of your business Calum.'

I waited.

'As if I was a b-baby. So I said – I said it's none of *your* business. Because I want to marry Nikki. S-so there.'

He rocked slightly, hugging his long shanks tighter. Calum came to see her after I'd gone to bed. She was still alive after I'd gone to bed. 'What did she say?'

'She started laughing. She said you c-can't marry her.' He drew a long gasping breath. 'She said, Nikki is your sister.' There was a silence punctuated by his shuddering breaths. 'Y-you can't marry your s-sister, Calum, even you know that. She l-laughed at me.'

'What happened?'

'I – I got angry. I just got–' He buried his face in his hands. I put my arm around his shoulders for a split second I couldn't and then I could try to comfort him. He cried terribly.

'Hush, Calum, hush.'

'I didn't mean – I didn't mean–'

'I know you didn't, hush now, hush.'

After a long time when he had cried himself out he asked me if it was true.

'If what?'

'You were Susan?'

'Yes.'

'She never said, she never, she never.'

'No. She never.'

He shifted his weight away from me and wiped his nose on his sleeve. The wind from the sea was freshening, the water in the shallows was forming almost-waves. It came over me that I was very very cold. My teeth had started chattering. My clothes were wet through and the wind made it worse. 'I'm cold–'

Calum hauled himself up. 'We'll l-light a fire.' We went up the slope and down into the dip again, out of the wind. He led me to the central cottage, where embers still glowed against a wall and a charred beam had been pulled up as a seat. His stick and rucksack lay in the corner.

'You were here last night?' I had walked past without even noticing. He set about rekindling the fire with scraps of rubbish and sticks; sat me down in front of it and went off for more wood. He came back with a couple of dead branches which must've been washed up because there were no trees but the rowans on Durris. The wood made a fierce blaze. I moved as close as I could. 'Have you got any food?'

He shook his head. What was I thinking of? Some sort of hideaway, we could be like shipwrecked sailors and live on the little island without anyone ever knowing? Eating fish and drinking brackish water, become innocent savages again?

We sat there for a long time watching the red and yellow flames, the way they leapt and splashed like water. I thought of him sitting there through the night. Wondering what was going to happen. Listening for footsteps? 'Didn't you hear me when I came through earlier?'

'I – I – thought y-you–'

'Yes?'

'You would be mad at me. I was afraid.' There was a silence filled with crackling and snapping from the fire. 'I h-hid from you.'

He had come out when I was in the sea. When I was up to my waist he'd started shouting and running after me. Suddenly he moved so violently that the beam rocked. 'I'm n-not going away.'

'What d'you mean?'

'From the island.'

'Nobody's trying to take you away.' I thought he meant me.

Despite the heat from the fire now his face was white. I realised he must be in shock. But he was thinking more clearly than I was. Of course they would try to take him away. They would put him in prison. They would take him from his island where he'd finally made himself free and lock him in a box away from sea and sky and flotsam and jetsam of every kind, away from the rocks where ghosts and stories attached, away from the foam-grey faces of the Blue Men, away from the world he knew. Because of the death of that witch.

I started to revive with the warmth. A rush of energy flushed through me, as if something frozen had melted. Calum. They would arrest him. Put on handcuffs. Lead into a boat, an animal to slaughter. My head was fuzzy but the heat was clearing it, making the mist evaporate, drying me to something clean and sharp. Why should they take Calum? Calum had a life. Calum had a place to be and a thing to do. It was stupid if they took Calum.

I thought about how if he hadn't come blundering and splashing through the shallows after me I would've been drifting to icy nothingness by now. What'd he dragged me out for? I could have taken the blame to the bottom of the sea. *If you'll never leave me, I'll never leave you.*

My skin was tingling from the extremes of cold and heat. Calum got up. 'We need more w-wood.' I followed him away from the fire, up over the crest and down to the shore where driftwood might be lying. I found some splintered bits of pallet. Calum had gone off in the opposite direction. *Not now nor ever.*

I dragged my wood to the top of the rise and suddenly felt very hot. Calum was still down at the shoreline loading himself up. I sat to wait; found my tobacco tin reasonably watertight in my pocket and rolled us both a fag. He came staggering up to join me and we sat there beside our firewood, smoking and staring at the tinfoil sea. Gradually there was a creaking noise which got louder until two swans appeared from behind us, flying low, with effort, huge wings creaking at each beat. They swooped down past the shoreline and landed in the sea, scattering water a thousand ways, shattering the mirror. Then they sat quite still while it pieced itself together and reformed round them so perfectly that four swans floated on the sea before us.

'You know where the s-swans come from?'

Seven swans

I'd never seen swans on the sea before – nor any swans on the island. The island was practically a bird-free zone. These were huge and snowy in the grey-brown sea; perfectly at home, dipping their beautiful necks under the water, floating in a lazy circle.

Calum told me the story of where the swans came from:

There was once a king on the mainland and he married a shy young girl from the island. He made her his queen. She bore him seven beautiful children, one for each year of their happy marriage, and then she fell ill and died. After a year of grief the king decided to marry again. He chose a widow from the south, a striking beauty, very proud, as different from the island girl as a rock is from a cloud. She was jealous of the first wife's children, who were tall and strong and handsome and beloved of all who saw them. She herself had a son she was ambitious for, and she was soon pregnant with another child of the king's. Her stepchildren played with her young son, swinging him between them so his legs flew off the ground, and he squealed with laughter and screamed for more. But the sight of it tormented her because the other woman's children were taller and finer than her boy, and they were easy and friendly with him instead of submissive and respectful.

She went to see a wise old woman and asked her how she could free herself from the first queen's offspring. 'Because one day they'll have everything and my poor children will have nothing. When the king is gone they'll lord it over us, commanding both the islands and the seas. They'll do as they please and we shall be no more than dirt beneath their feet.' The old woman made up a special potion and advised the queen to pour it into her stepchildren's porridge one morning when the king was out hunting.

Kindly the queen called to them: 'Come and eat your porridge, children, before it goes cold. I've poured on the cream, just as you like it.' When the oldest boy had eaten his porridge he stretched out his neck and gave a kind of squawk. His stepmother watched in satisfaction. Then a repulsive ripple seemed to slither along his neck and extend it like a thick-muscled snake so shocking to behold that the queen nearly fainted. The long blind neck stretched itself over his boy's head like a stocking rolled over a foot and when the shape of his round head was swallowed a sleek white bird head formed in its place with piercing black eyes and strong shapely beak. And he raised his arms which had grown to six foot length each one and with a rustling and a susurration of sudden growth a thousand strong white quills sprouted on each side and the wind as he lifted them was enough to send the breakfast pots crashing to the floor. Slowly he began to beat them and the huge white wings dazzled and unbalanced the wicked queen who fell to the ground in terror and the drumming and creaking of his flight rang deafeningly around the castle until he gained the arched doorway and was gone. And one by one his brothers and sisters followed him, beating through the air and raising such a wind in the castle that it tore hangings from the walls and doors from their hinges and fanned the flames in the hearths so they leapt out to catch at the clothes of the castle inmates. And as the seventh swan soared up high above the castle to the freedom of the heavens, the castle exploded in flames, burning so fiercely that not a single soul inside it escaped. And the swans flew over all the kingdom and were lords of the land and the isles and the kyles, they went where they pleased and obeyed nobody's law but their own.

Calum and I dragged our sticks down to the ruined cottage, leaving the swans masters of the shoreline.

We made up the fire and Calum told me where the spring was, the spring the old islanders had used. He had two Pepsi cans he'd rinsed and used before. I went down past the last ruin to the bright green patch in the reedy grass, parted it and knelt to fill my cans. As I came back I saw Calum had moved closer to the fire – he was squatting, hands up to shield his face from the heat, long shanks bent. The patient shape of him made me think of an African.

Nobody except us knew who killed her. She was the only other person who knew and she was dead.

It was like stepping off a cliff. Either you can fly, or you will plummet. You don't know which.

OK. Go to the edge and look down.

To a bad place. Thick close walls, windowless, airless; a locked door, no escape. The clanks and shouts and cries and whispers and moans and sobs of hundreds of other confined souls; misery seeping in through the crack under the door. No dawn sky to put an end to the night's horrors, only the flickering of cold fluorescent tubes. A black tunnel of time stretching out ahead; the white dot of its ending invisibly, immeasurably far. The casual brutality of warders and other inmates.

But you were going to walk into the sea.

Consider Calum in a prison. They would push, mock, goad, torment, flay. If he didn't lose his temper they would break him and if he lost it he would kill someone.

Our mother lying there on her carpet. No longer controlling either of us. I can walk away onto the next boat if I want.

Calum bends his head and runs his hands over his hair and face as if he's trying to brush cobwebs away. He glances at me. 'We c-can stay here.'

'Here?'

'Repair one of the c-cottages a bit – I can grow vegetables . . .'

And catch fish and seagulls' eggs; and I can spin yarn from nettles and weave shirts for us and we can make beds from swans' feathers and every time anyone comes to Durris we can hide. No one will guess where we are and the police will be quite happy to blame Phyllis's death on an unknown passer-by.

I seize at it though. Imagine getting a boat – rowing across to one of the more distant uninhabited islands – getting out of reach of other people – could we? To live like shipwrecked mariners. If we could escape . . . He's still looking at me hopefully, waiting for a reply. 'They'll come looking for us Calum. They'll come looking.'

'But if we h-hide–'

'They'll have dogs to sniff us out.'

He straightens his legs and begins to pick his way backwards and forwards across the rubble-strewn floor like an agitated stork. He is wringing his hands. 'We need some f-food.' He begins to cry. 'I d-didn't even bring any food.'

'Calum. I'll tell you what we're going to do.'

I get him to sit down again. And I tell him what we're going to do. Once you've stepped off, it's easy, blindingly swoopingly soaringly easy. I can fly.

22 · Night sky

From that leap followed a thousand things quite naturally and easily which could never have come to pass if I had not jumped.

Even leading me to ask, could I have done this before? Could I have made this kind of leap when I was younger and saved myself a lot of trouble? But it seems I was never in a place like that before, from which a leap was possible.

Once I was airborne my only worry was that Calum himself might screw things up. We sat by the fire all afternoon until it got dark, while I talked to him. I tried to impress on him that he must do what I said, but he was so shocked and bewildered that I couldn't tell how much he was taking in. The story was this: I had come to the island in search of my birth mother, I needed to see her to understand why she had rejected me. Once I found her I was scared to reveal my identity because she seemed to think I was dead (as Calum could testify) and I waited a while before I plucked up the courage. When I told her who I was we were alone together. She accused me of being an impostor; then she told me I was dead; then that she wished I was dead. When I cried (naturally, as you would) she attacked me physically, saying she hated the sight of me. She grabbed up the flat-iron from the fireplace and tried to smash me with it – and in the struggle and terror I got it off her, and knocked her to the ground. When she fell I threw the flat-iron in the fire and ran away as far and as fast as I could. I didn't know how badly I had hurt her. I was distraught, devastated by her hatred and rejection, terrified about what I might have done to her. Then my brother, calling early in the morning, discovered her – and in utter shock, ran after me. He found me and told me she was dead. I was inconsolable.

Calum listened and stared and nodded as if he was hearing the shocking truth itself. Only once he stopped me, putting his hand on my arm, and whispered, 'But I-I-I–'

'No. I did it. Nikki did it. You tell them where you found me. Where did you find me Calum?'

You could have counted to ten before he answered. I could see the thought slowly forming behind his good eye. 'In th-the water.'

'In the sea. Yes. What was I doing?'

He stared at me.

'You have to tell them what you think I was doing, Calum.'

'W-walking into the sea.'

'Why d'you think I was doing that?'

Another pause, and he shook his head.

'What happens when a person walks out of their depth?'

'Drowning.'

'OK. That's what you must tell them. You saw me walking into the sea. I was going to drown myself. OK. Because I killed our mother.'

'B-but–'

'Yes?'

'But *were* you?'

'I didn't know what else to do.'

He picked at the ground, jabbing out little shards of pottery with a half-burnt stick, turning them over with his long spidery fingers, considering them. 'You w-won't do that again.'

'No.'

'P-promise.'

'I promise.' Not now nor ever.

When I was sure he'd got it, the whole story, I made him go over his own version of the morning's events; his exhausted sleep after our yesterday's adventure in the sea, his sudden early morning waking, his walk down to his mother's, his surprise at finding the front door open (as I had left it in my flight); his view through the open sitting-room door to his mother's body sprawled upon the floor. The disordered room bearing signs of a struggle. His terrified shock – he called for me and I wasn't there – he ran from the house in horror.

It was so close to the truth anyway. It was truer than the truth. I had gone there to kill my mother.

When I had finished we went back down to the crossing place. It was getting towards dusk. I thought of waiting there until they came to find us but we had to eat. Calum said the tide would be low again by eight, we could get back to the island then. There were deep gaps between the clouds and we saw the first stars come out. The size and depth of the sky gave me a giddy rush.

'What will they do?'

'What d'you mean?'

'T-to you.'

'Well I guess they'll question me, they'll question both of us, they'll probably take me to the mainland and lock me up until they hold a trial.'

'It sh-should be me.'

'No. You should be here.'

'You're doing it for m-me.'

'Well will you stay here for *me*?'

There was a pause and then he said, 'OK.'

We lay on the short grass and looked at the sky, waiting for the tide to go out. Even as we watched the clouds shrank and disappeared, we could see right into the universe.

I saw how big freedom was. All the stars. Gazed at by sailors on distant ships a thousand miles from land. By shepherds in hot empty deserts of black. By astronomers in dim observatories where they watch with sandwiches and flasks, and laugh quietly together over a shared joke the dumb sleeping world will never get. By children camping for the first time and crawling out of their tents to see that vast shining overhead. By night fishermen watching the light in sky and water, dizzy between heaven and its reflection; by drunkards stumbling from the pub, falling heavily but with surprisingly little pain to the close safe ground, rolling over and noting that the dark is littered with sparks of fire. By lovers who've steamed up the car and get out for a last cigarette before driving to their separate homes, who look up and think *this is for us*; by pilots at night and drivers at night and people who duck out of their warm fuggy houses last thing before bed to take their dogs for a pee – and chancing to look up, see the glory of the constellations and planets above. By doctors walking from their cars to the homes of sick people; by tired midwives, closing the doors softly on the murmuring cries of new sparks of life.

We got back to the house at nine. It was a lifetime later but it was as I had left it in the morning. She still lay on the sitting-room floor, nothing had changed, no one had been. I picked up the phone and dialled the police. Then Calum and I went into the kitchen and made ourselves scrambled eggs and a cup of tea.

I saved my confession for the officers on the mainland. They had no trouble believing I did it. My motive was impeccable (always has been hasn't it?) An open and shut case. Except that for once in my life my plight conjured a degree of sympathy. TWICE REJECTED DAUGHTER DRIVEN TO BREAKING POINT was one of the headlines. Her terminal illness and the way *she* had attacked *me* were both taken into account (as was the fact that I had stayed peaceably in her house for the nine preceding days offering her no harm) and the charge against me was manslaughter. My lawyer pleaded self-defence and diminished responsibility. My remorse was genuine, according to the judge: 'Must this young woman, whose whole life has in a sense been a punishment for the fact that her mother abandoned her – through no fault of her own – must this young woman endure further punishment at our hands, burdened as she is by terrible remorse?' He gave me two years. I served a year then got my automatic conditional release. I was in prison in Inverness.

23 · Viking Bay

And there's nothing I want to say about that. It was 365 days all 24 hours long. There were 60 minutes in every hour. I had time to think about each thing that had happened, each incident on the island, each conversation with my mother and my brother, each story that Calum told me. There's a bay just south of her house, Calum called it Viking Bay. I held that in my head a lot of the time, because of its black rim of stones. Because of its waiting. The story he told me there was all about waiting.

Viking Bay faces the north Atlantic. The shoreline is quite black, black boulders and pebbles, and the grass runs down to the edge. There's barely any height to the ground here, the merest wave would wash right into the field, and the flat sea stretches to the tiny flat islands of land and cloud that float on the distant horizon.

Late one summer a thousand years ago a Viking longboat pulled into this deserted bay. They had set off from Norway making for distant Iceland; Ragnar and his wife Freya and his brother Olaf and their freedmen and their slaves and their furs and their shields and axes and mead and supplies of barley and seed and dried fish. But they had run into a storm and then into days and days of fog. Ragnar knew they had lost their way – maybe even sailed in a circle – and on the first day the fog lifted he released the ravens and set a course to follow their flight to land. They moved into warmer air and he recognised the mild current that flows around the north-western parts of Britain. He had been down the Irish coast the previous year, raiding; had brought back rich plunder of goods and slaves, including an Irish girl.

They pulled the boat ashore and turned it over; made fire and food and settled for the night. During the night Freya went into early labour and gave birth to a tiny sickly boy. In the morning the fog closed in again.

All day and night as she lay huddled under the boat with the baby in her arms she listened to fragments of Ragnar's passing conversations. Arguing with Olaf about what to do: they should leave tonight, sail on for Iceland, before the winter prevented them. But they must wait for the fog to lift. The baby must be killed and buried here, no point in taking a sickly thing on such a journey. Later she heard her husband calling to the Irish slave girl; she heard him questioning the girl and copying some words of her language; she heard them laugh together. She heard the deep voices of the brothers murmuring together as they sat by the fire after their food; she heard the sounds of a man and woman lying together close by. But she did not know if the man was Ragnar.

They were stranded on the island for days, blanketed in fog. On the day it lifted five whales came past the bay and shoals of fish so thick the water glittered with them. The baby boy was feeding well and growing stronger, he had his toehold on life.

Viking Bay

The men argued about the wisdom of sailing on. The island was a safe place to overwinter. To make the northern journey so late in the season was becoming hazardous; better to bide here and sail to Iceland in the spring. There were rich lands to raid nearby and no enemies on the island. Freya listened to her husband and the Irish girl exchanging words and laughter in the Irish tongue. She listened to them gasp and moan at night. She held the small baby between her breasts.

The next day Ragnar split the party: half for Iceland, half to overwinter on the island. In spring he would return for his wife and his son, and the freedmen and slaves he left with them. Sailing with Ragnar were the strongest of the oarsmen and three slave girls including the Irish one.

When they had gone Freya walked the black stones of the bay with her baby in her arms and looked out as the dot of their sail melted into the distance. When they had gone she sat on the rocks and combed her long fair hair with the bone comb Ragnar had carved for her when she was still a girl.

The days began to shorten. It was dark when they woke in the morning. It was dark by mid-afternoon. On some days when the cloud was low and mist hung in the air the darkness never lifted. The dark was a mood which hung in Freya's heart, it contained the sounds made by her husband and the Irish girl, and the black finality of the stones of the shore. The island was damp and quiet and dark and held permanently in suspension between the black night sky and the inky depths of the sea. She thought her husband would never return.

After the turning point of the winter solstice she walked the west coast of the island every day, eyes fixed on the cold flat sea. The dark pressed on her, it bowed her head, it infiltrated her and filled her up and was only broken by lightning flashes of vision: her husband and the Irish girl laughing together, her husband turning away from her. In a rage of despair one day she flung the comb he had made her out into the sea. Her son grew strong and healthy.

Early in the spring, before anyone could have expected it, a sail appeared to the west. It was a low dark misty day, it had never been light since the autumn, it seemed they had lived a whole five months by firelight and torchlight, the world closed in to the small dim circle around them that firelight created. Now a bright sail coming out of the darkness, coming straight to them.

She sat on the rocks and watched it grow with both joy and terror in her heart. He had come back to fetch her, he wanted her still. She would step from the black stones into the bright keel of her husband's boat. But now that she must leave the island its safety and solidity rooted her to the spot. Those black stones demarcating the land from the sea; were they not protection? Against wild formlessness, against the unknown, against swamping waves and engulfing winds and being dissolved into a thousand thousand grains pounding sorrowfully on the shore? Against rekindled love, against the laughing Irish girl, against all the grief in store for her? Underneath the sea, the waves inched the comb in to shore.

When he landed she asked him, 'How can I be sure of you?'

'When they put me in my boat with all my prized possessions, my sword and my shield and my drinking horn and my wife—'

'Ah—'

'And pour oil over us and set us alight. Then you can be sure of me.' Flames would leap over their oil-drenched bodies, the long planks would spit and snap out of place, the vessel would burst on the water red and gold as the setting sun and their black smokes entwined would spiral up to the waiting clouds.

The island was a safe place. It was both prison and freedom. But it was time to move on.

She stepped from the black stones into the bright keel.

They let me out of my cell. I catch the bus and the train and the bus and the ferry, I smile at the old folk and the walkers with their rucksacks. I come to the island and follow the road to Tigh Na Mara. The sky is so huge it makes me dizzy, the blues and greens and soft purple-greys of the mist over the islands and drifts of cloud in the tree tops stop me and make me stare. The air is alive with scents and sounds that stretch back to the furthest horizon, that waver and shift and move constantly like the quivering lungs of a giant animal. I am cradled in a living breathing landscape which melts and reforms into new shapes every time I move. It is infinitely various. There is no danger in it, there are shadows and echoes of long-lost voices but they touch the earth they walk on the water they float through the air like the patterns forming and reforming inside a kaleidoscope, they are in the texture and colours of vision. I breathe them in, they swirl in and out of me, my senses my breath my blood.

My name is Nikki. Sharp, with fangs; angry. Outside all charmed circles all groups friendships families sops. You can't pull the wool over my eyes. When I first came to this island it was flat as a plate.

Something has changed.

I can hear. I can see.

Island

I live with my brother in our mother's old house. A social worker visits sporadically to check I haven't murdered anyone else. The house is dirtier than it was, it has heaps of stones and driftwood and sea treasures and tools and vegetable sacks blocking the hall and heaped in the sitting room. I have the upstairs. I emptied it. I burned her things, Calum helped me. And to begin with I just took up my bed. There's a little table now I bought from a house sale in the village, and a broken chair Calum found washed up a long time ago that he's made into a stool. On the windowsill is the little Viking comb, carved by Ragnar a thousand years ago. The soft grey light flows in the windows like balm, sometimes there is a rectangle of bright sunlight on the bare floorboards. I can sit and watch the light shift and change, I can wake in the morning and before I even open my eyes I can feel the gentle mist patient against the pane I can feel the way it bridges the space between my window and the sky I can feel touched and blessed.

Calum is slow chaotic maddening my brother. He tells me stories. He likes my tale of Fir Apple. He plants and tends his garden. Every day he roams the island and brings back treasures from the sea.

Sometimes I see it one way, sometimes another. I can still see who I was. Even, who I will be. Not here in this peace for ever. Not cradled and cocooned in island mists, caressed by island voices, bathed in soft island light for ever. It is a milky womb where I swim blind and protected as a foetus, where I hang suspended perfect and weightless. I am in a still safe place. I am in no hurry for what's next. While I wait, I rehearse the stories. As a baby floating in its amniotic fluid dreams the dreams of its past and coming lives, I tell Seal Rock, Bull Rock, the Ashplant, the Prayer Stones, Salt, Table Rock, and the Seven Swans. I tell Viking Bay.

I haven't discovered anything new I have discovered something old and always known, not lost, not forgotten, not rare, not difficult.

Only unknown to me.

I have discovered a brave new world with voices in it I did not have before. Each voice has stories, each story has voices. They radiate possibilities.

The first story Calum properly told me was Table Rock, as he led me through the fog on my second day on this island. The woman who leaves her child on the rock, the child which is not her husband's. Now I can tell it over again: Table Rock.

A couple want a child, but the husband cannot father one. They love each other, on cold nights they curl around one another for warmth, their gentleness and kindness together feathers their bed like swansdown. But there will be no child.

They grieve, each for the other's loss. When he sits on the cottage step in the evening, staring out to sea, she watches his face and her heart weeps for him, because she knows he is thinking of the child he will not have. She loves him. She thinks of a plan.

When he is out in the boat one day she takes herself to his brother, who is home waiting for the cow to calve. She tells him her problem and her plan, and she gives him a cheese she has made, in exchange for what she needs from him.

And as the months go by she barely conceals the swelling belly, she almost flaunts her new self to her wondering husband, who strokes her soft flanks with timid, gentle hands, and wonders but does not question, because he loves and trusts her.

When she delivers the child she lays it on Table Rock. He's a good man, he will look for it. When he comes in from fishing he will find it there.

And when he comes in that night to the neighbouring bay, because he had a catch to deliver there, so doesn't pass by Table Rock, she bites her lip till it bleeds but says nothing. He is a good man and she must let him freely choose. She trusts him.

He takes in her face, her body, looks into her eyes. They do not speak. After his meal he leaves the table almost hurriedly – glances back at her where she sits in the shadow, looking after him. Outside he raises his face to the evening breeze, sniffing like a dog. Hurries, stumbling, down the cliff path, until he comes in earshot of the sound his ears have hunted – wades, splashing and nearly falling in his eagerness, out to gather up the child. And as he makes his way back to the cottage the questions he did not formulate, because he loved his wife, are answered. He sees what she has done and why, and his heart swells with love of her. He gives her the baby as a gift of the sea, as she has given it him.

Closer to home there's another story. A woman who abandons her daughter and keeps her son, and ends up being murdered: Phyllis's story.

An unhappy woman was once cruelly treated by her parents. She was impregnated by her father and gave birth to a daughter. Her mother told her that this baby, fruit of an unnatural and shameful liaison, had died.

The woman moved far away from her parents and began a new life. She met a man and gave birth to his son. She lavished upon the boy all the love she had been unable to give her daughter. For a while she was happily married, but then her husband died. Although she loved her son she found herself haunted by guilt and sorrow over her lost daughter, she became increasingly withdrawn and unhappy. She told her son about his sister who had died so terribly young. She was fearful for the boy and tried to keep him close, she wanted to protect him from danger but she hurt him by taking away his independence.

When he moved away from her she tried to kill herself. He saved her life. Her sense of guilt and shame was doubled, as she realised the burden she had become to this boy whom she loved so intensely.

A young woman came to the island where they lived, and rented a room from the mother and her son. The girl paid great attention to the son, walking and talking with him for hours, until the mother became convinced the girl was trying to steal her beloved boy.

Then the girl confronted the woman and announced she was her long-lost daughter. The wretched woman was overwhelmed by conflicting emotions. She had believed the story that her baby was dead so the girl's claim was as shocking as the appearance of a ghost. She wanted to believe but she did not dare; she wanted to laugh and rejoice and hug the girl but she was petrified of this dead person who'd suddenly come to life. She was afraid that the girl still had a plan to take her son away, and that she might be mad. The girl was furious with her mother for abandoning her and warned her that she was going to kill her. When the girl stormed out the mother collapsed in terrible distress, not knowing which way to turn. It seemed to her that the girl was strong and would survive, that the girl was like herself and could endure as much as the mother herself had endured (which seemed to her to be a great deal – an infinity of suffering). Whereas the boy was different, more vulnerable. He was the one she must protect.

Soon after, her son came to see her and confirmed his mother's worst fears by announcing that he wanted to marry the girl. The mother spilled out the whole sorry story to him. But her son, instead of sympathising, grew angry with his mother for lying to him about his sister's supposed death. If the girl was his sister, as his mother claimed, then he could not marry her. Thus his mother would prevent him – as she had done all his life – from doing as he wished. In his rage he grabbed the nearest thing to hand and hit his mother, killing her with one blow.

Then there's Nikki's story, another way of seeing it.

A young woman gave birth to a daughter whom, through no fault of her own, she could not keep. The daughter grew up bitter and twisted. Everywhere she looked she saw cruelty and selfishness and she reflected this back in her own spiteful nature. She could neither love nor be loved; she was petty and vicious and destructive, she was cowardly and terrified of shadows. She had no lasting friends, no real pleasures, no hopes or ambitions, no faith in herself. Unable to shoulder any responsibility for her misfortunes, she laid the blame on her absent mother. She decided to visit her mother on the island where she lived and kill her.

To her surprise she discovered she had a brother who lived on the island with their mother. The brother was as sweet-natured as the girl was cruel; he loved the world around him and didn't know what fear was. He knew the stories of past islanders and they were still alive to him. He collected lost fragments of their belongings and their homes, and treasured them. He liked the girl but he didn't know she was his sister, he thought he would like to marry her.

The girl revealed her identity to her mother – who denied it, because she had long believed her daughter to be dead.

In the morning the girl discovered her mother's body and believed that she herself was responsible for the murder. She did not find any relief in the mother's death, and so resolved to drown herself. As she was walking into the sea her brother came running down and pulled her from the water. And then . . .

Well, well, well. You know this story, I've told you everything. The only question is where does it end. Here? Here?

Here?

We are living like castaways on the edge of the world but we live in peace. I have no Fear. I have escaped the terrible loneliness of hating everyone around me.

I could tell you how I'm starting work for my friends Sally and Ruby, who took Calum under their wings during my imprisonment. I could tell you that one day I'll go back to the mainland, as Freya stepping into the bright keel. I could tell you Calum and I have spoken to a museum curator at Fort William who is next month coming to look at some of Calum's treasures. But all these things spoil the shape of the story.

I could tell you I am here.

Think of me here, on this island, now. I am safe.